ONE MORE VICTIM

A CALLOW AND OAKLEY FBI THRILLER

DAVID VIERGUTZ

Building a relationship with my readers is the very best thing about writing. I send newsletters with details on new releases, writer-life, deals and other bits of news related to my books. And if you sign up to my mailing list I'll send you something I think you'll like, my thrilling novel, *Red Mud River - A Callow and Oakley FBI Thriller*.

Details can be found at the back of this book.

CHAPTER ONE

Her knuckles white, Genevieve Callow—Callow to her friends, Jenny to a chosen few—gripped the steering wheel of her aging 2004 Chevy Tahoe.

The Virginia sun forced its way through the front windshield, cooking her forearms and raising the temperature in the vehicle until Callow was swaddled in it. The road flew by, a superhighway of white dashed lines, with drivers hunched forward in their seats or sipping on steaming coffee from paper cups.

Callow's head drooped against the heavy, comforting rays of the sun. Her eyelids felt weighed down by cinderblocks, and her breathing became deep and rhythmic.

Callow was ripped from her stupor by the blaring squawk of a gold Camry as it flew by the right side of her Tahoe. Her stomach somersaulted and settled in knots, her heart rate launched into a breakneck pace, and she was overtaken by a hyper-alertness that only came when a person's survival instincts were kicked into overdrive.

The Camry pulled ahead in the outside lane.

Callow felt her face flush and the back of her legs grow warm with sweat. She shifted uneasily in the seat as she waved the Camry's driver off, hoping the gesture would convey her apology.

She'd barely been on the turnpike for twenty-five minutes.

In truth, she had faded away for a few moments, lost in some memory somewhere, into a purgatory-like chasm somewhere between asleep and awake. Fighting off sleep was like pulling a snake out of a burrow; as soon as you had a grip, some sense of reality, it wriggled away and left you in dreamland.

Callow cranked the volume. Two of the Tahoe's speakers were blown, leaving only the rear speakers functioning, creating a hollow effect that reminded her of being underwater; like the sound was far away, behind a door. It didn't help with her exhaustion at all.

At Quantico, Callow had learned there were two types of tired: physical and emotional. Physical exhaustion came from lack of sleep or after strenuous exercise. Emotional exhaustion came from great mental turmoil that required focus and calibration to work through and comprehend. Most people who say they need to *"work through something"* are most likely emotionally exhausted.

Genevieve Callow was working through something.

She sighed and rolled down the driver's side window, letting the wind whip through her hair. That would be enough to stave off the nods for now.

A plastic bag on the passenger seat fluttered from the incoming breeze. Callow eyed a half-eaten sandwich—the same type of sandwich from the same shop she and her partner, Marcus Oakley, had eaten while on a case not two months prior. Hunting down another similar sandwich was turning into an adventure. The drive was a twenty-four-mile round trip—and the sandwich wasn't even very good.

The turkey was bland and tasteless, the cheese slightly sour, and the bread had an unidentifiable crunch to it.

The sandwich was an excuse to drive; the airport, a destination.

Genevieve Callow was working through something.

But unlike those who manage to decompress from their memories, Callow was trapped by hers. And like the subject of the memory, it had just tried to kill her.

Not with its hands pressing the life from her throat, but through the emotional residue it left behind that could peel her attention away from reality in an instant and run her off the road.

He can't hurt you anymore. You caught him. It's over.

But it didn't feel over.

Three weeks ago, Callow had nearly lost her life to the serial killer she'd been tracking. To compensate, her superiors at the FBI had given her three weeks off.

She'd taken one.

Upon returning to the fanfare from her co-workers, complete with the mandatory cake, balloons, and a medal, she had also been slapped with a new assignment. Callow didn't buy it. No matter how ASAC Jedediah Gold, her friend and mentor, dressed the position up as an "opportunity," she saw the assignment clearly for what it was—a distraction.

There was a reason Callow had only taken a week off. Her work wasn't done.

She couldn't focus on a new assignment—not when another unsolved case weighed heavily on her mind.

A case where the killer called out to her by name.

A dead-end case that only she could solve.

Her latest obsession.

Callow shifted uneasily in her seat, her rear going numb, and tapped her foot anxiously. With her other foot, she pressed the gas pedal, inching closer and closer to I-77.

Her eyes narrowed as rays of orange and yellow sunlight blasted under the sun visor, growing so bright that all Callow could concentrate on was the space between her hands on the steering wheel where the leather was cracked and worn. It was all a bright slipstream.

Once her eyes adjusted, Callow looked out over the highway. With the absence of any cars, it resembled more of a deserted runway. There was no Camry. There was only the road.

She felt her heart racing again. A wild recklessness washed over her; the same inexplicable insanity skydivers must surely feel moments before leaping from the plane and testing fate.

She yearned to feel *something*.

Callow jerked the radio knob sideways until it was five notches from full blast and mashed the gas pedal. Hard rock filled the SUV, but blood pounded in her ears, drowning out all other noise. The highway seemed to stretch into the distance, long and narrow.

The screaming vocals over the speakers became unintelligible, seeming to meld with the roar of the engine as Callow pushed the speedometer further.

Ninety. Ninety-five. One hundred.

She was a blur, her eyes barely able to keep up with the speed. A satisfied smile spread across her face as adrenaline poured into her veins like a shot of nitrous. For a moment, she thought she might have laughed.

But as she pushed the Tahoe toward one hundred and twenty, the vehicle began to veer to the left, buzzing over the lane indicators. Once again, that sinking feeling of falling tore through her stomach, and she backed off the accelerator.

Heaving, huffing, she sucked frigid, recirculated air between her teeth, down her throat, and into her lungs.

Why did I just do that?

It wasn't insane—it was just stupid.

To feel alive, Jenny.

A familiar voice answered her thoughts. The tone reminded Callow of her father scolding her.

You died in the mud in El Paso, Jenny. You died—you just won't admit it. Now, you can't feel anything.

But she didn't *feel* dead. She felt tired—no, *exhausted.* Emotionally and physically.

At least the dead have a reprieve from the pains of the living.

The Tahoe continued to coast, and once the SUV was back within the speed limit, she pressed on the accelerator again. With the large green road sign drawing closer, she blinked rapidly, trying to make out the letters. She surely must have missed her turnoff after her little stunt.

Suddenly, she became acutely aware that she was not alone on the deserted strip of highway. She could see cars—red, blue, gray, all staggered behind her in the other lanes. She had the feeling they had all recently moved over.

She swore, then finally dialed back the music as one car approached quickly from behind. She could make out a black grille guard, a white hood, and an ultralight, thin light bar on its roof.

Now you'll get it, Jenny. He'll impound your car for reckless driving.

A parade of red and blue lights ignited in her mirrors, and a siren chirped twice. Callow flipped on her blinker and slowly drifted toward the left-hand shoulder. She squeezed over to the left as far as possible, hoping the officer had room and wouldn't be too angry about having to walk the thin line between life and death as cars screamed by.

She came to a stop directly in front of a speed limit sign. 65 MPH.

She felt completely out of place. The flashing headlights and light bar seemed surreal, as if they were part of the dreamlike state she'd been in a few miles back.

But this was no memory. This was real.

Real police. Real speed. Real consequences.

Callow rolled down the window before locking her head forward, her hands pressed firmly against the steering wheel.

Her heart performed some sort of Riverdance against her chest. Her palms began to sweat, and her foot tapped along to the beat of her heart.

She couldn't stop it. The rhythm created an uncomfortable shake in the car, the Tahoe's aging suspension creaking as she fought against herself, praying that the officer might be lenient.

But why would he? She deserved whatever was coming.

Ticket. Impound. Jail. It was all her fault.

Callow had no good excuse for speeding like a madman.

You did it to feel alive, right, Jenny? You died. Tell him you died.

The officer approached on the left, squeezing between the SUV and the Jersey barriers. There wasn't much room on the shoulder, and Callow could hear the many accoutrements on his duty belt clanging, rustling, squeaking. His footsteps crunched on wayward stones and long pummeled car parts left over from crash after crash, pounded by the incessant traffic until they were no more distinguishable than the gravel kicked up by large trucks.

Callow could feel the officer just outside her door—then came the unmistakable odor of sweaty, sunbaked polyester. She could smell the salty remains of winter on his water-soaked boots and the hint of gasoline on his sleeve. The smell of frigid winter cold stood out the most. The snow had mostly melted, leaving a slushy, muddy residue.

The officer cleared his throat.

Callow turned her head slowly, stifling a gasp by clamping her mouth shut just in time, resulting in a painful knot that built underneath her chin like a sneeze she had forced back. The officer was tall, standing nearly a head above the roof of the Tahoe. The brim of his campaign hat shadowed his face, but his prominent chin and thick lips defined his chiseled face. He had to be in his fifties, his light blond hair trimmed neatly above the ears protruded and suggested he combed it lazily to the side. He wasn't a young trooper. Retirement seemed to be quickly approaching.

A thin bead of sweat ran down his cheek.

"Good afternoon, ma'am." His voice was deep and melodious. "My name is Trooper Tony Mackeras with the Virginia State Police. Do you know why I stopped you today?

"I do."

"And what reason might that be?"

Callow considered how to reply, worried about incriminating herself, but the admission of guilt was irrelevant. She was caught, and she didn't plan on fighting the consequences.

"I drifted off," she conceded. "When I realized, I got spooked and overcompensated. I know it doesn't excuse it, but I've been through a lot these last few days. Few *weeks*, actually. I'm sorry for putting you in this position."

The trooper cast a suspicious eye around the inside of the car. He looked past Callow like she didn't exist, then his eyes met hers. They were cool gray, almost like stone.

"'Drifted off?' I've been following you for *miles*. You didn't just 'drift off,' ma'am—you were driving at a speed of up to nearly 110 miles per hour, according to my radar. Most of the time when people drift off, they get slower and nearly wreck out. But you didn't slow—you *sped up*, crossed the center line, and damn nearly crashed into a Camry. Some might call this reckless driving; an arrestable offense in the Commonwealth of Virginia. Now, if you would, could you please hand me your license and insurance?"

Callow's eyes darted to the glovebox, where her service issued Glock 19 and her FBI badge and identification sat neatly next to each other. She glanced back at the trooper, looking to formulate the words needed to explain herself—and feeling exactly like a child in the principal's office.

"They're in the glovebox," she said. "Along with my pistol and my credentials."

The trooper raised an eyebrow. "Are you a cop?"

Callow nodded. "Yes, sir. FBI."

The trooper's hard façade melted away. "My kids call me 'sir.' Call me Tony. Grab your badge and ID and I'll get you out of here." His eyes darted sternly to the rubberneckers cruising past as he spoke, then he frowned. "You said you've been through a lot. Tell me about that. Does that have anything to do with what's going on here?"

Regardless of the trooper's generosity, Callow didn't feel any more at ease. She had prepared herself mentally for a ticket, or worse. She hadn't prepared herself to open up about her recent trauma.

Struggling to meet the man's gaze, she reached into the glovebox for her identification and badge. The officer stood up, stretching his back as a cohort of cars rushed by.

"I'm part of the Behavioral Analysis Unit," Callow offered, holding out her information. "We're in charge of profiling serial killers."

The officer took her credentials and looked them over. "Callow? As in *Genevieve* Callow? You're the analyst … sorry, the *agent* who caved the face in of the Red Mud River Killer. Shit, I heard he nearly killed you."

Callow pulled down the scarf around her neck to expose the green and brown bruising that remained there. Her tormentor's mark—bruising that followed the shape of fingers.

Callow realized the trooper, Tony, was only asking her name as a courtesy. Her name had been plastered all over the local news, and conversations about her encounter with the Red Mud River Killer followed her everywhere. The scarf did little to stop the hushed whispers behind her back. The entire Bureau knew who she was at this point. Recognized her, too. She'd contemplated cutting off her hair, but she hadn't been able to bring herself to do it. A moment of clarity had told her that only time would make the difference.

Time, and someone else seizing the limelight.

But there was another image portrayed of the events with the killer—one that didn't garnish pats on the back, but rather nervous glances. When Callow had apprehended the killer, she had been accompanied by a uniformed officer, and his body cam footage had revealed *exactly* what she'd had to do to survive.

That, too, had been plastered all over the news—blood and all.

"Heard you bashed his face in; left him sucking teeth. But you also saved that El Paso police officer's life. I can't believe the media tried to crucify you for leaving that asshole's prosthetic in the mud," Tony continued. "One girl was literally *hog-tied* a few hundred yards away. The officer's leg was caught in a bear trap, and the killer nearly ripped your head clean off—and they want to get mad over a prosthetic?"

"I'm just trying to forget it," Callow replied. With a long exhale, she sat back in her seat and dropped her hands from the steering wheel.

"Survivor's guilt?" Tony asked, rapping on the roof of the Tahoe.

"What?" Callow asked, facing him.

"Survivor's guilt. I can see it all over your face. I was in a shooting when I first got started, nearly twenty years ago. Three months in. My training officer didn't make it. I did. Are you seeing a grief counselor?"

"No."

"Well, this little stunt won't fix the hurt. It might go away for a bit. You'll try skydiving. Then rock climbing. Then something else equally dangerous and stupid. If you survive all that, you'll eventually come around to looking for answers at the bottom of a bottle."

For reasons unknown, tears swelled in Callow's eyes. She could just imagine the new trooper, young and baby-faced, wasting away in his misery. For a moment, *she* was the trooper.

In brief flashes, she saw herself mountain biking, then skydiving, then going one hundred and twenty down the highway. But instead of smiling, her face was twisted into a baleful mourn — an ugly, speechless cry. The tears fell down her cheeks, leaving salty streams in her faint trace of makeup. She sniffed hard.

"Hey, now—I didn't mean any offense," Tony backtracked. "Listen, let me get back to my car and I'll get you a card. We have a survivor's group. We meet on Wednesdays. Trent used to cook, but somehow he manages to burn damn near everything, including spaghetti. We mostly have pizza. You're welcome to join. No pressure, though. Just a bunch of us talking things through."

Trooper Mackeras walked away without waiting for her answer.

Callow shook her head at the thought of sitting in a room with a bunch of strangers, spilling her guts to expunge her demons. She imagined it'd be like a stuffy Alcoholics Anonymous meeting where everyone called her Genevieve.

"Hi, everybody, my name is Genevieve Callow, and I'm a survivor."

"Hi, Genevieve," they'd repeat, and that would make her wince. Nobody called her Genevieve.

She sniffed a few more times, then dabbed her eyes with a soggy napkin from the sandwich bag. A moment later, Tony returned, holding a crinkled card. He handed it to her, along with a long, thin piece of paper that said "WARNING" across the top. Callow took them both.

She lifted the warning up. "Thank you for this."

"Meet with us. Or meet with a therapist. Do something other than this." The trooper dolefully looked the vehicle over as if it was a loaded gun.

Callow could see something on the man's face—something just under the surface, beneath the budding wrinkles and five o'clock shadow. She could see some sort of incarnate recognition, like he didn't just understand, but had been through exactly what she had.

"The mountain biking. The skydiving. The drinking. Was that you?" she asked softly.

A truck passed by in the opposite lane, its exhaust drowning out his response. He clamped his mouth down and nodded solemnly. Callow nodded back.

"We need more face bashing and less drinking and drag racing," he said with a smile. "Take care of yourself, Agent Callow. Hope to see you on Wednesday." Suddenly, his face darkened. "And watch your back. There's another wacko around here, and something doesn't taste right."

Callow nodded firmly. *How right you are.*

Tony rapped on the top of the Tahoe again, tilted his hat by the brim, and walked back to his cruiser. Callow watched him climb in, turn off his lights, and chirp his siren once before pulling into the stream of traffic that was slowly building with evening commuters.

Callow continued to replay what had happened in her mind, then she glanced at the warning and moved to readjust the scarf around her neck.

Her eyes caught the outline of the fingers, the little light green lines. She counted eight smaller impressions, then two thumbprints that created a butterfly-like shape over her windpipe. She reached up slowly, crossing her arms over her throat but not pressing. Her hands were smaller than the killer's. Colder, too. She remembered how his hands had been strangely warm despite the frigid winter temperature.

Though she didn't squeeze, her breath caught in her throat. Her lungs refused to expand, and her vocal cords refused to contract. She couldn't scream; she could only watch as the memory of her ordeal strangled the life out of her from the inside.

Her eyes grew wide in panic as she bucked in her seat,

arching her back as the air in her lungs was depleted of oxygen.

You died out there, Jenny. Or at least, some part of you did. That part of you suffocated.

She began to beat her fists against the steering wheel—first as an involuntary reflex, then in desperation. Over and over, she slammed her palms and then her balled fists against the wheel. Her vision grew blurry at the edges, and sweat formed on her forehead from the struggle.

Slowly, everything began to fade.

Then, the killer was on top of her, reaching down, wrapping his fingers tightly across her throat, choking the life out of her.

She could feel him. Smell his sweat. Feel his hot breath against her face. See his face, twisted into an animalistic snarl.

She imagined herself prying at his fingers one by one—until a lifesaving breath of air filled her lungs. She heaved once, held it for a moment, then blew it out sharply. She repeated this maneuver—the one she'd been taught while in recovery at the hospital—until her vision slowly returned: a wash of colors becoming a clearly discernible highway, a fading sun, row upon row of red taillights, and the mute gray interior of her Tahoe.

Slowly, she came around until she could stand to look at herself in the rearview mirror.

Callow realized then, in those moments, that the voice in her head was right. Some part of her hadn't escaped the Red Mud River, and no matter how fast she drove or how reckless she became, she could never outrun her memories.

No matter in which direction she drove—north, toward the airport for a turkey sandwich, or south, back to her home—she could never outrun her memories.

Genevieve Callow was working through something.

CHAPTER TWO

Callow pulled her Tahoe around the jet black Crown Victoria parked against the curb in front of her house. The unmarked police car was a relic that served as a red flag to crooks casing the streets of her quaint, white picket suburb. The car screamed *"Cop over here!"* —and had been left there for that exact reason. Marcus wasn't one for subtlety.

The other car in the driveway was a modest Camry she'd bought a few years prior with what meager life insurance money her father had left her. The payout was so little, it was almost insulting, but the Camry had been put to good use by her little sister, Rebecca. At the time of the purchase, Rebecca was nineteen and a manager at a local fast food restaurant. Recent events had also warranted that she take the Camry to work, no matter how content she was taking the public bus.

"When some asshole flays a girl and leaves her in the parking lot, taking a car is the *least* of the changes we're making," Callow had told Rebecca after being discharged from the hospital. Her voice had been hoarse back then, and she'd hoped Rebecca could see the difficulty it brought her to speak at all. She hadn't replied, but she had nodded, and as far as Callow was concerned, a single nod from Rebecca was ironclad.

Callow glanced at the clock on the dash. It read 6:00 P.M., which meant Rebecca had been home from work for about thirty minutes. How long Marcus had been there, she didn't know, but even though they'd ended their exclusivity months ago, he still had a key to her townhouse.

Marcus wanted to be more than friends — and had made that clear on many occasions. He often stayed the night, and they sometimes had sex, too. From the outside, their relationship was a complicated mess, but from Callow's perspective, she was protecting Marcus from losing his job by keeping whatever they were behind closed doors. As Senior Special Agent, the Bureau wouldn't take kindly to her relationship with a subordinate.

Still, complicated or not, she was happier with Marcus around.

She turned and smiled softly at the Crown Victoria, a dark knight vigilantly guarding her home. Her pistol and credentials weighed heavily in her arms, and heavier in her heart. Her fondest memories of Marcus were coming back. In a few moments, she'd walk through the door and find him cooking with a confidence reminiscent of someone who'd spent years in culinary school and was at home in their own kitchen. Rebecca would be at the kitchen table, humming along to soft jazz playing from the TV and plugging away at her college homework. Marcus would be humming along with the low notes, smooth and classy, and as she got close, she would feel his voice rumbling in his chest. He'd crack an egg and toss the shell into the sink, or twirl oil in a wok, or tip spices into a boiling pot, working on intuition alone, all the while having a full conversation with her kid sister. The thought of Marcus like that made her heart flutter.

Nervously, Callow checked her reflection in the wing mirror of the Camry. Her eyes were slightly puffy, her hair hastily pulled back into a messy bun. She worked to smooth down the curls to either side of her head to no avail. She gave up, huffed once, walked to the front door, and slipped her keys into the lock, disengaging the dead bolt with a hollow *thunk*.

She was immediately greeted by a blast of cool, refrigerated air tinged with the scent of fresh garlic, steeping tomato sauce, peppers, and wet noodles. Beyond the car and the fresh cooking, his telltale insistence on the frigid temperature and hum of the air conditioner as it struggled to keep the house at sixty-seven degrees cemented Marcus was there, just as she'd imagined.

Callow lifted her nose, like a dog catching a scent, and caught the remnants of bleach in the air. That was a marker for her cousin Shannon, a neat freak, who often stayed at her house to help take care of Rebecca whenever Callow was away. Sure, Rebecca was an adult, but besides Shannon, Callow was all the family she had. She had stressed the importance of keeping family close, and to her surprise, Rebecca didn't disagree.

Shannon, however, was reluctant at first. The conversation was always a version of:

"Why does a full-grown woman need a babysitter? Not that I don't love Rebecca, but do I really need to stay here?"

"Do you need *to? No. Should you? I think so. We need to stick together. With things the way they are … it's not safe."*

Shannon didn't have to be reminded of exactly what Callow meant by "*it's not safe.*" Home wasn't safe.

Callow shook her head, ridding herself of the memory, and twisted the doorknob—once, twice, a third time, each time making sure that the dead bolt had sunk perfectly into the strike plate cavity. She kicked her shoes off by the door, where two other sets waited on a plush mat. She walked through the living room, past the TV, which played a video of a crackling fireplace on a loop.

As she'd expected, Callow saw Rebecca hunched over her book, her legs tucked up under her and balanced on a stool. She didn't look up.

Marcus hovered over the kitchen island across from her, a large butcher knife in hand. An onion rested on the cutting board in front of him, ready to be diced up with expert precision. He looked up and smiled at her out of the corner of his mouth.

The townhome was small—only two bedrooms—but made up for it with a large living room and kitchen that stretched all the way to the master bedroom at the back. But with Marcus in the kitchen, it seemed smaller in size, like a cave some giant had long since outgrown.

Callow stopped and met eyes with her partner. The slight upturn at the corner of Marcus's mouth slipped and spread across his whole face. He set the knife down and smoothed his black hair back from where it had bunched together in waves.

Callow loved the way he ran his fingers through it. As he did so, she could see the outline of his muscles through his gray pullover. Marcus Oakley could command a room with his presence and charm a woman with his thoughtful words and devilish looks. But it was his voice, that *resonance*, the thundering baseline that made him terrifying once angry.

"Feel like helping me cut up this onion?" Marcus asked. "They always make my eyes water."

Transfixed by the chemistry between them, Callow realized that she still stood in the living room. She kept her eyes locked on his as she plopped herself down at the table beside Rebecca.

Her younger sister looked up. "It's the acid. Onions are acidic."

Callow eyed her sister. She and Rebecca shared similar features, though Rebecca's eyes were dark brown with flecks of gold, and she had higher cheekbones and a smaller frame.

Callow considered herself stocky, "*filled in.*" Rebecca, by contrast, was quite dainty.

Rebecca turned back to her book and brushed her silky black hair behind her ear. "He's been here for an hour … *cooking*." She spoke the last word while delighting in her use of air quotes to accompany it.

Marcus twisted the knife in Callow's direction. "That's not *entirely* true. I wanted to make sure I was here when Rebecca got home."

His comment caused Rebecca to look up, shake her head, and reply with a blank face, "He's lying. He just wanted to make dinner for you. Shannon left about forty-five minutes ago, meaning he had already started cooking while she was still here. Honestly, I wish you two would just admit you're together, rather than claiming you're not."

An awkward silence followed, broken only by Marcus's renewed chopping.

"I got a call a few minutes ago," he said, changing the conversation for Callow's benefit as well as his own.

Callow raised an eyebrow. "From whom?"

"A trooper."

She rolled her eyes. "So what?"

"So, he said he's worried about you. What happened?"

Callow twirled a few rogue strands of hair. "Nothing you need to worry about." She frowned, unable to mask her irritation. "Are there any cops you *don't* know? I hate that he even called you."

Marcus appeared deep in thought, calculating the right words to say. He knew he was heading into dangerous territory. Callow knew it, too.

"Look, Tony and I go way back, and all he said was he's worried about you. Is that really so bad? He said it seemed as though you had a lot on your mind. He said you were driving *way* too fast. Somewhere near a hundred miles an hour."

He slid the knife down the cutting board and dropped the onions into a pan of boiling water.

"I *do* have a lot on my mind, but it's none of his business. None of yours either." She feigned defensiveness, but Marcus wasn't buying it. His eyebrows were still raised, and worry lines cut across the unblemished skin on his forehead.

"When are you getting married?" Rebecca jeered.

"You're not the first person to ask that," Callow said, throwing her a death stare.

She recalled the same question being asked by Detective Hank Juarez of the El Paso Police Department. He'd worked with Callow and Marcus on the Red Mud River case and had been exposed to similar banter between them. "Hank ..." she recalled, her mouth twisting into a genuine smile.

"Speaking of Hank," Marcus said, drawing a glass of water from the tap and sliding it across the granite countertop toward her. "He also called earlier."

"Called where? The house? You?"

"The office. He *claimed* he was asking for information about recruitment, but at thirty-six, he's way over the cutoff age. Bet he knows it, too. Plus, he called down directly to your office and left a message. He had to skip Recruiting to reach your line."

Callow released the hairs she'd been toying with while they spoke. Now, they were just frizzy and drifted annoyingly against her cheek.

"I'll call him back," she replied. "I reckon he wants to talk about the case."

Marcus gave his best impression of the Cheshire Cat's evil grin. "There was one more message." Callow rolled her eyes as he continued. "Apparently, Kennedy has finally made some headway on the Icebox Killer, but he wants a consult. He wants your eyes on the case. Jedediah agreed."

Callow sat back hard in the chair and nearly tipped it over behind her. She tucked her knees up to her chest.

The Icebox Killer. The one who hit too close to home. The one who not only struck home, but had called her out by name.

"Ol' Jed isn't going to make you primary—you have to know that—but a consult means he recognizes your value, even with how personal things are."

But Callow couldn't hear him—she was trapped in a memory. A red and white cooler, its top open and stained with blood, staged as the head on a decapitated woman's body. The cadaver wore jeans, a cream sweater, and black mid-rise boots, and her arms and legs were sprawled out in the snow as though she was making a snow angel. Her skin was frosted over—bluish in some places, black and decayed in others. A simple silver bracelet on her wrist. A charm on the bracelet— half a heart marked with her initials…

Carmen Watts was her best friend—and one of the Icebox Killer's victims.

Callow hugged her knees. She could feel Rebecca's eyes digging into the side of her face—and Marcus's, too, as he looked down on her from over a pot of homemade tomato sauce. Desperately, she forced her mind to clear; to remove the image ingrained there of her best friend's remains, on display for all the world to gawk at.

"Is Jedediah going to apologize for El Paso? For not trusting my intuition?" Callow asked, muffled by her knees. She stealthily sniffed back her tears and realized the day's odors were permeating through her clothes. She desperately needed a shower, but she couldn't get herself to move. At least Marcus and Rebecca were here. She was grateful for that.

"It sounds like he's going to apologize, but not for missing your calls while on the case. He said he was in briefings with the bigwigs at the time, catching them up on whatever leads we had."

"What about the box with the message? The one Icebox sent to the hospital."

Marcus chuckled, but it sounded forced. "We couldn't pull any trace evidence from the charm or the box it was delivered in. It seems Icebox wiped it all clean. Smart little shit."

Marcus turned the burner off.

Callow recalled the package she'd been given while recovering in the hospital: a small, innocent box containing the matching half of a charm she'd given Carmen years ago. Inside the box had been a note.

See you soon.

But Callow had been doing her job long enough to know what the charm and the message really meant. It was a threat.

"See you soon" actually meant, *"Back off. I see you. I know who you are. I know who your family is. Stay away."*

Callow wandered down the hallway as Marcus began divvying up the pasta and ladling sauce while Rebecca set the table with fresh silverware. He didn't call after her, and Callow didn't offer an explanation. Everything hurt. Her neck hurt. Her fists hurt. Her heart hurt.

Closing the door to the master bedroom, she set her mind on a shower. One step at a time. A shower, then dinner.

But as the warm water ran off the back of her head, over her face, and down her chest, so, too, did the tears.

CHAPTER THREE

Callow wiped away the fog that now obscured the mirror. A plush maroon towel was wrapped snuggly over her breasts. Bubbles she'd missed crackled in her ear. She smelled of lavender rather than sweat, and her hair was no longer greasy and unkempt. She swiped lower on the mirror so she had a clear view of her neck.

The hot water had reddened her skin, effectively hiding the bruises until they were only faint outlines of fingers, like little half-moons. Though they were fading with time, in her mind, the marks were still fresh. The man who had given them to her was Theodore Carson, and now, no matter how hard she tried, she would never forget his face.

Pronounced chin. Permanent stubble. Neatly combed hair. Almond-shaped eyes. Eyebrows—thick, bushy.

There was nothing remarkable about Carson. He was the next-door neighbor. The average commuter. The innocuous stranger.

And so, when Callow saw anyone, she saw *him.*

She eyed the scarf laying across the toilet seat. She'd gotten used to wearing it now, even in her own house. It was as much for her as it was to avoid prying eyes; the half-assed looks of pity that said, "*Oh, honey! Do you need help? Oh, honey, did someone hurt you?*"

Callow hated the pity. She'd not only survived being strangled to death, but she'd escaped and pummeled the would-be killer until he sucked on his own teeth. If she focused on that last part, she felt a sense of accomplishment, a triumph over evil, a swelling in her heart that said, "*go back to work. You can survive anything now.*"

But it wasn't so simple. You couldn't just walk away from a life-or-death confrontation and go on about your merry way, could you?

Callow liked that version of herself compared to the scared victim mentality. A part of her *wanted* to chase down the Icebox Killer; the same part of her that knew she couldn't stand to watch someone else cave his face in. She wanted it to be *her*.

The scarf loomed over the toilet, a limp blue snake that spent most of the day draped around her throat, claiming it for its own.

She shook her head. Despite surviving being strangled, she sure spent a lot of time reminding herself of what happened.

Hands propped on her hips, Callow huffed air out of her nose, reached for the scarf, then stopped herself mid-grab. She retreated, taking a step backward. Every fiber of her being called her to reach for the scarf; to remember its comforting grasp around her neck, the itchy wool fibers that stank when they got wet or sweaty, her shield against gawkers and neck-benders who wanted a quick peek. But she didn't give in.

Show them off, survivor. Show them off.

Her mother's voice dominated her brainwaves, injecting directly into her thoughts.

Someone knocked three times on the door. Judging by the weight behind the knock, it was Marcus.

"Yes?" Callow asked, turning her back on the scarf.

The door opened slowly, a respectful crack. "Are you okay? You've been in here a while."

"Does Rebecca know you're in here?" Callow asked, one eyebrow raised.

"She fell asleep on the couch. I tried to coax her up, but she wouldn't budge."

Callow's heart thumped twice out of step, and her stomach twisted into a knot. She opened the door slowly. Marcus stood in the doorway, a bowl of noodles and a spoon in his hand.

"I brought you this. I figured you wanted to be alone. There's plenty more if you want it."

Callow took the bowl. It smelled of sweet tomatoes, garlic, and beef. "Thank you."

Marcus turned to leave.

"Wait. Where are you going?"

He offered a kind, tired smile. "Despite what Rebecca said, I'm actually here for more than making dinner. It's my shift guarding the house."

Callow was taken aback. "Wait, what? Since when? Who else is pulling overwatch?"

"Me, Jedediah, Kennedy, Samson … Oh, and Wainwright, too."

"Who's Wainwright?"

Marcus smiled mischievously. "Your rookie, whenever you come back to work. He's been assigned to Samson for now. We've been pulling overnights. Locals are tied up and can't spare us a uniform. We'll keep it up until Icebox is caught."

Callow was speechless. Providing her with extra security was surely dragging the team down. She hated the idea of being responsible for long overtime shifts. She hated being in the limelight and in the media, and she hated the lasting effects the events at Red Mud River seemed to have on her, despite the fact that Carson was rotting away in some cell somewhere.

"I didn't ask for any of this," Callow said simply.

"And we didn't ask if you wanted it. We volunteered, unanimously. Once we confirmed the match on Carmen's bracelet, we knew it was a threat against you and your family. You'd do the same for us."

Callow felt a swell of adoration for her team. They had pulled together to ensure her family's safety. They were working overtime to protect her, missing out on time spent with their own families in order to do so. She thought how she might word her thanks, but nothing seemed good enough to explain how she felt. What came out seemed overly simplistic.

"Thank you … for everything," she finally managed to say.

Marcus gave a curt nod. "I'll be in the car. It'll be a few hours until I'm relieved."

Callow chased after him and grabbed his hand. "Stay inside? At least on the couch?"

Marcus shook his head. "Jedediah was specific: outside and vigilant. Oh, don't give me that look—you know where I'd rather be." He lifted her arm to his lips and planted a single soft kiss on top of her hand. "Besides, I've got an audiobook I need to finish. Trust me, I'll be okay."

CHAPTER FOUR

The following morning brought a stark contrast to Callow's dreams. Outside her bedroom window, an ancient oak with brown flowers scratched at the glass, dew hanging on the skeletal branches as the unabashed sunlight cast hopeful golden rays throughout the room. But while the new day seemed to signal hope, Callow wrestled with her pillow and sheets, fighting for a comfortable position.

It'd be impossible to sleep, anyway. For every time she closed her eyes, Callow saw Carmen's face, petrified in a forever look of terror, her head placed inside an icebox. The image taunted her again and again until eventually, after she had scrunched her eyes and rolled over, Carmen became Rebecca, and all hope of rest was truly lost.

6:00 A.M. came quickly, a sharp wail from the alarm clock notifying her that it was acceptable to get out of bed and start the day. Callow kicked off the sheets, swung her legs over the side of the bed, and lifted her arms in a deep stretch. A dizzying yawn followed, and she groaned.

Today is going to be a long day.

Peering out the window through the white Roman blinds, she spotted a white unmarked Charger parked a few yards back from the house's mailbox—an ominous sentry, hidden behind tinted glass. Callow didn't recognize the car; most agents used Crown Victorias or Tahoes, like her. But a Charger wasn't entirely unusual, and it wasn't uncommon for the FBI to buy old police cruisers and outfit them for their needs.

Callow stepped out into the hallway and walked toward the kitchen. She moved about the kitchen like a drone, locating coffee beans, a filter, and a cup, all in a robotic stupor. She added water to a set of three succulents—little green sprouts that could survive even a nuclear fallout. They were the perfect houseplant: small, slow-growing, minimal effort. Perfect for someone who was gone at odd hours on a moment's notice.

Within minutes, the aroma of steaming fresh coffee filled the bottom floor of the townhome and Callow sat at the end of the kitchen table with her phone, ready to scroll through its various applications until the day presented her with something more to do.

By the time she'd gone through her emails, Callow was caught off guard by Rebecca wandering down from her upstairs bedroom with narrow eyes and an oversized hoodie. Callow eyed her, then pretended to watch a video on her phone. Tension rose to a palpable level until Rebecca pulled open a drawer built into the table and tossed a plain manila folder down like a fish needing to be scaled.

"I read through this," Rebecca said in her usually cold, dry tone. The way she spoke and the words she chose were purposeful. She always assumed that same tone when she was inevitably drawn back into Callow's case. It sounded so odd coming from a young woman, to sound jaded beyond her years.

Callow glared at her. She knew what was in that case file—the images, the reports, all of it. They each painted a lucid picture better meant as a script for a horror movie. In a way, the file *was* a horror movie, for the synopsis—the brutal butchering of women and the systematic placement of their bodies—was more akin to a George Romero picture than reality. Nobody ever thinks, *"This can happen to me."*

"Why? Why on earth would you go through that?" Callow said heatedly, untucking her leg from under her, which had started to go numb.

"To help," Rebecca countered. "Fresh eyes. New ideas. That sort of thing."

Callow felt ashamed for leaving the file out; she should have known better. Rebecca was inquisitive—a problem solver, like her. Even as a child, she would rather have worked on a complex math project in complete silence than play outside. In third grade, she'd established the pattern by which the teachers assigned homework classes, allowing her to finish the entire school year's worth of homework in three months. This, of course, didn't exclude Rebecca from the assigned work, but it was never about that. It was simply a matter of proving she could.

Callow sighed, realizing that if Rebecca was confessing to reading through the packet and was giving it back, it meant she'd learned something.

"Did you figure something out?"

Her sister nodded, reached over the table, and held out the file. Callow hesitated to look, contemplating the manila file folder like a poisonous spider sat waiting on top of it, then gave in and gave it her attention. She *had* to know.

Rebecca shared the same stubborn blood; the curious drive of an investigator. She was calculated and practical, almost to a fault, leaving behind what some would call a cold, callous exterior. Callow knew her sister better. She had a very direct way of conveying her emotions: her unwavering gaze, her expressionless face, and the slight flicker of a twitching eyebrow said it all.

She had found something, and Callow needed to know.

Rebecca flipped the folder over with practiced grace until she landed on the first evidence photo—a young girl, mid-twenties, her arms spread out to make a snow angel. Pools of congealed blood formed a dark circle near where her head was supposed to be. It was an image that shouldn't exist, and looking at it was like a photo of someone with hundreds of eyes within a single eye, or hundreds of holes pockmarking the bottom of a heel. Trypophobia, it was called—categorized by an irrational fear of clusters of holes.

Irrational. Was she being irrational not wanting to review the evidence packet again and again, looking for evidence? Or was it irrational to leave stones unturned when she was one of the few who could help deliver answers to Carmen's family?

Avoiding looking at the photograph of her mutilated friend wasn't irrational. It epitomized self-preservation. Carmen's death was something that shouldn't have happened. The irrationality came from not being able to separate the personal from the professional.

"Show me," Callow said.

Rebecca dutifully reached across the table and turned the folder around so Callow could look at it right side up. Rebecca flipped through several reports detailing the state of Carmen's body and the evidence collected, then a medical examiner's report which outlined in detail all that had been done to her, both while she was alive and once she was dead. Finally, Rebecca turned to a map of the area showing the city limits of Colleyville.

Callow looked over the page. On it were two crosses in red marker at two different locations. She immediately recognized the crosses as the locations where the victims' bodies had been found.

"This isn't part of the evidence packet," Callow observed.

"It's not, but it might be after I show you this." Rebecca dropped her finger on the first cross. "The first victim and the second." She followed the crosses in a clockwise motion, indicating the points on a compass. "Two victims, four points on a compass. Your next victim might end up around here." Rebecca circled the southeast area with her finger. "This is a five-mile scale map, so your perp…"

"Unsub," Callow corrected. "Unsub" was a term for the unidentified subject of the investigation.

" … *Unsub* might live within the radius of the four points. I admit it's a long shot, but what if he's following the points on a compass?"

Callow's eyes narrowed on the page, then her shoulders drooped. "It's a good idea—except for this." She pointed to the intersection of Cooley and Smith, nearly ten miles south from the first dump site. "Carmen's body was found here, on the south side of town. There's a mistake in the report. Someone put her home address as the crime location."

Rebecca slid her finger off to the left on the map. It looked so strange, separated from the other marks on the page; an outlier that meant Rebecca hadn't really found anything at all. Callow looked at her sister. For once, she could see the powerful emotions running roughshod across her face, breaking apart her hardened exterior like drought wrought clay, cracking and crumbling.

"I hate this, Jen," Rebecca said, dipping her head. Callow immediately grew concerned; this wasn't usual for her. Callow hadn't seen her sister cry in a long time. It was almost weird in a way, like a double rainbow or a mirage from sunbaked concrete. She'd begun to think Rebecca didn't cry at all.

"I'm sorry, Bec. I really am. I know it's dangerous, but…" Callow tried to reach out, but her sister pulled away, her face torn by a scowl.

Rebecca's eyes swam with tears that had yet to fall. "I'm not scared, Jen. I'm *angry*."

"'Angry?' Why?"

"Because you *could* catch him. It's what you do. You're happy at work. You're confident at work. I can tell you're miserable—and don't even try to blame it on Carmen. You're pretending staying away is honorable, that you're protecting me or Shannon when, in fact, you're just running away from your responsibilities."

Callow was taken aback. Rebecca had never said this much in one sitting, especially not lit by such emotion.

"Whoa, now, I'm not running. I'm a consultant to the case …"

"That's bullshit, and you know it, Jen! Even if you're consulting, you have the same access to all the files as anyone else on the case. I'm not even an FBI agent and I know that to provide any consultations, you need access to the facts. You're on the case, but you're not. You're here, playing Suzy Homemaker with your little boy toy. It's been *weeks* since the Icebox Killer called you out, and instead of going after him, you cowered in your castle."

"That's unfair, Rebecca! You don't know what I'm going through." Callow's hands had begun to shake, and she gripped the table for support.

Rebecca sniffed hard and wiped away the free-falling tears with the back of her hand. "Don't I?"

She swung her black purse around the back of the chair she was sitting on, opened the top, and dove her hand to the bottom. She withdrew her hand quickly and slammed down whatever she was holding onto the table between them.

Callow stared down in disbelief. She was looking at the butt of a snub-nosed revolver.

"Smith and Wesson .38 Special … This was Dad's."

Callow sniffed. She could see Rebecca's stony face returning by the second.

"You can't carry this, sis," Callow warned. "You're not old enough, and you don't have a license."

"What's that shit you used to say when you hid a pistol

under the seat of Dad's old jeep? You'd rather be judged by twelve ..."

"... Than carried by six. This is different, Bec." The expression *"I'd rather be judged by twelve than carried by six"* was a proverb that meant when a person finds themselves in a tough situation with an impossible decision, it is wiser to act decisively and be judged by a jury than killed through inaction.

"How? How is it different? As far as I'm concerned, things are worse now than they were then. Ten years ago, you didn't have a serial killer dropping bodies in the drive-through. Ten years ago, when you were in high school, you weren't a hotshot FBI profiler. Now, you have a real chance of fixing things. Instead, you're wallowing in your own self-pity and hiding when you could be out doing something."

"It's not that simple." Callow started to reach for the gun, but Rebecca snatched it up, popped open the cylinder, and ejected the five silver rounds into her palm.

"I've been practicing. Call it in yourself. Hell, arrest me for carrying it if you want—because I looked it up myself. It's a class B misdemeanor. Way I see it, either I risk a class B misdemeanor, or I risk being a victim. At my age and without a criminal history, I won't even be prosecuted for illegally carrying a firearm and using it to defend myself, so go ahead and try. Yet one more example of you doing nothing when you could have been doing something."

Callow was stunned. Her voice choked up in her throat, jammed beneath a knot of emotions. She remained silent, struggling to find the words that would accurately convey how she was feeling. She felt deep sorrow for Rebecca, accepting the realization that her sister wasn't just growing up, she was being *forced* to grow up, quickly and in the worst possible circumstances. She also felt anger toward her, but she knew the anger was misplaced. She wasn't mad at Rebecca for carrying a gun illegally; she was mad at herself for letting it happen—for leaving her sister in a position where she felt she *had* to defend herself. But most of all, she felt a despair that only came from failure; the firsthand witness of opportunity slipping through her grasp like catching a handful of water from a hose. That opportunity was Rebecca's innocence —her childhood, ruined. And rather than working to fix it—she was doing nothing at all.

Callow met Rebecca's eyes.

"That's what I thought," Rebecca said.

She balled her fist, dropped the rounds into the chamber, spun the wheel, and pressed it shut in a practiced movement. She tucked the .38 into her purse.

Callow's knees felt filled with cement, her mind a blank slate. She watched her sister leave—not storming off, but walking up the stairs confident and secure. Rebecca had made a decision—a decision to act, to protect herself rather than play neutral and hope for the best. She had taken back some control from the Icebox Killer, where the payoff was sweeter.

If it ever came down to her using the gun, no jury would ever convict Rebecca of the charge. But to Callow, it came down to much more than that.

Rebecca had chosen to act.

"Judged by twelve or carried by six," she said, repeating the age-old phrase under her breath.

Leaving the case file open on the counter, Callow walked out the kitchen door in a haze and sat on a wicker chair facing out onto their postage stamp yard.

On the other side of the subdivision, the sun was beginning to rise, cutting at the chill that had sunk deep into Callow's bones.

CHAPTER FIVE

Callow's mind was a whirlwind.

Snippets of her conversation with Rebecca and random pieces of evidence from the case file mixed into an amalgamation of confusion. Going back to sleep with a belly full of coffee was an impossibility, while an early morning run gave a sense of productivity, as though she was accomplishing something very few people could or would want to do. Perhaps then her mind could rest.

Callow slipped into a pair of black leggings and a yellow hoodie marked "FLORIDA!" and tied her running shoes. She'd never been to Florida; the sweatshirt had been a gift from Marcus after he'd spent a training week in the Florida Keys while Callow was assigned as an attaché to Richmond Homicide. Marcus had given it to her wrapped in a garbage bag, and it smelled of the same cheap plastic. She didn't remember much about unraveling it other than the shit-eating grin on his face and his budding tan.

She thought it was only fair to sweat in it.

On her way out the door, Callow swiped the spare house key on its pink lanyard from a rack on the wall and tucked it under the sweatshirt, pressed her ear buds into her ears, and took off from the front porch at a leisurely jog. The air hummed with crickets, and the exhaust from a weathered gray Crown Victoria pumped fumes into the air. A subdued white light from inside the car indicated the agent within was watching a movie on his cell phone. Callow ran around the front of the car, waved, and kept moving. The driver flashed his headlights in acknowledgment.

The crisp morning air stung as it slipped into her nose and cooled her lungs. A cold fire brewed in her chest, demanding all her attention to maintain her pace. Deep, thoughtful breaths, in her nose and out her mouth, became a pace-setting cadence, her footfalls the baseline, and soon, Callow was running to her own music. She fell into the pace quickly, letting the key bounce off her neck.

She ran two blocks north, cutting left on Sheffield so she could run past the big house at the end of the street. It was the largest of all the houses in the neighborhood, set on a double lot, and towering above the rows of townhomes, it sat like a king amongst its subjects.

Callow felt the freeing sensation that came with a run. If she kept her pace, she couldn't think about work, Rebecca, Marcus, or anything else. Her steady breaths acted as a mental shield, allowing her mind to free itself. Sleep should have been her reprieve from what would soon come with the day, but her body had betrayed her—her mind, too, refusing to wind down and instead fizzing with things she wished she'd said to Rebecca. Now, her mind was forced to concentrate on nothing other than the chill creeping its way up her sleeves and the burning in her lungs.

Passing the big house, Callow prepared for a sharp left that would bring her onto yet another quarter mile stretch. Combined, the three left turns would eventually lead her in a circuit straight home and equal nearly a mile in length. Now that she was in a rhythm, the second mile would come much easier.

Callow banked left, her feet darting as she narrowly avoided a brick outcropping and several potted plants. She corrected and returned to the sidewalk, forced into a comfortable but narrow posture to avoid elbowing the mailboxes on her right and the brick flower gardens on her left. Each house seemed to be set on a hill, with steep driveways that gave the impression they were turning their nose up at simple passersby. Callow ignored the snobbish homes and instead focused on the second left-hand turn.

No more than ten steps past the big house, a set of ultra bright LED headlights illuminated her backside, silhouetting her in the dark and casting shadows that bounced off every mailbox. Though the car was coming up behind her, Callow tried to ignore it, but the ultra bright lights ruined her night vision. She counted the paces in her head.

One hundred. One hundred and fifty. Two hundred.

Still, the headlights illuminated her backside. They didn't fade as they would if she were running away and the car was standing still. No, they kept the same brightness, the same intensity, maintaining the same distance behind her.

No worries. Left-hand turn coming up. Then they'll move on. They're just being curious and don't want to pass.

Callow removed her ear buds and listened intently. She heard slow rolling tires crunching gravel; the ominous hum of a radiator fan; the angry squeak of old brakes as the car slowed to maintain the distance between them. She had a fleeting thought that the vehicle was just one of the agents following her on her run, but then she remembered that none of the vehicles in the BAU fleet were equipped with high-intensity headlights. Once this thought came to mind, Callow increased her pace.

The distraction caused her to throw off her count and rhythm, and consequently, when she rounded the second left-hand turn, she clipped her elbow on the mailbox on the corner, resulting in the hollow *thunk* of sleeve-covered bone on aluminum and a wave of pain that broke her concentration.

Callow winced, hobbling awkwardly as she cradled her elbow. She massaged it in circles, but every heartbeat sent a wave of burning pain shooting up her arm and into her shoulder. Her pace began to suffer, and she slowed to a jog. Still, the car followed her, maintaining its position a hundred paces or so behind.

She suddenly wanted to be home—not cutting across yards, not running up to the house, but inside, warm, and safe behind a locked door. Her pacing couldn't keep her worries at bay. Soon, gradually worsening images invaded her thoughts.

A man in a ski mask, hopping out of his car and tossing her into the trunk.

A figure whose face is no more than a shadow, chasing her down in the dark, wielding a scalpel.

A man who ignores her, passes by, and makes it to her house, dragging a screaming Rebecca by her hair across the front lawn and into the trunk of his car.

Or a man with neatly combed hair, a pronounced chin, and thick, bushy eyebrows reaching for her throat …

These morbid thoughts only prompted her to speed up more than she could maintain. Soon, her lungs were filled again with frost, her legs growing heavy with lactic acid and starting to burn, her heart screaming for a break. Callow's maintainable pace became a tear-laden, babbling sprint. Snot flowed from her nose and over her lips, and each outward breath blew it over her chin.

She began to pray. She prayed for Rebecca—and for herself. She prayed that whoever was behind her would just get it over with—take her, and let this be done. She prayed she could stop running, as her body was wrought with panic-inducing pain.

The final turn came into view, yet the car still kept its

distance. She felt a glimmer of hope as she saw the wisps of the Crown Victoria's exhaust fumes rising in the distance, but she couldn't scream for help. It took every fiber of her being to keep up her pace and repress the anxiety of what might happen.

Why is it just following me? Is it waiting to see where I go? Isn't it obvious I'm heading home?

Callow was two hundred and fifty strides away. Upon seeing her house, she felt a quick burst of rejuvenating energy that invigorated her lungs. For a moment, nothing hurt quite as bad.

Two hundred. One hundred and fifty.

She counted the paces in her head. Her home grew larger, rising from the small hillside—a castle at the end of a long, perilous journey.

Callow watched the surrounding shadows grow, stretching, widening, as the vehicle closed the distance. This was it. She'd need to cross the street in front of him. If he was going to take her, this would be it.

She could only hope the last of her energy would be enough to outrun her pursuer.

One hundred. Seventy-five.

Callow could see the front door. She pulled her key out from beneath the neckline of her sweatshirt. Fresh tears left salty streaks down her face. Fresh snot ran from her nose and coated her lips.

This is it. Cut across the Crown. Let him see you!

With a final breath, she increased her stride, sucked in a shallow breath of frigid air, and cut across the street, aiming for the hood of the Crown Victoria. The awaiting car hummed gently, spewing fumes out the tailpipe. She hopped the curb with feline grace, giving a split-second manic wave to the agent in the car and barreling for the front door.

Her world was a blur. In an oxygen-deprived stupor, she slammed the key home and twisted it in the lock, whirling around the door and slipping inside, an image of the killer sprinting up the front lawn to meet her, the agent's dying body strewn over the hood of the car, the attacker with a scalpel, glinting in the early sunlight.

But as Callow turned and seized the door with both hands, preparing to slam it shut, she saw none of these things. She caught a glimpse of the car with the bright headlights, its red taillights illuminated as it pulled up at a stop sign at the intersection a block away. In its back window was a little neon-colored sign.

Uber.

Callow fell back against the wall, allowing herself to slide down, unable to control her breathing from the breakneck pace. Adrenaline coursed through her veins, warming her from the inside out and making her forget about her bruised elbow. Through the war drum beat of her heart pumping blood through her ears, she heard the distant but familiar squeak of old hinges and the slamming of a car door. She twisted over, hand over her heart, as a figure walked up her front lawn and knocked twice.

"Callow? Jenny? Are you all right?" a voice said through the door, boyish and unfamiliar.

"Who … are … you?" she asked between ragged breaths.

The man on the other side of the door pushed it gently open and stepped into the dark, moonlit hall. He smiled. "I'm your new partner."

CHAPTER SIX

Callow remained in a crumpled heap on the floor. Hair disheveled, her breath came and went in short, unsatisfying draws. She wasn't so much physically hurt as she was embarrassed. Call it stress or paranoia, it didn't matter. None of what she'd thought was happening had been real. Instead, her mind had created a construct to fit her perfect, terrifying paranoia, flooding her body with adrenaline and pushing it beyond its limits at a breakneck pace that should have been reserved only for life-or-death scenarios.

Her face was flushed from the run, an opportune mask hiding the embarrassment coursing through her. The sting of the elbow she'd clipped during her mad dash was nothing compared to her bruised ego.

The boyish-sounding man stood in her doorway, tall and lanky. He turned on the lights in the foyer before offering his hand to help pick her up.

Callow met his eyes, then grasped the hand and allowed herself to be yanked to her feet. She immediately began righting her hair and clothes.

"I'm Wainwright. Curtis. But my friends call me Kurt. You must be Genevieve."

Callow winced. "Callow. Everyone calls me Callow."

"Ah, yes, ASAC Gold did tell me that. I apologize."

Callow eyed her elbow, then brushed herself off. It was a clerical act, meant to say she was done recovering. There wasn't anything on her besides pools of sweat under her armpits, staining the yellow hoodie. "Well, Kurt, I need water and a shower. You can stay for the first part."

She twisted around and made for the kitchen without checking to see if he was following her. She gathered a glass from the cabinets and filled it from the refrigerator.

She turned back around to find Kurt standing over the open case file on the kitchen table. She took stock of him in an instant. Tall, skinny—a runner, perhaps? He had a mop of blond curly hair, a squared jaw, and emerald eyes that looked down a large, sharp nose. His skin was fair, and his cheeks were rosy from the chill. The woefully apparent absence of the hint of a beard gave him an even more juvenile appearance.

Callow sipped the water. Kurt looked up casually.

"So, why the BAU?" Callow inquired over the glass. She saw no reason not to jump straight to it. "You're young. There's much more going on in the field."

The water only helped her scorched windpipe a little. She was trying to appear hardened, weatherworn from years of long hours and takeout boxes in seedy motel rooms. That way, she could see if he mirrored her behavior in an attempt to fit in. Then she could see if he was a fake.

He walked cautiously, heel-toe, his shoes clicking on the tile floor. His fingers draped lazily over the granite countertop.

"I accept I'm younger than most agents. I'm twenty-six. But it makes sense, really. The FBI is moving away from the seniority-trumps-logic mentality and is now placing people where they belong." He stopped in front of her and narrowed his eyes. "I scored top of my class in criminology, definitions, math, and the sciences. I'm fluent in French, and I have a degree in digital forensics."

"But …?" Callow asked, one eyebrow raised. She knew there had to be one. She took another disinterested sip of the water, clearly defying the young agent's showboating.

"But I was the lowest-scoring agent in combatives, marksmanship, physical fitness, and control tactics."

Callow snorted. "So, you're a brain without a body."

Kurt shrugged, prompting his bony shoulders to appear through his black corduroy sweater. "Don't use a hammer when you need a computer."

Callow instantly felt a palpable dislike for his attitude, but knowing Jedediah handpicked all members of the BAU from the Academy or from the field, there had to be a reason for Wainwright's appointment to the position. Computer or not, he would have to learn the basics of field agent work through her, as well as the specialized criminal profiling techniques each member of the team mastered and made their own.

Callow decided to ease off the interrogation a bit to see what she could glean from him, and therefore, Jedediah's thinking. A new agent wasn't uncommon, but a new agent assigned to the Senior Special Agent was. Assigning her a rookie added yet another piece to the enigma.

Yet a final piece of information really muddied the waters. "Why me? There are other agents who aren't nearly as … *indisposed* as I am."

Kurt didn't shift his eyes. She could see his mind at work, formulating, calculating. She felt as if she was looking at the inner workings of an electron microscope rather than a person. She turned away and gathered up a glass of water for Kurt.

"You've been involved in the capture of more than four serial killers in the last six years, three of whom were because of your own investigative skills. The other agents can't come close. You're the best. But you run on intuition. I've seen body camera footage of your techniques." He slid out a bar stool from under the countertop and sat down. "I want to see if logic beats intuition."

Callow's hand hovered over the sink. Two could play his little game of cat and mouse; this test of mental might to see who might gain the proverbial leg up on the other. Kurt was showing he was well researched and testing her ability as Senior Special Agent. He was throwing facts like fireballs, and it was up to her whether to defend or attack. But what was most impressive was his willingness to do it right in her own living room.

The kid has balls, I'll give him that. But does it come from capability or overconfidence?

Callow set the glass down in front of him and pressed it forward, so it slid across the surface with a shrill grind. "So, why not work in a think tank? Or go to college and study medicine? Why the FBI?"

"Maybe I'll do those things next. I like problems. I like solving them. Finding more unanswerable problems and solving those, too. Tell me, Callow, why do serial killers do what they do?"

Here it was—the philosophical test, the moment where Kurt would test her mettle. But to Callow, it worked both ways; now, she'd be able to test his, too.

"I think it's simpler than most people believe. Psychoanalysts, doctors, criminal profilers—they all think of it like a switch. Something curable, fixable, or preventable. I believe it's much less complicated than that. It's good and evil. There are those who are called upon to do good, and others who are commanded to do evil."

"Interesting," Kurt said, dipping his finger in the glass and then running it around the rim so it hummed. "So, you don't think it's mental health related? No trauma-induced psychosis or religious dogma that festered from a young age until it became a brain-eating amoeba? Your simple solution is that God and Satan are warring for space within someone's heart, and now and then Satan wins, leaving someone to run amok with a scalpel and their lunchbox?"

For the first time since they'd met, Callow smiled. "That's where you have a lot to learn, rookie. Our job isn't to figure them out; our job is to *find* them and try not to fall apart along the way. 'Good versus evil' helps me explain it to myself. Good and evil means I have a choice. I choose to do good. Take away that choice, and all you're left with is people doing unspeakable things for no reason at all, and that is truly terrifying."

Callow let her statement rest. She could see from the expressionless look on Kurt's face that he was desperately putting together something to say that would close the loop on the conversation—something highbrow that would leave her with something short and translucent like *"maybe"* or *"we'll see."* But after fifteen seconds of staring, Kurt's eyes wobbled, and he picked up the glass and drank from it.

Gotcha, you smug bastard.

"I'm going to take a shower. Would you like to continue this *enlightening* conversation in the bathroom?" she asked, her tone clear *she* was shutting the conversation down.

Kurt rolled his arm and lifted the sleeve of his sweater. "My shift is over. Agent Oakley should be on next." He got up from the stool. "Thanks for the water."

Callow walked around him to the living room. Kurt followed and paused by the front door. He towered over her by nearly a foot.

"What should I tell Jedediah about when you'll be back?" he asked as Callow opened the door.

"Tell him I don't know."

"And about your little ... *marathon*?"

Callow sighed, hoping he was going to let it go in his defeat in the kitchen. She'd still have to explain why she ran like a frightened fawn across her front lawn and then collapsed inside the door.

"Have you ever had someone try to rip your head off?"

He shook his head.

"There's no logic when that happens. There's being alive or there's being dead. If you're lucky, you're alive—but some shit sticks with you. Better get your weight up and hit the gym, rookie. You can't logic your way out of a fight, and sometimes, that's all there's left to do. If you manage to survive, you'll never be the same."

Kurt slowly crossed the threshold like a wounded puppy, stiff from his waist up. The bitter morning cold was nothing more than a peaceful chill now, and it seemed the sun would rise unencumbered into full glow.

"Come get me in an hour," she said, just before closing the door.

"What for? I'm off duty."

"You're never off duty, rookie, and if I'm going to teach you anything, then that's the first lesson. Come by in an hour, ready to roll."

"Sure thing. Where to?"

"I need groceries," Callow replied, slamming the door before he could reply. She imagined him standing on her porch with a finger up, mouth agape. She threw the lock, then walked to her bedroom.

You won this battle—but only just. He's sharp. Watch your step, Jen—especially if half of what he said about the FBI is true.

CHAPTER SEVEN

Callow stepped out onto the front porch and was blasted by enthusiastic rays of sunlight and a warm breeze that felt out of place for what should have been a heavy winter. The crusted, compacted remains of ice and snow exploded beneath her black knee-high boots. She wore dark jeans and a brown parka, concealing her service pistol underneath. Admittedly, there were times when she didn't carry her Glock, and thinking back, it was foolish not to. The gun wouldn't do her a lot of good in the car if she needed it. So, with a practiced twist-and-pull, she shuffled the weapon in its holster into a better position directly in line with her hip and yanked the front of the parka down a bit to conceal it.

Kurt Wainwright was standing by the driver's side door of an older model Chevrolet Impala only an inch from the curb. He stared blankly as Callow followed the sidewalk to her Tahoe. She took her time parking it in the garage. She recalled a text message she had received while in the shower that said Shannon was taking Rebecca to work and then would be gone for the day, volunteering at the local animal shelter. Callow knew her cousin would arrive back at the house covered in various stains and smelling of wet dog, but she'd be at her happiest for a few days and not nearly as vocal about staying with Callow and Rebecca when Rebecca really could handle her own. Callow wished she could find something to zip her mood up that quick.

Kurt glanced at his wristwatch. The young agent reminded Callow of a praying mantis: large, watchful eyes, overly long, thin arms, and a rigid, upright posture that surely spelled back problems in the future. She pulled on the handle of the passenger's side door and fell into the car. It was sickly warm and humid inside and smelled of hot rubber. The dash showed the defroster was on. A droplet of sweat rolled down her side from her armpit.

She turned the defroster off and stopped. The car was immaculately clean—not a single hair, fingerprint, or stain. It was as if the car was fresh from a lot.

Great. A neat freak. This is going to go well the next time we have to search a sewer for fingernails.

Kurt slid into the driver's seat. "Where to?"

"There's a grocery store a few blocks down. Take your time. Let's talk."

He put the car in drive. "Listen, if this is about earlier …"

Callow put up a hand to cut him off, and his mouth clamped shut mid-sentence.

"If we're going to work together, there's something you have to know," she said. "This isn't a job; it's a *burden*. It's a responsibility and a calling. The hours suck, but the memories suck the worst. You will not be the same person you were the day before. What you have to decide is how much of this will become a part of who you are, or just something you do for money. Don't answer me now; I don't need to hear it. This is between you and whatever deity you call God. It's my job to teach you the skills to stay alive. It's on you to figure out how much weight you can carry."

Once Callow finished, silence hung in the air. After a minute, she looked at Kurt. She saw a softening in his face, a brief flash, a microexpression of sadness or humility, maybe. Perhaps it was understanding or commiseration. Whatever was there, it was fleeting, and it gave Callow hope that Kurt Wainwright was more than a machine assigned to solve a complex problem. A brief flash of emotion, then his cold shield wall returned, staring back at her with callous green eyes.

He gave a nod, indicating that he'd heard her and was processing her advice, then he pulled away from the house and turned right.

"I can tell you care a lot about what you do," Kurt said. He shifted stiffly in his seat. He looked too tall for the car. His bushy hair rubbed against the headliner.

"I care about what happens if I don't. Do you know what's most brutal? It's not seeing a stranger being lowered in the ground; it's when it's your friend in that box and you have to explain to their grieving mother why you didn't catch the killer in time. It's her tears and her wailing, an unconscionable cry of a mother's broken heart that keeps you up at night. What these murderers do is sick, and you compartmentalize what happens to the victims in order to cope, but the everlasting pain is for the family who look you in the eyes and ask you, '*Why didn't you catch him?*'"

Kurt exhaled loudly. "Did that happen to you?"

Callow's mind forced her to remember Carmen, her brown hair freshly curled and resting over her shoulders. Snow swirled in the air and fell into the hole, resting upon her face. It didn't melt. That's what Callow remembered most clearly.

Snow didn't melt on a cold body.

"Carmen hit home," she replied.

"And then the Icebox Killer threatened you?"

She nodded, then lifted her sleeve. She had a small, circular tan line around her wrist where she'd worn her friendship bracelet to the beach over the summer, and the shadow seemed to be taking its time to fade.

"Carmen wore a bracelet—the other half to my own. Icebox mailed it to me while I was in the hospital. It's amazing how such a simple thing can take me out of commission."

Kurt turned into the grocery store parking lot and navigated the cruiser to a parking space near the back so he wouldn't have to back up to get out. It was also far enough away from the other cars that they could see clearly in all directions.

"It wasn't the bracelet. The unsub wanted to torture you; to manipulate your mind. He saw what happened in El Paso. He's worried you'll do the same to him."

"Well, it worked." Callow looked down at her hands. A single line of scar tissue ran up her pointer finger between the first and second knuckles. The doctor had plucked an incisor from her flesh where it'd been lodged in the bone. For a moment, while she'd fought for her life in the sticky, cold mud, a piece of the killer was *in* her. In response, she'd released a violence from deep within; the kind of violence she never thought she was capable of.

A piece of him was inside you. His blood mixed with your blood. Will you do the same to the Icebox Killer? Will you unleash the same rage? The same violence? Step into the mind of a killer, they said ...

You almost became one.

"I'll be right back," Callow said. "Wait here."

"You don't want me to come in?"

"Do you want to help me pick out tampons?"

"I'll wait."

Callow shut the door and went inside. Her feet felt large and awkward, as if her shoes were a few sizes too big. She realized then that what she was feeling above all else was guilt. She felt responsible for Carmen's mother, who'd cried out, *"Where were you?"* She felt responsible for Rebecca, who felt as though she had to act and carry a gun. It was all too much, and so Callow did what all people who can't process their emotions do—she went numb.

The feeling of emptiness consumed her. Her feet were numb, and her heart was numb. For once, pounds were lifted from her shoulders, and she felt as if she could just float away. It made her stomach twist in knots and her breath shallow. She hated how she felt.

With uneasy hands, Callow reached into her back pocket and flashed a membership card to the store clerk waiting just inside the double doors. As she moved to put her wallet back, she noticed a white card poking out from the money pocket. Curiously, Callow retrieved it.

It read: TROOPER TONY MACKERAS. VIRGINIA STATE TROOPERS.

On the back was a faded and smudged handwritten note: *Wednesday, 8:00 P.M. Herman Public Library.*

Callow had forgotten about Tony's invitation. Were there others who felt the same way she did right now? Could they understand this nauseating, sickening feeling?

It can't hurt, right? Go once—because you're a mess. Remember your morning jog? If Kurt reports what happened, Jedediah will want to know how you're taking care of yourself. Go. *It can't hurt.*

Callow faced a clock on her left. Herman Library was on the other side of town. She didn't need tampons, really; she just needed some time alone. But maybe being alone wasn't such a good idea ...

"It can't hurt," she said under her breath, then, with uneasy steps that gradually grew in confidence as she headed back through the parking lot, she solidified her plans for the night.

Before she got to the car, Kurt stepped out and looked at her over the roof. "Change your mind?" he asked.

"I've got a meeting."

"Mind if I ask what kind of meeting this is?"

"One you should be grateful you don't have to attend," Callow replied curtly, climbing back into the car.

Kurt followed suit and drummed his fingers on the steering wheel. "Jedediah asked me to report in on you. You know, how you're doing."

She turned to look at him. "He asked you to *babysit* me?"

"He's concerned. You haven't told him when you're coming back."

"Never mind his babysitting—I'll deal with that later. Don't worry, I won't say you told me. But you can tell him I'm not sure if I'm even coming back. I've never really said it to myself before, but it's a real possibility." She sighed. "I'm not mad at you, rookie. You're only doing your job. Just tell him to give me one more day. I'll know more tomorrow, depending on how this meeting goes."

"Job interview?"

Callow shook her head. "I'm just going to sit and talk to some folks. I'll call you tomorrow." She eyed the young man up and down, and a realization hit her. He'd divulged confidential information about a direct order from a superior, all in her best interest. He had confided in her.

"Hey, Kurt?"

"Yes, ma'am."

She smiled. "You're not as big an asshole as I thought you were. You're smart, and I respect that. But what I've got to teach you can't be learned from a book. Drop me off at the house so I can grab my car and I'll call you tonight."

"Yes, ma'am."

With that, a mutual unspoken understanding seemed to blossom between them. They'd both shared their reasons for working in the BAU. They were miles apart, but one thing was clearly established: respect for the players in the game, because it takes a lot out of someone to make it as far as she had and not lose all sense of who you are.

CHAPTER EIGHT

Kurt left Callow at her mailbox. He leaned forward in his seat, pulling himself up by the steering wheel as if about to say something. Instead, he pursed his lips, gave the short nod he favored so much, and drove off, turning left on Jefferson.

A flurry of conflicting questions and incomplete opinions brewed in Callow's head. She wasn't sure exactly what to make of her new partner. Kurt was quick on his feet, prideful, arrogant, but there was an air of calculated intelligence about him that could bring balance to the BAU. She used her intuition and experience. Marcus was cunning—and a brute, at times. Kennedy was a curious blend of diligence or obliviousness—either on his game or lost in left field. Each agent filled a gap. Perhaps she wasn't giving Jedediah enough credit for his selections. So far, each member of the team had their place.

Callow trudged up the driveway to the front door, let herself in, and pulled her car keys off the hook on her way to the garage. The Tahoe sat like a sleeping gray beast, dormant and mellow. It had a particular smell that permeated the garage: the scent of gasoline, hot plastic, and worn rubber mixed with the dust particles that clung in the air.

She regarded the Tahoe like an old friend. Department-issued, she'd driven it since she first arrived at the BAU. It had seen mad dashes across the city and romps through the high plains and swampy lowland muck. At one point, it'd protected her from a baseball bat in an unrelated road rage incident. The Tahoe had seen a lot.

"Who will drive you if I quit?" she mumbled, trailing her hand around the taillight as she made her way to the driver's seat. She unlocked the door and climbed in. The interior was a few degrees warmer than the garage, but still pleasant. In the coming months when the snow melted for good, the worn leather seats would act as frying pans for unfortunate areas of uncovered skin. The air conditioner would work twice as hard, and the enormous radiator fan would kick in, bringing with it the rushing, roaring sound reminiscent of a helicopter blade.

Callow turned on the engine and opened the garage. Backing out, she realized it was silly to think that such material things would last forever, as if she'd just continue to build memories with the vehicle and it would be safe from the decay of time. Eventually, the transmission would go, and then they'd total the vehicle and throw her in a Crown Victoria or a Charger with rubber flooring and a stiff metal dash.

There was heart to the Tahoe. Character. That's what her memories with it represented. And with those memories came the feelings they elicited; like oil separating from water, the feelings were just below the surface. Memories, then feelings. She'd learned to compartmentalize them, but as of late, things were stirring the mixture until it created a slopping, churned mess.

Powerful emotions and awful memories. The two didn't mix. And when poured into an engine, the results were catastrophic.

Callow shook her head, clearing her mind, and drove two

blocks in silence until she couldn't bear the sound of her own breathing anymore and she turned on the radio. She breached the intersection of Caldwell and Jefferson when the light turned green, merging into the right-hand lane and taking the on-ramp to the freeway. She drove ten miles across town, occasionally singing along to whichever songs she recognized on the radio and humming to the beat when they were new. Along the way, the sun dropped below the horizon, and the last dregs of light guided her into the parking lot of a small square building nestled in the historic heart of Colleyville. The red lettering on the wall read: HERMAN FREE LIBRARY.

There were three other cars in the parking lot when she arrived. Light from inside lit the sidewalk through a glass door. Callow shut off the SUV and made for the front door.

Once inside, she was guided by a sign to the left toward a large open conference room filled with worn leather couches and silence. She counted three heads, all facing away from her. One sat on an old couch, the other two on folding chairs. The smell of fresh coffee permeated the air.

Callow paused before entering the room and contemplated turning around. She didn't much feel like reliving all the things she'd seen over the years. Once she revealed who she was, she'd be expected to answer burning questions—some in admiration, others born from curiosity. The same thing happened whenever she taught basic profiling at the Academy. Every recruit wanted to hear the war stories. She couldn't handle that right now.

Callow fingered the keys to the Tahoe.

"Jenny?" a familiar voice asked from the doorway behind her.

Callow turned to face a kindly blond-haired man with soft blue eyes bracketed by crow's feet. She recognized the trooper from the other day, but he looked different now that he wasn't wearing his uniform—younger, more approachable. He wore a plain blue polo shirt that showed the first stages of a gut. She also spotted the imprint of a pistol on his hip.

She gave a weak smile. She'd forgotten his name. She supposed she could check his card, but that would be too obvious. Instead, she cocked her head, as if formulating a question.

"Tony. Tony Mackeras," he said, holding out a hand. In the other, he held a steel coffee cup. Callow gently accepted the handshake.

"Hi, Tony. I guess I made it."

His smile grew as he nodded. "I'm glad you're here. The coffee's fresh, and we're just about to get started. I was just checking the parking lot before I lock the doors."

"Why do you do that?" Callow asked, intrigued.

"Because each of us in this room has been in an encounter in which two people came together, but only *one* person walked away. Every one of us has killed someone. Each one of us is a survivor of that encounter. A locked door is the start to taking back control."

Callow was taken aback by the sincerity in Tony's voice. Nothing on the side of the road—except his generosity at waiving the ticket, perhaps—could have hinted about the compassion and truth to his words. He was proving to be far more than the uniform.

"I know the look on your face. You were contemplating leaving. No, it's okay. I think we all go through that. I know I do it each and every meeting. Listen, if you want to go, of course we won't stop you. But I'm willing to bet you won't meet anyone quite like us. We're the few who have tangled with death and are able to talk about it."

Callow was stone-faced. Tony was speaking truths, but each sentence seemed to pluck stitches from her heart. A lump was forming in her throat by the second.

"I can tell it was tough to even get you here. I'll tell you what— I'll let everyone know you're here just to listen, and then you can make your decision. Is that fair?"

Callow nodded.

"All right, then. Follow me. Cups are on the table. I bring my own because I'd be filling those Styrofoam cups every three minutes. One thing I'll say, I should have invested stock in coffee with how much of the stuff I go through."

Tony walked around her and looked over his broad shoulder to see if she was behind him. Despite her reservations, she was, but she couldn't shake the feeling of being led to a carnival ride she didn't want to be on.

Tony left the hallway and pointed toward the coffee table. Callow shook her head. Her mouth had run dry, but holding a cup meant the other attendees would be able to see just how shaky her hands were. She walked toward the circle of chairs and saw Tony carrying over the last chair for himself from near the door. It creaked as he sat and even more so when he leaned over to place his tumbler on the floor beneath it.

Callow stopped outside the circle.

"Folks, this is … Callow. She's just here to listen unless she says otherwise. Boyd, Martin, do you two mind sharing a couch so she has a spot?"

A man with colorful full sleeve tattoos, a chiseled jawline, and a military haircut sat next to a black man with a full beard nestling atop his worn military style jacket.

Callow drifted around the seat and sank into the cushion.

"Great," Tony said. "Well, Callow, the part I didn't mention was I'm a licensed therapist. Call it a previous life. What I will say now is that this is *not* a therapy session. Our focus is on community. Comradery. Finding strength in those who share similar situations that very few can relate to. We don't take notes. We don't tell war stories. We just talk about what interests us. If things arise in the midst, we follow the rabbit hole as far as it will go. I'm simply a facilitator for the conversation. Does that make sense?"

She nodded.

"Tonight is Martin's night to start us off, but before we begin, is everyone okay with introductions?" There were nods from each of the men in the room. "Callow has asked that she doesn't have to share …"

"I can," she offered.

"Are you sure?" Tony asked. "No pressure."

"Yes. It's okay."

"Excellent. Well, for the sake of tradition … I'm Tony Mackeras. Virginia State Trooper for seven years. U.S. Marine Corps for twelve."

He lifted a palm to the black man, who cleared his throat. "Cory Martin. Dallas PD, retired."

"Cal Boyd. Florida State Game Warden. Medically retired," said the man with the sleeve tattoos.

"Floyd Carroll. U.S. Army Ranger, six tours. Eight years. Retired."

"Genevieve Callow. FBI Behavioral Analysis Unit. Seven years. Call me Callow."

"Excellent! Welcome," Tony said warmly. "Well, introductions aside—Martin, mind getting the conversation moving?"

Martin shifted on the couch and cleared his throat again. "I visited my daughter today. Brought her flowers I grew on the back patio. First time I've been able to do that. Normally, I buy them from the store, you know? Casey always wanted to grow flowers. It took me a while to get the soil fertile enough."

"Orange and banana peels for fertilizer," Boyd said into his cup before taking a sip.

"That's right. Thanks for that idea," Martin continued. "Anyway, I brought her the flowers, but there was already another set there, which was weird. Nobody leaves Casey flowers but me. I spent a few minutes reading *Goosebumps* to her. Chatted with her doctor for a minute before taking off. That's when I ran into *his* mother."

Martin stopped after nearly spitting out the last couple words, leaving Callow confused but eager to listen in. She also found it soothing that the conversation wasn't what she'd expected; it was casual, like it was between friends at a barbecue. Mundane, almost. Perhaps she should have listened closer to what Tony had said about the group.

"And how did that go?" Tony asked.

"We locked eyes from across the lobby. I was going to ignore her and keep moving, but she stood in front of the doors. Then she hugged me. I didn't know what to do. Normally, she just cries. Sometimes she waves. So, I hugged her back." Martin gave a heavy sigh. "I felt better. Just better. Not content, not happy, and definitely not angry. Better."

Finally, Martin turned to Callow and said, "The woman I'm referring to is the mother of the man, Paul Porter, who tried to kill my Casey and left her brain-dead. She's been trying to talk to me for months."

Callow nodded as the pieces came together. Paul Porter had made the national news for breaking into a police officer's house after being released from jail for drug possession. Cory Martin had been the arresting officer. Porter had snuck into Casey's room by accident, looking to kill Martin. When he was challenged by the officer, he'd pulled a firearm, missed, and hit Casey. Martin had returned fire. Porter had died at the scene, but Casey had been left in a coma. Callow felt her heart swell for Martin.

For the next twenty minutes, the conversation flowed in every direction and from every member of the group, but none in the direction of survivor's guilt. The talks became gossip, joking about bad dates, gripes about wives, and frustration with pensions. Then, at a natural lull, the members of the group began dismissing themselves, clapping hands and offering hugs before walking out one by one.

Eventually, Martin was the only attendee left besides Tony.

He tried to drink from his Styrofoam cup, but it was long since empty. He looked inside it, disappointed.

"Well, I think that's my cue," he said, standing up. "Thanks for everything, Tony. And thanks for listening, Callow. I hope you find a home here."

"Thank you for sharing," Callow said. "I can't imagine—"

"Don't," Martin interrupted. "We don't do that here. We just listen to the parts that need to be heard and move on. If you need someone to listen while you share your feelings toward someone else's situation, that's what Tony's for. Me, I just need a hug."

With that, Martin stepped forward, patted Callow twice on the back, and offered her a sideways hug. She appreciated the friendly gesture.

"Tony, I'm out." Martin left the circle, veering toward the stale coffee dregs left in the bottom of the brewer but leaving the library instead.

"This was unexpected, to say the least," Callow said.

"It's different. There's a psychotherapeutic term for this type of therapy, but generally, I prefer the term 'venting.' These people all harbor a monster within them—something fashioned from survivor's guilt, anger, confusion. Venting keeps the monster at bay, maybe even deflates it a little."

"I like it," Callow said. "This is every week?"

"Every week."

Callow considered what it'd be like walking in next time. Now that she knew what the meetings were about, she was less nervous than before. She even felt a level of comfort in knowing the members of the group shared at least some commonalities. Military, law enforcement, survivor's guilt—they were all on a similar, if not the same playing field, and there wasn't any pressure to talk about anything that didn't need to be said in those moments. Callow even began to wonder what it'd be like to talk about Carmen for the first time.

"Well, I've got to rearrange the library and lock up," Tony said. He flipped his chair around and folded it.

"Thanks for everything. I think I'll be here next week."

He looked at her with fatherly eyes. "Good. I'm glad. Drive safe, Callow."

"You too, Tony."

Callow walked through the hallway toward the front door. She crossed the parking lot to the Tahoe, and for the entire drive back to the house, she rode with the windows down and the music just a little louder than before.

CHAPTER NINE

Callow crossed the threshold a few minutes after 10:00 P.M., but she was anything but tired. She felt energized, as if the survivor's guilt meeting had had a recharging effect on her heart and mind. It was reminiscent of how she'd felt fresh out of the Academy. *Bring on the world's problems, come what may. I'll solve them all!*

Energy was energy, misguided or not, and it was best not wasted. In the kitchen, Callow went to work wiping down the countertop and put on a kettle for tea, hoping it'd help to pass the time, weening her off her second wind. She brought her work laptop over from a bag in the living room and set it on the counter as well, waking it up.

The screen of the worn computer lit up sky blue. Lights blinked and flashed their acknowledgment from near the bottom of the screen, and the FBI logo appeared against the ominous background. Callow entered her password and nonchalantly opened her emails while she went to pour steaming water over a teabag.

She returned and saw that she had four missed emails: one from HR regarding parking space allocations and birthdays; another from Marcus about an old case; an email from

Jedediah that she could probably guess the contents of; and a final email with no headline from an unknown sender. She frowned at the odd message and double-clicked it.

At first, she couldn't tell what she was looking at, then slowly, she twisted her head. Like the dribble of sand in an hourglass, realization hit her; a deep-memory recognition, not quite *déjà vu* but near enough to make the hairs on her arm stand on end.

The image was of a dark but familiar parking lot, a few cars, and a square brick building. The picture cut off the building's sign, but there was a recognizable red glow.

She was looking at a picture of the Herman Free Library.

Despite no indication of the date it was taken, Callow knew the image was from earlier that night. The picture, too large for a single screen, required Callow to scroll down. She did so with a shaky, twitchy finger.

Slowly, the image appeared as the computer rendered the high-resolution photo. She set her mug down and covered her mouth as her heart was driven up into her throat.

The rest of the picture showed the rear of a vehicle: a large SUV with the trunk open. Laying on her side, hogtied and gagged with duct tape, was a blonde woman with heavy dark makeup around her blue eyes.

Eyes that screamed. Eyes that were begging.

Pinned to the girl's chest was a piece of paper on which words had been written in black marker:

YOU'RE BOTH SO ALONE.

Callow was frozen, sickened. She suddenly felt vulnerable, as if whoever had sent the photo was watching her from the shadows right now and any second would send another picture of her to her email address. She spun around, but of course the room was empty.

Upstairs, she could hear soft music playing from Rebecca's room. She turned back to the picture and scanned it again. She didn't know the girl, but she desperately wanted to say she did.

YOU'RE BOTH SO ALONE.

Callow scanned the photograph left to right, until her eyes fell upon a tear in the upholstery of the back seat. An all-too-familiar tear.

"No fucking way," she said, her voice no louder than a whisper. The sickening reality of it all came crashing down at once, like a wall of frigid water.

That's my car.

She didn't think.

She didn't breathe.

But she had to do *something*.

Years of practiced training and muscle memory took over and she yanked up her shirt, sliding her hand over her belly and down onto the grip of her service pistol. She rose and drew the Glock with precision, thrusting it forward and activating the weapon-mounted light attached to the barrel with her finger, aiming it down the hallway in a two-handed stance.

Somehow, she knew who had put the poor girl in the trunk of her car. Was she still there? Was the sick fuck responsible waiting in the wings, tucked into the shadows? Or perhaps he was in the back seat, watching with cold, still eyes. She knew who *he* was without saying it.

She made for the front door of the house, swinging the Glock around into blind corners, flicking on light switches along the way. She took the key fob to the Tahoe and stopped at the door. She realized how much of a dangerous position she could still be in. She took a second to dial 911 on her phone and left it ringing in her back pocket before heading back outside.

The air outside was cooler now, the ghostly moon in full display. Her breath came in little gusts of fog in front of her face and the chill fought to distract her, but nothing could keep her eyes off the back of her SUV. She moved around the trunk of the vehicle, the Glock's tac light illuminating the headrests and confirming that the seats were empty.

Unless he's laying down?

Even if an attacker was in the vehicle, she had the advantage. She eyed the truck like she would a casket. She knew that what she was about to find would shock her to her core, injecting her with that same icy sensation that came with the discovery of every vic.

Weapon in hand, Callow used her off hand to double-click the button on the key fob to unlock and automatically open the rear hatch. The Tahoe's lights blinked red twice, the lock popped, and the tailgate began to rise. Callow crouched into a supported firing position, ready to defend herself if someone came barreling over the back seat.

But as the lift gate rose, she saw that the trunk was empty.

She sprang off her heels.

In quick, jerking movements, Callow circled the vehicle, ripping open door after door, jabbing her pistol into nooks and crannies like it was a red-hot poker looking to drive a rabid fox out of hiding. But there was no one in the vehicle.

She panted, then groaned—not from disappointment, but exhaustion.

She came around to the trunk again. No girl. No letter. Nothing. Nothing but that icy injection in her veins.

This was the Icebox Killer.

It had to be. Just as he'd taunted her in the hospital, he was taunting her now, fiendishly dangling the carrot.

Stowing her weapon, Callow fished her cell phone from her back pocket, tapped on her contacts, and dialed Jedediah. He answered on the first ring.

"Genevieve. How are you?" Her superior didn't sound tired. He liked to work late.

"Not good. I'm at a crime scene. I need the technicians, Kennedy, Oakley, and the rookie."

"*Jesus*. What happened?"

"Come see for yourself," she said. Her mouth ran dry.

"Where are you?"

"My house."

"*Your* house? Is Rebecca …?"

"We're fine. I don't have a body, but we will if we don't move quickly."

"Hold on. Let me send a message. Okay, the chips are falling. Here comes the crew. Oakley is drunk—his night off—so it's just you, Kennedy, and Wainwright. What do you think you have?"

"Icebox."

Jedediah swore. "I need you back, Jenny. Is this you coming back?"

Callow should have anticipated the question. The Icebox Killer had just played a tune and she'd danced to it. He'd infected her private life in so many ways, to the point that staying away seemed impossible. Callow thought about him when she didn't want to, and when she finally could sleep, she dreamt about catching him.

Then she remembered the hogtied girl and the streaks her makeup had made as it ran down her face. She imagined her screaming from the trunk of her car while Callow had been cutting it up with other cops, talking about gardening and sipping stale coffee.

If the Icebox Killer had wanted her to stay away before, now he was calling her out of an early retirement. He'd called her out before, but this was next level. He wanted someone to play his sadistic game. He held the clock, and the timer was set.

Icebox was going to kill the blonde girl in the next two days.

On the third, he'd leave her body and a cooler roadside for some kid on a bicycle to find. For that not to happen, Callow would have to be all in.

"Yeah, I'm back. There's no sense in hiding—and Icebox doesn't want me to. He wants me to play. So, here I am. Let's play."

Within seven minutes, the serene façade of Callow's quaint neighborhood was broken by the wail of police sirens and the strobe of emergency lights. Soon, neighbors in nightgowns emerged on their stoops, hugging themselves or recording with their cell phones. Callow waited on her front porch, her head resting on her palms.

Jedediah was first to arrive. The Assistant Special Agent in Charge parked his 1998 red Jeep Wrangler half a block away. Callow watched him cross the street, a giant among men. He wore a pair of plaid shorts, sandals, and an oversized Hawaiian button-up. A ball cap marked "FBI" covered his head, and a pistol in a black leather shoulder holster bounced off his ribs.

"Genevieve?" he asked, stopping in her yard and looking around. He eyed her pistol next to her on the concrete patio. "What happened?"

She eyed the trunk of her SUV. "He was in my fucking *car*, Jed. Icebox was in my car."

"How could you have been followed? You're being tailed round the clock."

Callow frowned. "What do you mean? The team only watches the house."

Jedediah shook his head. A cruiser turned off Jefferson and accelerated in their direction. The officer deactivated his siren as the car drew closer.

"The surveillance team are supposed to tail you no matter where you go, for as long as your sister and cousin are gone."

Callow sighed and pushed herself to her feet. "Well, somebody fucked up. Let me get my computer." She ducked inside and returned with her laptop. She held it for Jedediah to see.

"*Jesus*. I'm assuming that's your Tahoe?"

She nodded. "Same tear in the carpet. Forensics need to take the car apart. Digital forensics need to do the same with this." She shook the laptop and then showed him the message with no sender or subject line. "How the hell did he send this?"

"Technology can be manipulated. That doesn't worry me half as much as him following you. First, he didn't want you on the case, and now he does. That's what worries me."

The approaching cruiser parked at the curb, and the officer walked up the front lawn.

"Get me a perimeter, twenty feet, around the SUV," Jedediah instructed. "Nobody talks to the media. I'll call our PR guys."

"And who the fuck are ya?" the officer asked.

Jedediah growled and dug in his shirt for his badge. "FBI. Perimeter. Now."

If the officer had something smart to say, it was too quiet for anyone to hear. He stalked off toward the trunk of his car and dug around within, appearing a moment later with crime scene tape and traffic cones. He began to string the tape around the SUV, using sticks driven into the cones as pylons.

"Wainwright said you were out and about. Let's see if I have this right—you get home, the unsub sends a picture, and you check the back of the SUV?"

"Pretty much. Drove all the way home, then checked my email. Searched the SUV after that," Callow summarized.

More officers were arriving with flashing lights and squealing sirens. A black box truck with the words "CRIME SCENE" written on the side in white lettering was close behind.

"Internal Affairs are going to want to talk with you," Jedediah said. "They'll probably say you can't be on the case. I'll let them know, *technically*, you aren't. Not as a consult."

"Thanks, Jed," Callow replied.

The door behind her opened and Rebecca poked her head outside. Her eyes were still puffy and narrow from sleeping.

"I'll be inside," Callow said. "Tell Kennedy to drag Oakley out of bed. I don't care if he's drunk. I'm not doing a profile with Kennedy, and I'm damn sure not doing one with a rookie."

Callow walked inside and shut the door to the growing commotion. It barely stifled the sounds of idling engines, radios squawking, and Jedediah barking commands. She went over to the couch and fell back into the seat, exhausted. Rebecca appeared beside her.

"Is there a dead body in your car?" she asked.

Callow answered without opening her eyes. It felt good to let them rest. The adrenaline had worn off, the initial shock settling in. "Yes. No. Maybe there was. I don't know. But it means I've got two, maybe three days before the killer adds another notch to his belt."

"'I've?' You said *I've*. Does this mean you're working again?"

Callow bit her lip. Who else could take this one when she'd been singled out at the dance? She'd been picked as prom queen, and it was her duty to dance with the Devil himself. Duty, responsibility—destiny, maybe. It seemed something as simple as declaring herself ready to come back to work was a momentous task, like the decision to climb Kilimanjaro or swim with sharks. She didn't feel confident. No, she was scared—and rightfully so.

Come what may. She heaved a heavy breath in, expanding her chest, and breathed out.

"Yes. It doesn't seem like I have much of a choice. Icebox called me out, and if I don't answer, he might escalate his timeline. Things are different this time—for the both of us." She faced her sister. "Still have your pistol?"

Rebecca didn't answer.

"Keep it on you at all times. I was supposed to have a

protective detail and the unsub still managed to drop a live body in the trunk of my car, take a picture, leave, and send it to my email using some sort of anonymous software all within the space of an hour."

Home isn't safe. Callow's voice of reason echoed. Whatever Rebecca's thoughts were, they didn't move her. She was rooted in place, her eyes locked on Callow's with a fierce determination. Her eyes glistened, but no tears fell. Her brow came together, forming harsh lines, and then she skirted behind the couch. Callow felt her sister's hand trail softly across the top of her shoulders. It was such a simple gesture, but so much was delivered with so little touch. It said, *"We're in this together."*

It was Callow's turn to fight back tears.

Outside, red and blue lights swept across her driveway. Rebecca could commiserate. So could Jedediah and Marcus. But nobody could feel quite the same. Icebox chose her, and by doing so, he'd secluded her, just like he wanted.

YOU'RE BOTH SO ALONE.

How right the Icebox Killer was.

CHAPTER TEN

The next day, Callow entered the briefing room five minutes before it was supposed to start. She sat down near the back of the room at a polished aluminum and black glass table and stared blankly at the white projector screen, her thoughts intermingling with waking dreams. She reached for the soft spot of skin between her thumb and forefinger and pressed. The quick jolt of pain livened her senses, only for her eyes to settle into a hazy lull, half asleep, half awake.

All night, agents had passed through her house to use the communal bathroom. Callow had given herself the task of keeping fresh coffee flowing. She'd shown the agents where to find more cups, but they'd ended up washing the same one after each use and placing it on a nearby towel to dry. After pouring out the second untouched pot, she'd taken herself to her room. She hadn't said a word after she'd spoken with Rebecca.

Throughout the night, the crime scene technicians had scoured and cataloged while Callow tossed restlessly under the sheets. Her body had been screaming for rest while her mind had run like a hamster on a wheel. Exhaustion had taken over sometime after the devil's hour, but despite her body's pleas for rest, the hamster was soon on the wheel again.

Callow had eventually pulled out of the driveway in the morning hours in Rebecca's car with heavy bags under her eyes and an obnoxious yawn that never went away. The technicians had continued to work diligently even as she left, little worker bees in blue field jackets following a scent trail of coffee inside only to return to work, revitalized.

"You look like shit," Marcus said, sitting down next to her and sliding a manila folder under her elbow. He leaned over and opened the blinds along the briefing room's far wall to allow the sunlight to stream in. Callow hissed and turned away.

He held a Styrofoam cup filled with black coffee out to her. Above the aroma came a sweeter, softer scent. She looked at Marcus and noticed he hadn't shaved, and there were wrinkles in his suit. The scent meant he hadn't showered, either, and had just spritzed himself with cologne instead. He also hadn't changed. *Has he been up all night as well?*

She cradled the coffee and spoke into it, as if its murky depths held some deeper truth. "Where were you last night? You don't look much better."

The door to the briefing room opened. Lanky Agent Wainwright walked in and sat near the windows. He was almost rigid in his seat, his FBI-monikered notebook and pen placed obnoxiously straight in front of him.

Marcus leaned in and whispered, "Jed had me combing through everything the techs found, which wasn't much, but it meant a lot of waiting. Wainwright delivered all the trace evidence to the lab in person. He looks like he slept plenty. Rookie energy—that's my guess. Anyway, there wasn't any—"

He trailed off as the briefing room door opened again. Jedediah stormed in, followed hotly by a distraught-looking Kennedy carrying a box of files. Kennedy sat the load down, pulled out a laptop, and connected it to the cabling on the floor near the screen. His stringy blond hair hung in his face, covering his wrinkled forehead and revealing an ever-growing bald spot he went to great lengths to hide. His suit was sagging, and his tie was loose in his collar. He looked exhausted. He drained a water bottle in one breath while Jedediah hustled out of the room.

Nobody said anything to her, and Callow wasn't surprised. Agents were threatened all the time. Emails. Texts. Phone calls. But it wasn't every day a victim was staged in an FBI fleet vehicle. The sourness to the case brought a sourness to the room.

Kennedy seemed in worse shape than she was. He was struggling to insert the power cable into the laptop. His hands shook, and sweat had broken out across his brow. He was disheveled, and his blond hair hung in greasy clumps. His suit hung loosely on his frame, and his tie was wrinkled.

"I've never had that problem," Marcus said to Kennedy, sneering.

"Fuck off, Oakley. This case is a shit show. *My* shit show. Jed's been up my ass all morning. I'm briefing the brass today and they're going to expect us all to know the answers, so I hope you're ready. That includes you, too, Callow."

Callow frowned. "Why is leadership interested in the BAU? They always run the politics."

Kennedy slammed the laptop down, prompting a wince from Marcus.

"Are you back or what? Because I'm sick of listening to Jed bitch at me for your absence! You kicked ass, you saved that girl's life, and for that, you should be proud. But if not, and if you're going to stick your head in the sand again, you may as well drop your badge off on Jed's desk on the way out. While you've been sitting on your ass at home, I've been struggling. So what if you're not primary? Do you want to catch this guy or not?"

Callow turned to Marcus. Kennedy wasn't normally this much of a dick. And what was up with that comment about her having her head in the sand? She opened her mouth to ask Marcus what she'd missed, but someone stiff-arming the door drew her attention.

In walked three people, of whom the only one Callow actually knew was Jedediah. Callow recognized the other two newcomers—a man and a woman with the same, emotionless expression—from photographs on the wall near the Stars and Stripes at the entrance to the building.

Jedediah stepped to the front of the room with the new faces in tow.

"Team, this is the Chief of Staff Wendy Bryant and Deputy Director Samuel Goforth. Sir, ma'am, this is the BAU. I'm sure you've seen their names all over and maybe their faces a fair few times. I hate to introduce you in the wake of these circumstances, but I assure you that my team is the best."

Callow raised an eyebrow. Sensing she was about to speak up, Marcus kicked her foot under the desk and fixed her with a warning look. In the meantime, Jedediah introduced each of the BAU team by name for the benefit of the higher-ups.

Deputy Director Goforth cleared his throat into his hand. He was a tall, imposing figure, aged but not elderly. His shoulders were broad, and he spoke with a distinguished clarity that screamed 'trial lawyer.' He ran a hand across his face and over his head, a practiced movement that left oil in his already wavy hair.

"Thank you, Jed. We, of course, know of your team's many accolades. We've been following each of your careers closely. Now that we've been introduced, let me tell you how my job works. Director Acres himself receives his official counsel from me to ensure the agency looks wonderful on paper and screen. Special Agent in Charge Adam Friedman reports to me, ASAC Gold reports to him, and you report to ASAC Gold. So, when I get woken up at 2:00 A.M. with a phone call from Mr. Friedman telling me that one of our agents had—and I wish to stress—*had* the body of a victim in the trunk of her car, I grow a bit concerned. ASAC Gold has requested this briefing to bring me up to speed."

Amid the ensuing silence, Callow sat on the edge of her seat. A vein throbbing in her right temple, she felt as though she was sitting through an intense war briefing, but it was asinine to think that way. This meeting was clearly meant to be a threat—an "ass-chewing," as Jedediah would call it. Jedediah's boss's boss was here. That meant they'd all stuffed up.

Bryant, the Chief of Staff, cleared her throat, which sounded more like a tiny dog's *yip* than anything. She looked to be in her fifties, her shock of blonde hair cropped just above her shoulders and starting to intertwine with gray, and her face bore the onset of wrinkles around her eyes, mouth, and forehead.

"Agent Callow, glad to see you back," she said in a singsong, petite voice.

Callow nodded. Bryant appeared meek—sounded like it, too—but Callow knew this was only a façade. Wendy Bryant was the former head of the BAU, and she'd fought hard to become chief of staff. A nickname for her had circulated around the Academy, as she often gave the commencement speech for graduating classes: Barbarian Bryant. The sobriquet was well-earned.

In 2003, Wendy "the Barbarian" Bryant had been responsible for the arrest of the Coppin State Killer, after a five-month, twelve-body killing spree. The Coppin State Killer's case was so impactful on rural communities in the Southwest, the president himself had pleaded with the FBI to catch the killer. Bryant tracked him down herself. When the arrest took place, the killer, Tony Smeg, had fought with Bryant, picking her up and tossing her over his shoulder. Whispers around the watercooler spoke of Bryant biting into his jugular vein, ripping a hole in his neck in order to escape. The local PD had followed the blood trail to his body.

The story had made national headlines, and the nickname stuck. Callow saw a brief glimpse of "Wendy the Barbarian" in the woman's eyes, and together, they shared a bond that traversed words. Eye to eye, they commiserated in that moment.

"I know what you've been through," the look said. Callow couldn't share these feelings with anyone; not Jedediah, or even Marcus. To stare death in the face, whether he be named Tony Smeg or Theodore Carson or their recognized media monikers was irrelevant. What mattered was what remained of who you were when all the blood washed away. Callow felt an immediate respect for Bryant.

"Special Agent Kennedy, it is my understanding you are primary on the Icebox Killer case?" the chief of staff asked.

Kennedy stood up frigidly, nearly choking, mid-sip, on his coffee. "That's right, ma'am. Special Agent Callow is available for consult due to her relationship with one of the victims."

"Fair enough. Give us a rundown, Mr. Kennedy, and make it brief."

Kennedy walked stiffly to the podium where his open laptop was waiting. He continued to fumble with the cabling for a few tense moments before giving up and rolling up the display screen to a map of the city underneath. He used a red marker to circle three intersections a few miles apart.

"To date, Icebox has taken three victims. In each case, same M.O., same circumstances. Young. Early twenties. Petite. Always in broad daylight and crowded areas, suggesting the unsub blends into his surroundings and draws his victims in close through trust and charm. He's manipulative. Smart. Calculated."

Kennedy circled a fourth location Callow didn't recognize, then a fifth that she did.

"The photograph of the latest victim was taken here, at the

Herman Free Library. The victim, Ms. Marissa Marley, was taken from Main and Martin Luther King Boulevard. This is out of Icebox's normal range, based on the previous incidents, meaning he made a special trip to the library just to take the photograph. The unsub sent an email to Special Agent Callow. Digital forensics are all over it, but haven't turned up anything as yet."

"Any other developments or leads?" Bryant inquired.

"Nothing notable. PD have doubled their night shift roster and administration are out working days. The mayor will announce a curfew later this afternoon. The whole world is watching."

"We're working diligently," Jedediah said quickly. Kennedy was sweating, and his mouth hung open while he shuffled through his paperwork and notes. Callow understood why; there was a lot riding on this investigation, and the entire team carried the weight of it. "We believe the killer's strategy is changing. He's emboldened ..."

"Why Callow?" Bryant interrupted, prompting Jedediah to clam up. "Why her? Why now? I thought he wanted her to stay away? Isn't that why he sent the bracelet? As a warning?"

"It's control," Callow stated. All eyes rested on her. She stared pensively at the table. "Or maybe it's not. Maybe it's a simple case of 'he can, so he does.'"

"And what do you make of it?" Bryant asked her.

Callow shrugged. "I wish I knew. Perhaps he discovered my connection to Carmen while assessing her suitability as a victim, and that gave him something new to play with. I was ... *convenient*."

Callow's words flowed despite her intention to stop them. She was speaking unprofessionally, which was unusual for her. There was only speculation in her words. No fact, nor logic. It was unfitting for the kind of work they did. It didn't fit her profile.

The tension built. Jedediah stirred, and Callow didn't want to meet his eye. She'd see the fury then. An ass-chewing was imminent—but she didn't care. She'd spoken the truth—or so she believed with what little they had to go off of.

"Fair enough," Bryant said. "Kennedy, please continue."

Kennedy adjusted his tie. "The latest trace evidence we have came from examining the coroner's reports across all victims. The coroner noted the presence of HDPE—high-density polyethylene—the same stuff found in grocery bags. Tox results negative. Stomach contents inconsequential."

"And the follow-up on the polyethylene?"

"Interviews at two local medical supply companies. It's believed the HDPE transfers from whatever Icebox stores the instruments in—bins or whatever, maybe a protective case. Microscopic cut patterns on the victims show evidence of precision rather than hacking or slashing, which supports our theory that he has medical or surgical training, or at least familiarity around blades. This is a new development. We'll be following up with interviews into local medical supply companies immediately. Locals are available to assist with this one."

The room fell into ominous silence. It was a reach. They were all agents seasoned enough to know that chasing down "suspicious activity" at local establishments was clutching at straws.

Callow couldn't help but feel disappointed. She wished for so much more, something—*anything*—more substantial than field interviews, and she began to regret her time away from the office. She felt out of place, aloof from the case, a casual observer with little to offer. And by having little to offer, she felt like Carmen's death was being exasperated tenfold. What little peace she hoped to have was slipping through her fingers, only to be compounded by the bodies piling up in the morgue.

"Very well. Thank you, Agent Kennedy," Deputy Director

Goforth said. Everyone gave him their attention. "There's no sense in re-stating the obvious. Keep on it. We're watching, and you have our utmost faith and support. Use your wits. Be smart. Watch your backs. This team is more than capable, and I trust you will put an end to this Icebox Killer. We'll be waiting in the wings. I've read the case file: we've got two days until we've got another body. Don't let that happen. Dismissed."

Callow pushed back from her seat first, but Jedediah was already at her back. She could smell his aftershave — bourbon-scented, warmed by the heat in the room. Marcus wasn't far behind.

They made for Jedediah's office, where an ass-chewing was imminent.

CHAPTER ELEVEN

Any mention of Carmen was enough to bring Callow to tears. She sat, defeated, in Jedediah's office while he paced. The door was closed, and Marcus fiddled with a pen cap.

"*'Maybe it's a simple case of 'he can, so he does,''*" Jedediah hissed, finally placing both hands on his desk and leaning across it. "I've got the deputy director and the chief of staff in the room, and you shrug and give me *that* bullshit?"

Callow was numb. She wasn't hearing Jedediah; instead, she was attempting to connect some of the dots in her head about where the victims had been found; their ages; names—anything at all. It was a mind-numbing activity, and she didn't expect a positive outcome, but it enabled her to avoid focusing on the here and now. If she did that … Well, she'd feel worse than she already did.

Hopeless. Alone.

YOU'RE BOTH SO ALONE.

"Jenny! Say something!" Jedediah snapped, louder and closer this time.

She looked up slowly. "What do you want me to say, boss? I've got *nothing*. Polyethylene? Plastic? What do you want me to do? Make a profile from that?"

The ASAC huffed and sank into his chair. "I don't get it, Jenny. Not that long ago, I couldn't get your nose out of the case file, and now you're giving up? Help me to understand. I bring you on as consult and ..."

"And *what*, Jedediah? What? Did you want me to lie to make you look good? This is all so *fucked,* I couldn't even *pretend* things are okay. You were worried I wasn't being objective? Well, maybe you're right—I'm not. But I can't sit around and do nothing. Icebox won't let me, and neither will you. Maybe I *am* alone."

"Why would you say that?"

"I didn't—Icebox did. It was on the note in the picture. 'You're both so alone.' He's right. I am alone."

Jedediah's face assumed a softer appearance. "Now, look, this wasn't meant to go this way ..."

Callow was already on her feet and turning to leave.

"Where are you going? Is that it? You're quitting?"

Callow whirled around. Tears clung to her eyelashes. One blink later, and they fell to the carpet to be absorbed amongst the worn fibers. "*Quitting?* How could I? Isn't anybody listening to me? I couldn't quit even if I wanted to. Icebox needs me as much as you do. Hell, I probably need this job, too, otherwise I'd only sit at home and tear myself apart. Do you know what it feels like to have this weight on your shoulders every day? The pressure? Not because of the FBI's image or some director breathing down your neck, but to know Carmen, my friend—my *best* friend—will have no justice, no *peace,* until I catch this guy. And it has to be me. You know that as much as I do."

Callow finished her tirade. There were no more tears. That would be too easy. Instead, she breathed heavily, her fingernails digging into the back of the leather chair she had just been sitting in.

Marcus looked up at her with a sullen face. Jedediah maintained his composure. His eyes didn't show anger;

instead, he seemed to shrink himself down, back to her level, back to the father and friend she knew she had in him.

"What will you do now?" he asked sincerely.

"The same thing everyone else is doing: I'll hit the pavement. We'll canvas the area, conduct interviews, and spread out. Fancy cognitive connections and intuition won't solve this one. It looks like a job for boots on the ground."

Jedediah's mouth twitched at the corners. "Sometimes, the best thing to do is start from the beginning."

Callow remained silent.

"Find the facts, Callow. He'll slip up. They always do. Marcus ..."

"Sir?" Marcus replied.

"Keep her safe. You're assigned as a permanent watch."

"Sir, I don't know if that should ..."

Jedediah raised a hand. "Sometimes, we just need someone close by. You knew Carmen, didn't you?"

"I did."

"Then you're the only one besides Jenny who can dig deep enough to figure out why she was chosen. Conduct your canvases, interview, be vigilant, and review the case file. We'll catch this bastard."

Callow left Jedediah's office. Marcus didn't lag behind. She could tell based on his slightly invigorated pace and the more relaxed swing of his arm that he found his new placement at her side enjoyable. She had to admit, they worked well together. Trust Jedediah to find a way to give her what she needed most. He always saw beyond the uniforms to the humans underneath; the people who were affected no matter how hard they tried to steel themselves against reality's icy grip.

The two agents entered an empty elevator. They got off on the parking lot level and strode along the familiar long glass walkway. Despite the coolness of winter, heat radiated off the sunbaked windows as cars buzzed by across the street like a line of sugar ants.

They walked in silence until they reached Rebecca's car and both of them got in. When the car started, the radio played, and Callow immediately turned it off, preferring to drive in silence.

"That could have gone worse ..." Marcus offered as Callow drove onto the turnpike and joined a long line of cars caught in traffic. "Listen, if you want to talk ..."

"I don't," Callow replied dryly, reaching to restore the radio. She didn't want to talk; she wanted to *work*. To engross herself in the case. To act, rather than watch from the side-lines. Anything to not feel stagnant. She wanted to feel like that, even if she wasn't finding the slot to fit the puzzle piece, she was still hunting for the appropriate piece to begin with.

She cycled through the radio stations twice over before shutting it off again completely. She sank back into the seat and sighed. "Canvases, for fuck's sake? We're really lost, aren't we?"

"Not entirely," Marcus said. He perked up a little. "We probably missed something."

"Forensics scoured the library parking lot, my car, and my laptop. We would have picked something up by now." Callow thought about what that must have looked like: men and women on their hands and knees, searching, the bright floodlights drawing more people to that little library than it had seen in a lifetime. Agents with magnifying glasses and cameras, and looky-loos with cameras to watch the men with cameras. Callow felt a nervous twinge in her gut, just above her navel. It nagged and nagged, pinching uncomfortably enough for her to notice. *Cameras ...*

"Did Forensics mention camera footage from the library?"

Marcus reached into the back seat for his bag and with-drew the manila case file. Callow started forward, merging into the middle lane while he rifled through the papers.

"Only that the image was too blurry. 'A dark-colored truck' is what they wrote. The locals pulled video from three stores along the same road. Two faced the front doors. One faced a tree."

Callow's heart sped up as she neared the toll station. "Did they check the toll road cameras?" she pressed. "Maybe we can get a list of dark box trucks."

Marcus looked up and around. "Shit. It doesn't say if they did. But that's a stretch, too, don't you think? You know how many dark trucks probably pass these every hour?"

Callow veered off, hard to the right, taking the exit ramp and cutting across two lanes, resulting in angry horns being leaned on for a little too long.

"Where are you going?" Marcus asked. "We're supposed to be canvassing medical supply stores."

She snorted. "That was Kennedy's bright idea. I told you he was an idiot. I told Jedediah, too, but he still wouldn't listen."

"What are you getting at? If Jed figures out you're veering off course, he'll can us all."

Callow shook her head. "He can't. Not yet, at least. He needs us to solve this thing."

She slowed the car as they arrived on the service road. There was little else ahead of them. Six blocks down, she could turn right and arrive right back at the library parking lot again.

"Will you at least fill me in? I'm getting worried."

She threw the car in park in the middle of the access road. "Remember what you said earlier about cameras?"

"Yeah, they were all too blurry. The geeks tried to enhance the footage. Didn't work."

Callow turned in her seat, her heart racing with excitement. Not a lead, nor a hunch—just a feeling. It could be her intuition, or just another wild goose chase. Either way, it felt better than the default "canvas" approach. She pointed out the windshield toward a steel overhang with metal trusses divided into four separate lanes. Two were for credit cards, one was for a pre-paid fast pass, and the other, cash. A lone attendant opened a glass window and took a handful of change from a man in a red minivan.

"There."

Marcus's eyes reflected realization. Callow nodded furiously even as a car buzzed by, leaning on their horn. Now, he could see what she meant.

"The toll road camera …" he said.

"The toll road camera. Clearest pictures in the world. And we have approximate times courtesy of the other cameras on the street."

"Would Icebox really be stupid enough to take the turnpike?"

Callow shrugged. "Let's put in the request. We'll send a uniform to talk to the attendant, too. In the meantime, let's head to the library."

"Forensics didn't find anything. What are you looking for?"

"Forensics didn't speak with anyone *inside* the library. There were at least four people there with me that night, and everyone came and went at different times. Maybe one of them saw something. Let's go down the rabbit hole."

CHAPTER TWELVE

Callow didn't wait outside the library for long; there was no need. Evidence of crime scene technicians told the whole story, and the groundskeeper lived only a few miles away. In the far corner of the lot, near where she'd parked her SUV, there were deep, muddied tire tracks in the grass. Cigarette butts, wadded strips of duct tape, and the chopped ends of crime scene tape were trodden into the grass. The parking lot was empty, save for the feeling of being watched—that abnormal paranoia that comes about late at night when the lights go out and irrational fears cause you to look over your shoulder coming up the stairs; that palpable fear that made you double-check the locks and leave a hallway light on.

Marcus seemed to sense it, too. His elbow rested on his holster, his arm occasionally bumping against it, reminding him it was there. Callow could feel his eyes hunting the darkness while she crouched where her Tahoe once stood.

"What are you looking for?" he asked.

Callow wondered the same thing. What could be revealed that the evidence technicians hadn't found? They could pull DNA from a strand of clothing fiber. What could she do?

Nothing. Not a goddamn thing—because that's what Icebox

wants. He's watching you, somewhere out there, between the trees and buildings.

Callow pressed up and her knees cracked.

"I hate this," she replied. "Just waiting. And thinking."

"About?"

She turned to Marcus. "I'm trapped, Marcus. Even if I wanted to quit, Icebox wouldn't let me go. This is what he wants. First, he forced me away, now he's brought me back. The whiplash is killing me. If I try to run now—if I try to quit and play Suzy Homemaker somewhere, he'll dump a body for Channel 7 News to report, knowing I'll see it. He has my focus, Marcus. How long until he takes more of me?"

Marcus studied her, and she wondered how silly she must look to him. Emotional, and losing her nerve. Could he understand what she was going through? Did he care?

Callow was about to ask him those very questions when the blue car arrived in the parking lot amid a din of screaming brakes. Marcus turned his attention to the driver, but his eyes said, *"I'm not through with this."*

Callow approached the car. The driver, an older black man with a graying beard and blue coveralls, stepped out and peered over the roof of the vehicle. He leaned over the top before setting a large ringlet of keys down on it. He chewed a toothpick and studied them both.

"I'm Earl. I keep this place running. Y'all the Feds?"

Callow nodded. Oakley strode forward, hand extended to shake.

"Don't bother," the old man spat. "Ya'll done enough to fuck up the grass. You should know, I ain't too happy to see ya. Tracked mud through the romance section and stopped up a toilet, too—and not the cheap toilet, neither. The good flusher."

His eyes were kind, though his words conveyed his frustration.

"You care deeply for the library," Callow said, "I can tell."

"Ah, see, that'd be the smartest damn thing said out of all your colleagues. This library was here when I was young—a great place to hide from the dope slingers, crooks, and whores. A good place for the young now, assuming they can make it inside without the thugs shaking them down. It's an old place with old books, but young blood."

Callow smiled gently. She knew exactly the kind of adoration Earl had for the building. She loved libraries, and old ones in particular. In her mind's eye, she could smell the aged pages of plastic-wrapped hardback books. She could feel the hardwood rocking chairs in the youth section and hear the whine of ancient computers working their hardest to load the most basic of internet pages. She could see the head librarian, gazing out over her glasses at youngsters who couldn't be bothered to take a book back to a chair before they began reading and simply lounged on the floor in the aisle.

"I used to read a lot," Callow said. "Agatha Christie. James Patterson."

Earl tapped his knuckles on the hood. "I can believe that. Things change, though, don't they? Well, agents, or officers, or whatever you are, I wasn't here the night the girlie got trussed up in the back of one of y'all's vehicles. Had a meeting that night, and ain't nobody stepped out."

"Sir ..." Marcus tried to interrupt, but Callow put her hand on his shoulder. She felt she was on the cusp of something. The aging caretaker seemed withdrawn. He hadn't come out from behind his vehicle, and he'd only been making small talk. Callow didn't believe he'd make a special trip to the library just to gripe.

Realization kicked in, and she had to suppress a smile. He wasn't just here to gripe; in fact, he knew *exactly* why he'd come back.

"Earl, you said you weren't here that night, correct?"

The man nodded and spat a yellow glob of spit next to the front tire of his car. "That's correct, miss." Callow caught a flash of a smile, and she realized Earl was playing a cheeky game. He wouldn't play with Marcus—that much was evident—but she realized he was testing her observation skills.

"But you said nobody came out of the building, is that correct?"

He didn't answer.

She smiled. "So, if you weren't here, but you know nobody came out from the meeting, then you must have witnessed the scene in another way."

"Possibly."

"You installed additional cameras around the building, didn't you?"

For the first time since his arrival, Earl grinned, showing a large gap in his teeth and a gold crown on one of his canines, the same way a mischievous grandfather would beam after playing a prank.

"Why wouldn't you turn that evidence over?" Marcus spat. "That's a felony, you know."

He was right, but Callow understood why Earl hadn't disclosed the additional cameras. "He didn't tell us about the camera because he knew we'd seize it as evidence, and since the CCTV cameras around the building are shit, I'm willing to bet he has a trail cam for a very specific purpose," she said, to nobody in particular.

She breezed past Earl toward a clump of trees that offered an unobstructed view of the side of the building, and in particular, two rectangular windows—the bathrooms.

Callow went to the largest of the trees and followed the height of the trunk upward until she spotted a piece of wood cut at an angle—with a plastic mount designed to point a trail cam downward still attached. She walked triumphantly back to a bewildered Marcus and a grinning Earl. Suddenly, his grin seemed as friendly as a snake's smile.

"Care to fill me in?" Marcus asked.

Callow sighed, a sour taste in her mouth. "I'm sure if we run Earl's criminal history, we'll find crimes against children, including pornography and other lowlife behavior. He loves the library because that's where *young* neighborhood girls come to spend their time—isn't that right, Earl? And this game camera is at the perfect height to peer into the far stall of the girl's bathroom. The camera's missing, but the holes for the mount aren't. I'm willing to bet the memory cards have since been destroyed?"

Earl continued to grin. Oakley looked ready to hit him.

"But you're a pedophile with a *conscience*, isn't that right, Earl? You didn't say anything about the trail cams until you'd cleared the images off them. I'm willing to bet when you took them home that night to download, you also discovered some *unsavory* behavior."

"*Unsavory* ..." he said, enunciating every syllable of the word. Callow's ears rang.

"And since you're a pedophile with a conscience, you brought the cleared memory cards with you because you'd hate to see a woman hurt, am I correct? If I'm not, the only reason it could be is because this victim is way older than your ... *tastes*."

"Very good, Fed. Very good. I ain't admitting to nothing, and what I do ain't hurt nobody. You're clever for a Fed, ain't ya?"

Earl ducked into his car, and Marcus instinctively jerked for his firearm. Callow stymied him with a gentle touch. Earl popped up a second later and slid a small square memory card across the roof of the vehicle.

"Ain't right what he'd done to that girl."

Marcus snorted. "Like you give a shit."

Earl frowned. "I ain't ever touched nor hurt nobody. I like to look. We've all got our tastes. What matters is if we *act*, and I do no such thing. Never have, never will. I'd just as soon hang myself in the closet before I touch."

Earl flicked the memory card with one fat finger so it spun off and fell to the pavement.

"Fuckin' pigs," he snapped before flopping into the car, starting the engine, and driving off, leaving the smell of burnt fuel and hot rubber behind.

Callow walked over to the memory card and picked it up. She held it up to the light as if she'd found a puzzle piece that had gone missing.

"Piece of shit," Marcus said, disgusted.

Callow smiled. "Let's hope he left us the footage of Icebox and not something else."

"And what about the other pictures? Are we just going to let him go like that? I can't stand pedophiles."

Callow's smile turned cold. "He can delete the images all he wants, but Forensics can recover them. I needed him to believe he was safe to hand the card over willingly, otherwise he never would have."

Marcus raised an eyebrow. "You're wicked …"

"And you've got a temper. Let's go. If we hurry, the squints can take a look at this before lunch."

CHAPTER THIRTEEN

Callow, Marcus, and a stiff-necked tech wearing a thin red tie and an obnoxiously clean white button-up peered over a large touchscreen monitor in the sub-basement of the FBI headquarters. The room resembled half warehouse, half computer monitor burial ground and smelled of grease and stale coffee. The evidence technician ran his fingers across the surface of the screen, adjusting resolution and applying filters to the best of a sequence of images featuring a dark-colored truck arriving in snippets as the trail cam took still shots.

Callow tapped her fingers nervously on her arm. It was all she could do to prevent herself from digging a nail into the soft lump of skin between her thumb and forefinger, a habit she did out of nervousness. It brought her heart rate down, giving her control of the feelings in her body rather than becoming a slave to angst and worry.

Marcus peered over the edge of a white box, one of many on a metal rack off to the side. He was attempting to appear inconspicuous. The tech coughed loudly, and Marcus jumped. Callow grinned.

"I think I've got it here," the tech said in a bubbly, know-it-all tone. Marcus and Callow approached the table, ready to take down the license plate number and a description of their unsub.

The tech pressed a button to enhance the image. He sat back, his arms crossed in triumph.

But Callow wasn't pleased. "How do I scroll?"

The tech pointed to an arrow at the bottom of the screen. She tapped it rapidly, flashing through the enhanced images, each one further contributing to her disappointment. It showed a dark-colored, square-bodied truck pulling up alongside the Herman Free Library, then parking with its back passenger door near Callow's SUV.

"Moving van, maybe. Refurbished?" Marcus questioned.

Callow sighed. "The plate is covered. No emblems on the doors. We've got bupkis." She tapped the arrow until the screen showed an image of the driver getting out of the vehicle. He wore a brown slicker—way too hot for the day—and dark leather gloves. His shoes were simple black boots.

Callow watched each still frame change as the unsub—the Icebox Killer—opened her trunk, then his own, and stuffed a clearly struggling, bound woman into the back long enough to take a picture. There was a flash from the back of Callow's car. A handful of frames later, the woman was returned to the cargo section of the unsub's vehicle, and it drove away.

"That's it?" Callow asked.

"That's it," the tech confirmed.

Callow groaned, pressing her palms into her already tired eyes. They were running out of time. There was a cost to all this, and she'd paid up, hoping the investment would be worth it. Now, she wondered if Jedediah was right and she should have been canvassing. This ... This all felt like a waste of time. They'd confirmed nothing. All they had was a vehicle. A *non-descript* vehicle.

Callow started to walk off. She couldn't stand the smell

anymore, or the quiet tapping of soft fingers on keyboards, or the frigid air from the air-conditioning unit that hummed angrily overhead. Everything drove her senses wild down here, and the fact that they'd gotten nowhere made it all that much worse. She felt like she'd hit another dead end.

"Wait, there's more on the card," the tech said. "There's some other evidence ..."

"File it under exploitation of a minor. I'll take the case," Marcus replied, tossing the tech a business card and struggling to catch up to Callow at the elevator.

She didn't wait to press the button. She just needed to get some fresh air. Some fresh air and a bit of a break.

Marcus stood next to her in the elevator in silence. They rode it three floors up, but when the doors opened, Marcus pressed the button to close them.

"Let's talk," he said. She could sense his intimate, caring nature for her transcending the case—but to her, they were one and the same.

Callow stared at her disheveled reflection in the aluminum panel of the elevator; four metallic walls that forced her to reconcile with one fact no matter which direction she turned. One fact written on her face in bold.

He knows the game, and he's got you chasing the carrot.

Callow didn't want to talk. She wanted to scream.

Marcus's hand traveled her lower back and pulled her gently toward him. Her shoulder pressed against his chest and she looked up hesitantly, knowing full well she was on the verge of crumbling. The constant letdowns; the hopelessness of the case; Carmen ... It all weighed on her, settling in her belly while pushing her emotions to the surface.

Marcus grinned. Not his sly, devil dog grin—there was no boyish charm or weathered dark humor. No, it was a genuine grin because he knew *exactly* how she felt, and she hated that. He could see right through her, as he was doing right now.

"We'll catch him," he said. "I promise. And when we do, I'll let you choke him out. That'd make you feel better, right? The rear naked choke? Tell me you know the rear naked choke."

That was enough to elicit a small, unwilling chuckle.

"Remember: one arm over the neck, grip that arm, and press. Don't forget to flex!" Marcus growled, mimicking the chokehold.

Of course she knew the steps, and the fact that she was so close to laughing and crying at the same time broke her shell and she gave in. The faces Marcus was making—tongue out, cheeks puffed, one arm wrapped around his neck—did that. The floodgates lifted, and she cried. It wasn't sniffling or pitiful; instead, a buildup of frustration, constant angst, and overall exhaustion. Her tears were more surface level than usual, and they dried up a little faster, too.

"What do you want to do?" Marcus asked, holding her at a gentle distance. She hooked her fingers into his pockets. It dragged his pants down, and he hated it. "Canvas?" he asked, twisting away, annoyed.

Callow shook her head. Canvassing was useless. Canvassing when you had no idea where to start generated mountains of useless leads—rubberneckers who might've seen this or that, hoping their descriptions ticked the right box for a handout. No, she didn't want to canvas. A sudden thought, unwarranted and unannounced, popped into her head.

Just start at the beginning. When in doubt, start over.

"What if we start at the beginning?" she vocalized. She wasn't asking for permission; she was brainstorming. "Establish a pattern instead of hopping around blind. Look for the crumbs that might have been missed."

Marcus nodded. "You know what that means. You know what you'll have to do."

She nodded grimly. "I'll have to revisit Carmen's case. Not just the case file—all of it. Walk in her shoes."

"If you're going to do this—and I mean, if you're *really* going to do this—stick with hers. I've been through the other vics. You can trust me when I say there's nothing that isn't in the case report."

Callow wiped her nose with her palm. "Why would you trust me to look over Carmen's case, then?"

"Because it's your intimate connection to her that will allow you to see something I can't. Nobody can. It's both what makes you detrimental and imperative to the case. Right now, we need a crumb. You don't need to be objective to follow a trail—and before you say it, even the best of surgeons nick a vein sometimes. Icebox messed up somewhere. Find out where, Jen."

Marcus leaned in before she could answer and pecked her on the forehead. She caught the hot air wafting off his chest, his cologne reactivated with the heat of the day. He smelled of bourbon and oak.

He pressed the button to open the elevator doors.

"Where are you going?" she asked. Part of her hoped he'd say he was bringing the car around. They didn't have time to fool around, though. The clock was ticking. Icebox had a captive, and that meant they were working to *his* schedule.

Marcus turned. Now, he smiled, and her heart fluttered. "Someone has to cover for you when ol' Jed wants to know where you're at. Go home, Callow. Grab the case file, and let me know when you have something. You can do this."

The doors closed, and Callow was left staring at her own reflection again.

This time, she didn't look nearly as haggard. There was something there, behind her eyes: a glimmer of light that hadn't been there before. She considered what that gem might be; a trick of the light, maybe? But she preferred to believe it was hope. It had gone away for a while back there. Now, she'd dug deep, felt the painful truth of it all, and, with that sacrifice, realized hope wasn't really gone. She had hope, and she had a plan.

Callow pressed the button for the top floor.

She had a plan.

CHAPTER FOURTEEN

Callow approached the door to her office as she would a door leading to a derelict mineshaft, for it had the same appeal. Since Red Mud River, she hadn't stepped foot inside, and imagining herself sitting at her desk, pecking away at reports while Marcus brought her hot coffee seemed too simple, too surreal, like a fever dream. She'd often wondered what she would feel upon her return. Would she feel anxious or excited? Would she feel worried? Or would she be numb?

Callow realized she'd already run through the gambit of emotions. She'd felt anxious when she'd gone to the meeting at the library and had admitted, just with her presence, that she felt guilty in some regard for things completely out of her control. She'd felt excited when she'd discovered the trail camera, despite being promptly deflated at its lack of results. And now she felt numb.

Her hand gripped the polished gold knob with the same confidence she might shake an infant's hand.

It said enough.

It said, "*You're not ready, Callow.*"

She sighed—a quick, forceful burst of hot air—and turned the knob. The office held a dusky appearance, brought on by the disturbance of the dust accumulated on the desk and the rays of sunlight that squeezed through the drawn blinds. A single manila folder sat centered on her desk, an empty leather high back chair behind it.

The folder seemed menacing, drawing Callow's eyes to it, left there by Jedediah or Marcus or … hell, maybe she'd even left it there after El Paso. It didn't matter. She looked at the file differently, the case differently. Everything had changed since it had been placed in her care. Her hand rattled the knob, and she drew it back.

She turned on the light.

She wasn't ready to come back, that much was clear. But what choice did she have? Running didn't work; the Icebox Killer had caught up to her. Hiding wouldn't work, either. She could stick her head in the sand and pretend he didn't exist, that it wasn't her responsibility, and that somebody—*anybody*—would eventually catch him. But then there was another feeling—*terror*—that invaded the numbness like a disease. Terror injected her thoughts with nightmare scenarios, where it wasn't Carmen's name on the file, but Rebecca's, or Shannon's—or her own.

Callow entered the room and drew her hand along the top of the desk so that the glass whined beneath her fingertips, then settled into the chair. It felt foreign to her, but it shouldn't have. The smell of boxed leather was long since gone, and there were little sections missing where the butt of her pistol had worn the fabric. No, this was *her* chair, and the file on the desk was a copy of the investigation into Carmen's murder. The clock on the wall was real, too, endlessly counting down until Icebox's deadline was met. It was all real, and there was no escaping that excruciating reality.

Callow pondered the case file and the letters morphed from "CARMEN" to "REBECCA" before her eyes. She groaned when the overwhelming desire to call her sister set in. She dug her work phone from her pocket and dialed her, knowing their conversation would be short. If she called from that particular phone, it was her way of letting Rebecca know she was all right, but on the job.

Rebecca picked up on the second ring. "Hello?"

"Hi, sis. How're things?" Callow asked, trying to sound casual.

The sound of sizzling oil and a spatula scraping a cooktop came through the phone. Rebecca was at work, too. Just a few weeks prior, the Icebox Killer had dumped another body in the parking lot of her place of employment. Back then, Callow had wondered if it had been on purpose—perhaps as a warning message to her, saying what he'd always said: *"HOME'S NOT SAFE."* But if that were his message, why did Rebecca seem so unfazed? She still got up in the morning just the same, studied just the same, and acted just the same—carrying Dad's revolver aside. How could she, without the training or obligations Callow had, be able to continue like nothing had happened?

"Busy. We just had a school bus full of high school football players come in, and I've had two people call in sick. I'm running the grill, the fryer, and the drive-through."

"Oh, wow."

"Yes, so I'm busy. I see the number. Are you taking a flight?"

Callow realized she normally called outside scheduled hours, as she did when she was being hurried away on an assignment somewhere. "No, I … I just wanted to talk."

Rebecca was silent for a few moments. "You called because you're worried. Don't be. I've got my pistol, and I'm in public. *He* wouldn't dare."

Callow winced. Rebecca was hardened beyond her years; forced to grow up quickly and react even quicker. As her sister, she was affected, albeit indirectly, by Callow's job. She carried work home with her, regardless of her attempts to lock the cases away in the office, and Rebecca somehow lived vicariously through her, via some sick kind of emotional osmosis. And after she'd found Gwen Hammond's body, the number of years such trauma could age a young woman was too terrifying to imagine. Her innocent view of the world would be gone in an instant. She wished she could shield Rebecca from it all, but when all they had was each other, that meant accepting the good and the bad. Though she might leave the paperwork behind, Callow carried the memories with her always.

"I *am* worried, and rightfully so. Can you blame me?"

Rebecca paused, the spatula scraping away. "No. But I can either ignore the reality that this will all come to a head or I can charge toward it, knowing full well it will sneak up on me when my back is turned. Frankly, I don't like either option. At least this gives me control again."

Callow stared at the manila folder, around it, through the glass to her feet. They jittered, bouncing on her heels. It was either that or she'd dig and rub at the soft spot between her forefinger and thumb until the skin was raw and angry. Rebecca was right: there was no limit to what Icebox was capable of, and if they fell on his path of destruction, it wasn't a matter of chance, but they could still take back some measure of control. Callow could appreciate that about Rebecca, even if the implications were shit.

"That's a good point."

"I know."

"Don't get cocky."

"And don't you get teary-eyed. I've said it before, and I don't mind saying it now: he *will* mess up—and when he does, you'll be waiting."

Callow froze, a cold shock to her system rearranging neurons and synapses so that nothing worked properly. "That's the problem—I'm always waiting, never doing," she said gravely. "I'm tired of finding bodies, Rebecca."

"Then *change* it," her sister shot back. "Do something

rather than nothing. That's all I'm doing—*something*. Do you think I want to flip burgers fifty hours a week? I'd rather not, but I need to do something. It sure beats waiting."

"I can appreciate that."

"Yes, big sis, I'm giving you permission to work more, despite what Mom would've said. Listen, I've got to go. I'll text you when I'm home. Be safe."

"You too, sweetie."

The call ended.

Callow realized she'd just had one of the longest phone calls with her sister she'd ever had. Rebecca was always so direct; coarse, almost. The change in her over the past few months was rapid and jarring, and Callow's brush with death at the hands of the Red Mud River Killer probably had something to do with it. Vaguely, the smell of damp mud—an earthy, wet smell—rose from her memory, where she thought it had been safely locked away. She shook it off, ragdolling her head atop her neck, listening to the bones crack and groan.

"That bad?" a voice said from the doorway. A familiar, unmistakable voice.

Callow smiled, her eyes still closed, rolled her head to the front, and opened them slowly.

Detective Hank Juarez leaned against the door to her office, confident and bold. He wore a modest gray suit and black cowboy boots. His skin was naturally tanned, and he'd recently gotten a haircut. His El Paso PD badge flashed beneath his coat.

Callow leaned back in her chair. "You're a long way from El Paso."

"Ain't that the truth."

"Still looking for a job on the fourth floor? Recruitment office is outside the lobby."

Detective Juarez pushed himself off the jamb and then dropped into the chair in front of her desk.

"Actually, I was at a conference. When that ended, I burned a few days of vacation. Figured you wouldn't mind the company."

Callow didn't mind the surprise at all. Juarez had turned out to be a valuable ally, following the trail of breadcrumbs that had eventually led to the Red Mud River Killer. If it weren't for him, the bodies probably would have kept piling up.

"I don't," she agreed. "But I'm more curious as to how you wound your way onto the fourth floor. There's a security code in the elevator."

He smiled flirtatiously. "You can get a lot of information just by asking. Oh, and by dropping *your* name."

Callow rolled her eyes.

Juarez looked over the bridge of his nose at the case file between them. Strangely, she felt better with him here, as if she was secretly sharing the burden.

"Guessing you're stuck," he said definitively.

"How do you know that?"

"You're in the office. Case file is closed. And there's dust on the shelf behind you, meaning you just got back. Only time you end up in the office is when your leads have run cold. Am I right?"

"As always," she conceded. Then, whatever she'd tucked away, hidden behind a veil, the compilation of frustration and rigid worry, rushed outward from her mind and made her eyes suddenly heavy. She felt them droop, what little energy she had stored up now gone. "I'm tired, Hank."

"We can't be tired," he said firmly.

She hadn't expected such an outward tone. He'd always been a bit more compassionate. They met eyes. "There's a message here, isn't there? Some story about when you were a kid or a rookie cop and how it changed your life for good, at which point it'll all click together and apply here as some sage advice."

Juarez blew a raspberry. "I wish I was that clever. No, the reason we can't be tired is because no good will come of it if we are. If we sleep, the only thing that'll greet us when we wake up is another body. Which, according to the headlines, will be in about a day or two."

Callow's heart twisted. "What are you talking about?"

Hank looked genuinely confused. "It's all over the news, Callow. Someone leaked your case. The one with the girl in the back of your car."

Callow's blood ran glacier cold. Her breath caught in lungs that refused to expand, and her mouth filled with the taste of black copper.

She turned in her chair and switched on the TV for background noise.

CHAPTER FIFTEEN

Callow's mouth hung open. She stared at her computer, playing a shortened reel of the day's headlines. It was the same across all channels. She'd made national news. Or rather, the Icebox Killer had, and she was the perfect vessel to highlight just how close to home the case really was.

She had the video muted, but the pictures said enough. Images of her house. Agents crawling like soldier ants through her vehicle and in and out of her house. Another short take of her, head in her hands, seated on the front porch. Another of a crime scene sketch, the line art depicting how a body could fit snugly in the back of the Tahoe.

Callow hadn't even noticed her old habit rearing its ugly head. Her thumb found the soft meaty part of her other hand, right between her other thumb and pointer finger. There, she pressed her nail, creating an indent in the skin, then began scraping, scraping, scraping ... The skin was raw and angry, the video long since over, before Juarez planted a comforting warm hand on her shoulder.

She drew her eyes upward. "I didn't leak it."

"I know," he offered reassuringly. "But does your chain of command trust you?"

Callow looked at the numerous awards on her wall, the various PR stunts where she'd shaken hands with leaders and dignitaries, the occasional police chief, and Jedediah. Jedediah trusted her; he had to. She'd never given him reason not to, and he was the first person she'd called when she'd discovered Icebox had gotten into her Tahoe. Quickly, the fear of media repercussions slid aside as her mind worked to put together the facts. She'd have to think like she was on a case—discover what facts were known and unknown, track down the flow of information, look for patterns, and imagine the worst possible fallout.

In this case, whoever had leaked the story to the media had to have intimate knowledge of the case. The reports seemed too sure, too *headliney,* to be guesswork by white-picket-fence rubberneckers in her neighborhood. Whoever had leaked the information had even described the crime scene in vivid enough detail for the channel to create a sketch. Perhaps someone driving by snapped photos and went to the news with it? Perhaps one of local uniforms has an in with one of the local leggy news anchor and was looking for kudos, unaware of damage such a leak might do to the case?

Callow flopped back in the chair, running her hand through her hair and fluffing it nervously. It was greasy, and she could smell her sweat. As she stared off at her feet again, unable to focus, there was a timid knock on the metal doorframe.

Wainwright held two cups of coffee.

He eyed the back of Juarez's head, who didn't bother turning around. Wainwright didn't wait for Callow to motion him in; he stepped into her office, placed the coffee on the desk, and sat.

Juarez winked at her and turned his head, offering a powerful hand to the rookie. Wainwright shook it. "Detective Hank Juarez, El Paso PD. I helped Callow ..."

"With the Red Mud River case. Yes, I read the file. Special Agent Curtis Wainwright. Most people call me Kurt."

Juarez grinned mischievously and turned to Callow. "They hire them pretty young, don't they?"

"Wainwright's a special case—and a rookie. Mine, actually. What can I help you with, Kurt?"

Kurt adjusted his tie. Thin and snakelike, it made his head appear like the eraser atop a pencil. She wondered how he'd passed the rigorous physical training standards at the Academy.

Callow read on his face that he had some news to break. She studied the microexpressions there—quick, fractional, fleeting indicators of true emotions one could become competent in reading if given a few moments to focus. From that focus, Callow saw excitement and perhaps a bit of nervousness, evidenced by his eyes darting about the room and the subtle raise of an eyebrow. Then, after all that, something odd … unfathomable malice, raw hatred that nearly drew her inward as she tried to spot it again. But just as she saw his young, soft demeanor transform into something monstrous, it was gone, and she was left with only the boyish looks again.

Perhaps she'd seen something that wasn't there; she was, after all, dealing with her own rocking emotions. Or maybe *he* was the leak, trying to ruin her by using the media as a cudgel to add even more stress to her clearly stressed life.

"I'm assuming you saw the news," he said.

"I have," Callow replied dryly. She reached for the coffee. It wasn't steaming. Marcus would have made it fresh. Kurt was definitely not Marcus. "Who do you think is the leak?"

Kurt sat back in his chair. "I am," he said boldly.

The words hung in the air, reverberating. Callow felt as though the snow had just slipped off the roof and ruined all the hours spent shoveling, as if she was trying to find a needle in a haystack but someone just kept moving the mound, ruining her progress. She was infuriated in an instant, which manifested as a single utterance. "Huh."

Nothing more, nothing less. No wasted breath. Her next step would be to march up to Jedediah's office and explain what Kurt had just told her; to let the cards fall where they may. It wasn't a political move, nor some attempt to rain hellfire down on Kurt's head. He'd effectively ended his career himself.

"With Jedediah's blessing," he added quickly. Then he smirked, and Callow felt her cheeks flush and a wave of heat suffuse between her breasts. She tried not to let her confusion show. If what Kurt was saying was true, he was here to gloat, sharing some strategy he'd approached Jedediah with behind her back to gain favor.

The only issue was, it came at her expense. It was *her* face plastered all over the news.

"I'll chat with him," she said curtly, pushing back her chair and breezing around Juarez. She let her hand drape lazily over his shoulder. "Hank, we'll get together soon. Wainwright, please close my office when you're done."

She left without saying anything more or looking back. She couldn't. Betrayal, anger, and confusion were driving her forward, down the hall to the elevator. When she got inside, she had a brief glimpse of Juarez leaving her office for the stairs, and Wainwright standing triumphantly in front of her office door. As the elevator doors closed, she swore his lips upturned into a smile.

Her own were a blank slate.

The bell dinged for the fourth floor, and her feet carried her to the opposite end of the hall. As she passed each door, heads looked up. Callow could see them from the corner of her eye, but she refused to acknowledge them. Senior leadership were based on the fourth floor, each one of them the next link in the chain and surely in the loop regarding Jedediah's twisted media stunt, knowing full well the pressure it would put on her life.

She tried to ignore the word *"betrayal"* popping into her mind in flashing neon red.

How could Jedediah go along with such an idea? How could he even *think* it was a good one? What could be gleaned from media attention toward what would surely be viewed as one of the greatest FBI fuck-ups of all time? She could hear the reporters now, swarming her front door like mice toward a fresh square of cheese.

"Agent Callow, can you explain where you were when the Icebox Killer left a body in your truck?"

"Agent Callow, do you know who the Icebox Killer is, or why he's reached out to you specifically?"

"Agent Callow, do you feel safe in your own home? Wasn't it just a few months ago that you barely survived the clutches of another serial killer?"

Are you sure you're competent for duty?

Are you sure you're ready to be back?

Are you sure?

"Genevieve?"

Callow came to the doorway to Jedediah's office, her hand poised to knock, but he was already looking at her from across his desk. He gave her a soft, sorrowful look. His mouth lined with permanent wrinkles, thick bags clustered under his eyes. He looked even more exhausted than she did. Suddenly, all demeanor and protocol melted away.

"How could you?"

"Genevieve, listen …"

"How could you do this to me? As if things aren't hard enough, you go and slip behind my back to the press. To the fucking *press*, Jedediah!"

"It's really not that simple. We have a plan."

A plan. Plans were built on logic. The media was designed to disrupt plans, muddy the waters, question authority and sources. There was no logic and no fucking plan that successfully incorporated the media.

"You just put Icebox in the spotlight! Where was that in the *plan*?" Callow hissed.

Jedediah sighed, wearily rubbed his bald head, and offered an upturned hand to the conveniently pulled out vacant seat in front of his desk. She sat, conveying as much frustration as she could. She folded her arms, tapping her elbow impatiently.

"The trail has run cold. You must know this."

She did. But she'd also felt like she was on the cusp of a breakthrough—some piece of evidence the techs combing through the fibers in her floorboards would find; something that would break the case and pull them a step ahead for once. She realized with a heavy heart they had nothing. She replied with her silence.

"Icebox wants you, Jenny. He wants you to live in fear; to worry. He's toying with you. We've identified the victim, but Wainwright and Kennedy pulled on that thread and nothing fell through."

"Let me see the case file. I'll conduct the profile. Wainwright is new. He probably missed something."

Jedediah raised a hand. "He might have, but Kennedy didn't. He's on his game on this one, Jenny, despite what you think about him. I trust Kennedy, and you should, too."

Callow glared back at him. "Why should I trust *you* if you're going to offer me up to the press like some sacrificial lamb?"

Jedediah appeared to be choosing his next words carefully, not through fear of Callow's mouthy retribution, but because that was who he was—calculated, as he'd taught her to be. Assuming his nature hadn't worn away, her anger begrudgingly piqued into curiosity as she wondered what sly plan he might have concocted.

"Icebox wants to play. He's got a captive, and as he has

her, the game is set. Our thoughts are, he wants to see you jump, squirm, and fight back. We're not going to give him that satisfaction."

Here it is. The big reveal.

"You're going to appear defeated and do nothing. Do not engage. Do not tempt him in any way. You'll be downtrodden and exhausted, pressured from the higher-ups to the point of failure. Icebox will become desperate. Now that we've given him a taste of media coverage, he'll feel more inclined to act out, and when he does, we'll be waiting in the wings with silver bracelets."

Jedediah sat back triumphantly, his words settling in the air as if the Gospel itself had been spoken. Callow immediately recognized what Jedediah was attempting to do. They were playing dead. After months of chasing their tails, they were rolling over, defeated. It was the equivalent of the negotiator hanging up on the hostage taker when he started making demands. A subtle power transfer.

It reeked of Wainwright. Underhanded. Sly. False.

"And this was Wainwright's idea?" Callow asked.

"The condensed version. He offered some analogies regarding hognose snakes who feign death or something obscure. About sums him up—*obscure*."

Callow grinned, her fury cooling a little. A brief memory played out in her head of her somber face, a moment of weakness when she'd rested her weary head in her palms—the moment caught by the television crew. It didn't feel right for the BAU to be so deceptive; their strategies and training were to spot deception, not to wield it. They were supposed to analyze, not manipulate. It was exactly the sort of unscrupulous bullshit a weasel like Wainwright would suggest. It only made sense that she would suggest a counter offer—devil's advocate and what not. It was *her* life, after all, and the life of the victim they were possibly endangering further.

A strange itch formed over Callow's ear at the realization of exactly what Jedediah was suggesting.

"You want to use me as bait," she stated, and her words stole the air from the room. It was just the kind of reckless plan that screamed "Wainwright." Young, and reckless. Though she would never admit it … she liked the idea.

"Yes."

"You think he'll try to contact me."

"He did before."

Jedediah was right. She remembered the unique bracelet she and Carmen had shared copies of, each charm half of a heart that clicked together to become whole. She remembered how exposed she'd felt when Icebox had sent her Carmen's half in a box after almost dying at Red Mud River. And how alone. She never wanted to feel that alone again.

"You'll have to remove the security shifts from in front of my house."

"Absolutely not," Jedediah said resolutely.

Callow stood firm. "Remove the security shift. Assign Oakley to my house. I don't trust anyone else alone with my sister."

Callow crossed her arms and sat back. *He who talks next, loses.* She'd come away from the Academy with some sales training, too—the art of negotiation, and she'd just finished her last stroke. All she had to do was wait.

Jedediah appeared to mull it over, rubbing at the white scruff on his cheeks that seemed to form by the minute.

"A good ol' fashioned sting."

Callow waited …

"I like it."

CHAPTER SIXTEEN

Callow found Juarez in the dining facility on the first floor. She wasn't hungry, but her office was stuffy and unappealing. She craved normalcy, and a cafeteria lunch offered that. He was waiting in line, an empty tray in his hands. She walked up beside him, feeling slightly more enthused than a few minutes prior. She felt good, regardless of the reality that there was still a missing girl and their plan could disastrously backfire. What if Icebox didn't take the bait? What if he simply stayed true to form and hacked a girl to pieces with surgical precision and then dumped her corpse for some poor kid to find on their way to the school bus?

"Something on your mind?" Juarez asked.

The line moved forward, and he dropped an apple on his plate while Callow sent Marcus a message to meet her downstairs in the dining hall. He responded back in seconds: *On my way.*

"Do you think the media attention will flush out Icebox? Embolden him so he makes a mistake? He has a strange fascination with me."

Juarez reached for a plastic-wrapped sandwich, then contemplated a bag of chips and had to force himself away from them. They stood in line to check out; half a dozen other blue or black suits queued in front of them.

"Might work, assuming he doesn't kill that girl first. He could flaunt the kill rather than use it to force you to react."

Callow was worried about that, too, but Icebox's timeline was too precise—it always had been. It was extraordinarily rare for a killer to change his M.O.—his modus operandi—halfway through. No, if Callow's training and experience told her anything, it was that these people weren't agents of chaos acting out of impulse. They were calm, calculated; true sociopaths who were experts at manipulating others and could not, by definition, feel real human emotions. That disconnect allowed them to push morality—general human decency—aside in order to commit their terrible acts of violence.

Juarez handed cash to the woman at the counter and led the way to a bench seat near the window. They sat, and he started on his sandwich with a disapproving sniff.

"I don't think he will," Callow said. "He's gone to a lot of effort to contact me via our secure server. He also sent me a box while I was in the hospital. And who could forget the incident with my Tahoe?"

"Why you?" Juarez said with his mouth full.

Callow shrugged. "I knew one of the victims. It added to his high, I guess—the rush. Not because I was invested with the job, but because I was emotionally invested, too."

"And are you still emotionally invested? I thought you BAU agents preach objectivity like it's the Gospel."

"We do in theory, and so far, I've been objective when it counted. Now, I'm thinking about my family. Jedediah wants to use me as bait, but that will put my sister and cousin in harm's way. Jedediah agreed it would be foolish to leave me unprotected, but he also stipulated we have appearances to uphold—more specifically, those of defeat. I'm already secondary on the case. Kennedy is primary. A lack of security at my house so close to the killer's scheduled time to act would give the impression of failure."

Juarez looked outside to the parking lot, and beyond that, the freeway, pierced by towers holding electrical wires, as if that was where he might find answers. Marcus sat down tiredly next to Callow before he could say something wise. He turned back to his sandwich unenthusiastically.

"Hi, Hank," Marcus said, his voice deep, gravelly, weary.

"Hey, Marcus."

"Long way from El Paso."

"I got lost and thought I might work for y'all. Heard the benefits are good."

"They're shit."

"So's the food."

"I know a good sandwich shop in the airport." Marcus said slyly, tossing Callow a wink.

"Would you two knock it off?" Callow pleaded. Their banter was jarring. It was bad enough that she was already having to plan the rest of the day and what she would do besides wait around the house for something to happen.

She decided she could comb the case files and evidence logs. Surely there had to be some findings a tech had declared useless but her mind would realize was of vital importance. That was what she was trained to do, after all.

"Jedediah wants to do a sting," Callow explained for Marcus's benefit. "He thinks Icebox will try to contact me if he thinks I've given up on the case."

Marcus's face became instantly serious. "You're the bait?"

"It wasn't my idea. Even worse, it was Wainwright's. Jedediah is going along with it. I had to fight him to move the security team away from the driveway."

"And I take it Wainwright is staying with you, then?" Marcus probed, the hint of jealousy not lost on Callow.

Not a fat chance.

"No, actually, you are. I didn't have to push Jedediah too hard for it."

"Jenny … I don't know if we should …"

She rolled her eyes. "*Please*. Don't think that highly of yourself. I need you there for Rebecca. She trusts you. *I* trust you. If anything happens to me … well, you'll need to be there for her."

Marcus peered off into a corner. "This is so … *off*, Jen. There's a lot of *hope* being invested here, and not a lot of *certainty*. We're running out of time. Tell me again about this … *plan* of yours."

Callow recounted her conversation with Jedediah, starting with Wainwright's reveal and leading up until this moment. Juarez listened intently, his sandwich caught in limbo between his plate and his mouth.

Marcus leaned back against the booth, his eyes set on the table. "When the options are this limited, and the trail has gone so cold we're out canvassing, perhaps something as out there as this plan is what's needed," he finally said. "I don't like Wainwright, though. Guy's a prick. Thought so since I met him."

Callow remembered her first interaction with her rookie—Wainwright's smugness, and his perpetual desire to be the biggest brain in the room, all of which did him no good now. He hadn't presented his findings, or a profile on the killer, but a simple plan—bait. Callow would have come to the idea eventually, but only when extreme recklessness was needed.

"I don't like him, either. He's smart but cocky. Full of himself. He strikes me as a boy with a bunch of toys who'd rather take them apart and make something new rather than play with them as is."

"Sounds like a kid I knew once," Juarez said, his eyes reflecting a memory. "Found him with a magnifying glass roasting a cricket he'd taped to the concrete behind his house.

A few years later, I arrested him trying to sell titty magazines in front of the same store he stole them from. Not too long after that, I got called to this house … Blood everywhere. Found the same kid in the living room—covered in it, too. He'd hacked up his grandmother. I could see the emptiness in his eyes. All those times I'd dealt with him before, he was just warming up, trying to feel something …"

Callow waited patiently.

"It made my stomach hurt to look at him. He was calm, never once spoke out of turn or cried, not even when he was sent to the supermax. Not a good place for a skinny eighteen-year-old kid." Juarez rolled his empty cup across the table and suddenly looked up. "I don't like him, either. The way he was with you upstairs? The guy's *loco*."

"Well, I guess you can't work for us, after all. He might be your boss by the time you get through the Academy."

Juarez snorted. His mood changed, the memory wiped away with a hopeful grin. "Shit, I've only got a few years until retirement. You won't catch me in this stuffy place."

"Speaking of which, why *are* you here?" Marcus asked.

"Red Mud River follow-up." The detective shrugged as if it was just another day.

But the events of Red Mud River hadn't been "just another day" when they were happening. Juarez had been instrumental in bringing Theodore Carson to justice, and Callow would always be grateful for his support. She could still remember Carson's cold, merciless eyes … empty, like the cold desert. She absently reached for the fading marks on her throat.

Juarez reached across the table and rested his hand on hers reassuringly. "Hey." Callow looked up. "Carson's still locked up. I just saw him yesterday."

She caught Marcus staring at her hand, covered by Hank's, and pulled away slowly, huddling her hands sheepishly in her lap.

"It's not Carson I'm worried about. It's Icebox. It's Rebecca. It's Carmen. All of it jammed together. And even though I've got the case at home, and even though I've got access to the files, I don't feel like I'm *there.* I feel distracted, spinning so many plates ... Only when I look up, there aren't any plates at all."

Callow felt a pang of guilt settle in her stomach like a sucker punch, slipping between the fibers of her muscles and driving out coherent thoughts. Instead, she was left with brief flashes of the case file—mostly bloodied coolers—and the intense desire to run. Her heart began to race, and the intensity grew until she suddenly launched to her feet. Out of respect, Marcus and Juarez followed suit.

"I'm going to the house," Callow announced. "I need to think. I need to do something other than pore over chips. If anything happens to that girl, I'll never forgive myself for just sitting here when I could've been doing something. Don't leave without saying goodbye, Hank. I'm a long way from El Paso."

She turned to leave. Marcus slipped out of the booth, giving her room.

"Callow?" Juarez said.

She turned.

"Do you want to know what I did when I found out I'd met the kid who killed his grandmother? You know, when he was covered in her blood?"

Callow remained silent, stalwart.

"I asked him why he did it. I shouldn't have even talked to him—technically, I could have ruined the case—but I couldn't help it. I couldn't understand how someone could do something so evil, so calmly, and to a family member, too. I would have preferred it if his brain were fried, or she'd abused the kid, or anything other than the actual answer he gave me. He looked at me from the back of my patrol car and said, *'Sometimes, people do bad things. Sometimes, good people can stop bad people in time. You're a good person, Detective. This wasn't your fault.'"*

Callow's eyes flooded with tears, and the slight shimmer in Hank's suggested his were the same. "Sometimes, good people can stop bad people in time, Callow. This wasn't your fault. The girl in the photo wasn't your fault. Carmen wasn't your fault. Do your best, do everything you possibly can—and if you do that and you still can't stop the bad person in time, it's not your fault. Goodbye, Callow. I'll be rooting for you."

Callow left the cafeteria, no longer feeling flighty. Her shoulders were depressed, anchoring her to the floor, turning each step into a miniature trudge through heavy mud. She continued like this until she reached her car and the Virginia cold snap nipped at the tops of her ears.

She huddled against the frost, uncomfortable. Perhaps she *deserved* to be uncomfortable. Maybe if she was uncomfortable, things would seem more pressing to her, more immediate, and her mind would work in mysterious ways to put the life-or-death puzzle together in her head.

As she drove home, Callow left the heat off and the window cracked, letting that same frigid air lick the side of her head. She drove with no music and no thoughts, and when she pulled into the empty driveway of the house, she wished dearly that someone would join her so she wouldn't feel so alone.

Inside, she walked numbly to the kitchen and yanked a bottle of red from the catacomb wine rack above the stove. The vintage didn't matter. Mid-pour, there was a double knock at the door, followed by the turning of a key in the lock, which Callow thought was an odd thing for someone to do if they had a key.

She turned her back, knowing full well who it was. She didn't want him to see her smile—or her tears—as she pulled two glasses down from the cabinet.

CHAPTER SEVENTEEN

Callow surveyed the damage.

Her pants were draped over a chair, her shirt near the bathroom door, her panties scrunched up near the foot of the bed. Two pillows had been knocked to the floor, and the sheets were wadded up under the footboard. The TV was on, but neither she nor Marcus knew what had been playing for the last half hour.

Marcus lay shirtless, arms above his head, staring at the swirling fan that did little to recirculate the heat pulsing off his skin. Callow laid her cheek on his chest, calm and content. They hadn't made it to the wine, which sat abandoned, open but full, on the nightstand. She was fully prepared to down the bottle, regardless of it being just after one.

She hadn't planned to spend the night with Marcus. As always, it had been sporadic, random—and welcomed.

Marcus's assigned post was her house. Her's was to wait for contact from the Icebox Killer. Marcus was her protection, and while she lay naked, her leg draped lazily over his, she'd never felt safer—and that *terrified* her. Did she deserve to have a normal life with him? Could it always be like this?

"I can feel you thinking," he said. She felt his voice rumble.

"I'm not thinking about anything, actually. I'm just enjoying this. You."

She felt him reach to the bedside table, and then there was the familiar *click* of a cell phone camera taking a picture. She looked up to see Marcus holding her phone, admiring the candid photo of him sneering boyishly and her with her eyes closed.

"There," he said, setting the phone aside. "Evidence that *the* Genevieve Callow, criminal profiler, can turn her brain off for once." He looked down at her, and their eyes met. "Well, not for long, it seems. What's on your mind?"

"Hank."

"We just had sex and you're thinking about *Hank*?"

She rolled her eyes. "Not like that. What I mean is, I'm thinking about what he said—about that kid and his grandmother. He absolved himself of responsibility in that case."

"I don't think so. I think Hank just realizes that blaming himself for things out of his control won't help anyone. I expect you're thinking about the time we just spent together and wondering if you've squandered precious minutes you could have been wringing out your hands with this case. I'd say the time wasn't wasted. You're doing your job."

"I could be doing more …"

"We could all be doing more. I'm not saying I don't think this case is important—I do—but what else could you be doing?"

Callow didn't have an answer. She felt run aground; no path left to turn to other than to handle whatever came next and hope someone didn't die in the process. The Academy never prepared her for this; the mental anguish of stretching herself so thin, she might snap, or risking having a personal life. She'd learned to be tough, to look for the small things, to follow up and canvas and interview … but they hadn't taught her what her life would be like living with those skills when they didn't work.

"Maybe you're right, but I can't help feeling I should be doing more."

"That's always the case. But if you let that feeling consume you, there will be nothing left of yourself. You'll only know the job, and that's it. What kind of life is that?"

He raised a lot of good points. They swirled in her head, each one a different thread to tug on and each one dedicated to untangling her life if she pulled on it too hard. Callow resigned herself to a simple, deep sigh.

"What if we gave it up?" she asked, briefly surprised by her own question. They'd been over this so many times before.

"I can give it up," he said, playing with her hair. "But I'm not so sure how easy it'd be for you. You know I'm dedicated to whatever holds my interest. There hasn't been much consistency in my life because of that—except for you. No matter how much we try to avoid it, we always end up like this—and I don't mean the sex. I mean this very conversation, where we talk about all the things that could be."

"I like these talks."

"Me too. But I can't decide this for you. You must make that choice. And if you do, I'll hold your hand when you turn your badge in and drive you to the airport. We'll catch a flight somewhere warm, where there isn't any snow."

"And then you'd get a desk job, nine-to-five, and we'd have kids and a dog and a white picket fence?"

She felt him stirring. "We'd have each other. The rest will come."

Callow felt that was a good place to leave the conversation. Her stomach growled, followed by Marcus's shortly after. She padded to the kitchen in his suit jacket and made eggs while he took a shower. He joined her a few minutes later, wearing a spare set of clothes from the bottom drawer of her dresser and drying his head with a towel. She munched on toast and eggs while she sat at the table, the Icebox case file open at her elbow. She slid him the plate and offered him her coffee.

"Midday breakfast?"

"It would have been more customary if all this had happened in the morning," she said, "but by tomorrow, I don't think my mind will be anywhere but with that poor girl."

Marcus sat across from her, cradling the coffee. He pulled an evidence log, one of seven that cataloged the investigation into her vehicle. *Black hair tie. Empty soda can. 2007 Chevrolet Tahoe manual. Nine millimeter Federal Gold Dot shell casing.*

Callow remembered that casing. It had slipped down her shirt, white-hot, at the range. Marcus had noticed her flitting around, shaking out her shirt, and had broken into belly laughs, making some wisecrack about finding it later. She'd viewed that moment as embarrassing, and not in the funny way. Looking back, there were lots of moments when Marcus laughed and she didn't. She was coming to regret those now. How many moments had she lost to seriousness when a little levity could have done her some good?

Looking over the half-inch-thick case file, guilt rode into Callow's mind on a white horse, ready to relieve her of her hope for a normal life. *White picket fence.* What if she could save one more victim? *Marcus smiling on a Florida beach.* What if she could save one more?

Thus continued the war with herself, wrought by her own desires to serve. Serving someone else, the thankless job motif, could be addictive. It made living in squalor, or pain, or guilt sufferable because to serve was to do something good, no matter the cost. In her situation, it was clear Callow was serving the FBI at a cost to her own personal life. In her vision, Marcus wandered toward the water, and when she looked down, she was dressed in a formal pantsuit and had a case file open in her lap, her feet naked in the sand. A blood-stained cooler stared at her from under an umbrella …

She hadn't noticed she was shaking. The evidence log Marcus had been holding was set aside in the neat pile of already-read documents. He was doing the dishes. The pots clanked in the sink.

"Can we talk later about what you said about us? About me leaving the FBI?" Callow asked. She flipped the page to a map marked with Sharpie at the location of two of the Icebox Killer's victims and, in red, the Herman Free Library.

"Sure. Can I get you to promise that you won't be thinking about a case when we do? I can compartmentalize, but you …" He softened his approach after he caught the look in her eye. "I don't think your judgement is impaired. I just think the job has a grip on you."

Marcus read her mind. He had effectively regurgitated what she was thinking in a scary, uncanny way.

"After the case, we'll talk. Lay out our options. Is that fair?"

Marcus shut off the water, then grabbed a towel to dry his hands. "After the case. And you won't take on a new one until we talk."

"Are you annoyed? About us, earlier?"

He shook his head quickly. "I know what we are. I have for a while. But I also know we can be more, and I know how that can happen. We're a *thing* that never stopped being a *thing*. You're my best friend, Callow. I know we can be more, just as we have been in the past, but I can't force you to give up all you've done—and all you'll go on to do—to be with me."

He strode over to the table, broad, confident, took up her hands, and kissed the tops of them lightly. "You need to give it all up for yourself or you'll live with regret, always wondering *'what if'* you'd stayed."

Marcus let her go, and Callow felt herself squeezing her

fingers just a little tighter, wishing so badly he wouldn't. There was so much riding on the case, she'd shut off her emotions to be *objective,* but there were still those rare moments of impossibility where objective thought and emotions connected. Those moments were where real behavioral analysis work was done: when you could draw the victim out of the equation, dump yourself in his or her shoes, and come out the other side with the facts that would break the profile wide open. At other times, objectiveness and emotions fought a bitter war.

"I promise, when the case is over, we'll talk. You, me, and no case file between us."

He kissed her forehead once. "Fair. I need my jacket back, though. We've got the day left. Let's find this sucker. Do you have a plan?"

Callow looked at the sprawl of paperwork before her—countless hours of meticulous data collection, maps, crime scene photos, victim reports, and more. It wasn't a matter of the efforts wasted; that would be selfish. No, the paperwork represented entire lives; unanswered questions that were her responsibility to answer for the people left behind. Somewhere in that packet was Carmen's case file, and like the families of the other victims, like Carmen's mother and half-sister, she, too, would never find peace without answers.

"Piece by piece. We've done it once before, but we can do it again. We've missed something. When we do, that's when the case breaks. When we find that missing piece, we'll run the profile and catch this monster. For the fallen girls."

"Hey, it's okay to say we'll catch him for *you,* too."

"Fine. For the fallen girls—and for *me.*"

CHAPTER EIGHTEEN

Callow's phone buzzed on the countertop, squealing an obnoxious corporate ring. Marcus scanned it, gave a confused frown, and handed it to her. The number was unknown.

Callow felt a sudden coolness flood her body as her nerves rested on the fine edge of a high-tensile wire. She looked at Marcus, then the phone. Could it be Icebox, reaching out to taunt her? Would she finally hear his voice—the cold callousness behind a man who could kill without a second thought?

With hesitant fingers, she picked up on the last ring. Marcus started an audio recording on his own phone, and she pressed the speaker button. He must have been thinking the same as her.

If Icebox can send an anonymous email, a phone call wasn't too outlandish.

"This is Special Agent Callow."

A pregnant pause.

"Special Agent Callow, this is Wendy Bryant, Chief of Staff."

Callow expelled a controlled breath, the one that had caught in her throat as she awaited the terrible, menacing voice of the Devil on the other end. Marcus raised an eyebrow. Callow waved him off, referencing the recording, but he shrugged and left it running.

"Yes, ma'am. What can I do for you?"

"Nothing, actually. The reason I'm calling is to offer what I can do for you."

Callow remembered the shrill, mouselike woman from the briefing in Jed's office, and wondered what mighty strings her tiny frame could tug on. Then she remembered how Wendy Bryant earned her nickname—by ripping a man's throat out. She could envision the woman, battered, looking as if she'd just seen war, blood dripping down her face, as she stumbled out of an abandoned warehouse. Everyone knew the story of Wendy "the Barbarian" Bryant. From a corporate position, that image must have done wonders.

"Yes, ma'am," Callow replied simply.

"I'm calling to encourage you. To offer up my condolences officially for your friend Carmen, and to urge you to be careful. It's probably no surprise that I don't approve of a … *plan* that requires our best profiler do nothing." She sighed. "But I can commiserate with what happens when a case runs cold. Putting additional pressure on you will not tune your skills, and it won't help. You know what's at stake, Callow, so I'll end our conversation with this: outside your door, across the street, is a media van."

Marcus pulled down the blinds, then nodded curtly.

"They are ours—independents, paid to live stream throughout the day. They're watching the house for us, and for your unsub, who I'm sure is paying attention to the feeds. When he sees you going about your business, appearing to be lost, he will mess up. He will relinquish a piece of evidence by mistake or on purpose, and then we will pounce."

"I understand," Callow replied.

"I hope so. Nobody will blame you if you don't succeed." The chief of staff scoffed, a short *pip.* "Well, nobody except the media. And perhaps you will blame yourself, but every reasonable person will see how the cards are stacked against us. Fear not, all the resources of the FBI are at your disposal. You have excellent training and an impeccable eye for detail, which is where you'll find the answers. Get him, Callow. We're all watching."

"Thank you, ma'am."

Wendy Bryant hung up. Her words were brash, quick to the point, but clear. Callow put the phone down, ready to share her thoughts with Marcus.

"I'm confused," she said. "What was the point of her call? I don't feel as if she helped me at all. She only told me what I already knew."

Marcus tapped his phone. "I was listening, and I'm sure there were others huddled around a conference room with her. It was a *threat*, which is why she said it wasn't."

"Let me guess, by offering 'all the resources of the FBI' and mentioning my training, she's going to bury me in the media if I fuck this up?"

"Correct."

"She just said the quiet part out loud."

"Yes. I don't feel helped or supported—and neither should you. That woman is not your friend. That meeting with the bigwigs—that was a message to all of us. This case must really be worrying the top brass. We've missed unsubs before. This is different."

Callow felt small, girlish, like a bully had just shoved her out of her place in line in middle school. No matter the effort to separate herself from the stress, it seemed stress, external or otherwise, was intent on making itself at home on Callow's shoulders. It was enough to make the strongest of mind and will crack, to fall to the floor and curl into a defeated ball. A weaker person might have done so, but Genevieve Callow was *not* a weak person.

"It doesn't matter," Callow spat. "Bryant wasted her

breath. If they were trying to make a case for me to stay after this, they suck at it."

"They don't know you're considering leaving. I only just learned of it myself."

Marcus grinned, and the smile was contagious. She grinned back, and no matter how much her anxiety tried to fight it, her mood was lifted a notch away from "defeated ball." Marcus gave her the confidence she needed with a few kind words and his presence.

Callow looked at the case file. It wasn't so irresoluble now, not quite so imposing. The pages seemed to hold hope, the pictures a puzzle to solve, as opposed to a painful recollection of despair.

"I'm going to go through this again. Front to back. Every page. You do it with me. If you see something, say something, or we'll keep going." Callow furrowed her brow. "We've got time."

Callow scooped up the scattered papers and arranged them neatly in the manila folder. She'd already sorted them into piles several times and had lost track of what was what; each time she'd sat at the table to comb through it all was a scatterbrained crapshoot. She needed to start at the beginning, and now that she had a place to start, the end of the pile was just that—the end, the place where she shouldn't only have answers, but a direction as well. The end of the packet was effectively a lighthouse.

Renewed with hope, Callow took a deep breath and tried to imagine the file folder had just been handed to her.

Gone was her kitchen and the smell of butter and cooked eggs. Gone was the hint of stale coffee and the trace of Marcus's cologne and sweat on her neck. Instead, she was in her office, where a wisp of frigid air snuck in through a weather seal, smelling like snow. The floors felt like stiff commercial carpet, and she could hear the echo of heels on granite floors, echoing down the chamberlike halls of Quantico.

She imagined Jedediah handing her the case file and her taking it with all the confidence of a trophy winner who'd just smashed the competition in half the time; the confidence that could only come from absolute surety that failure was not an option, and winning was only a matter of time.

Out with the old, Callow opened the case file anew.

"For each of the victims, potential witnesses were interviewed and the areas from which they were taken were canvased. Pathology also confirmed identical findings of marijuana."

"Which is no surprise. They were both of college age," Marcus replied quickly.

"Right. Coroner's reports are identical: all victims died of blood loss, then were decapitated. In each, a major artery was cut with a precision instrument, most likely a scalpel. Their tongue, eyes, and teeth were all removed postmortem and placed inside the cooler next to the victim's head. Nothing notable." Callow slid the paper aside to Marcus.

"Let's go over it again. The victim and the location. Carmen Watts: Cooley and Smith. Gwen Hammond: Second and Broadway. The third victim is a Ms. Marissa Marley, Main and Martin Luther King Boulevard. All in the morning hours before lunch. Coroner confirmed our suspicions that there is an extended time between time of death and the placing of the bodies based on the elemental decay."

"Nothing notable about the locations, either. Rebecca's 'four points to a compass' theory is null since two bodies were found in the south. What about the victim's places of residence?" Marcus asked.

Callow retrieved a second map, this one with blue circles

showing home addresses for Gwen, Carmen, and Marissa. From what either agent could tell, there didn't seem to be a pattern. The only thing worth noting was each of the victims lived in and were taken from Colleyville, a city of fifty square miles.

Callow sat back, alternating between twirling a pen and nibbling on its cap. "What we have is this: the victims were taken in the morning, without any witnesses or camera footage, suggesting the unsub strategically identified locations from which to conduct the abductions. He takes the sedated victims to an unknown location, tortures them, and then dumps their bodies between twelve to fourteen hours later. The unsub is most likely a white male, mid-thirties, with medical experience or training. He's likely …"

Marcus held up a hand. "Let's wait on the full profile. We don't want to risk you repeating what you've said and letting it get ingrained. We need more."

Callow didn't disagree. For the past hour, she and Marcus had combed over every document they held, including those relating to Carmen, but unlike her first experience viewing her autopsy report and crime scene photos, Callow didn't feel the abject urge to scream. She was more focused now; truly objective. She prayed silently for Carmen, Carmen's family, and herself, wishing retribution on the unsub and peace as a result. Then she moved on because, like with all the other crime scene photos, there was nothing more to offer.

"What about the forensics on your email?"

Callow turned her laptop around to show the email from the digital forensics team. The message from the Icebox Killer had been sent using an encrypted messaging service with a burner email address tracing back to the dark web, an email address that essentially cannibalized itself after the user was done with it.

"Is it worth noting the unsub knows how to access the dark web?" Marcus asked.

"Doubtful. It's almost commonplace now. Most people just avoid it because of how dangerous it is."

"Our unsub doesn't care about that."

"Which follows our theory of his sociopathic tendencies," Callow continued. "He lacks the capacity for feeling human emotion, which is why he turns to violent behavior that most would deem unconscionable. I think the icebox is a metaphor for his heart. Cold. Empty. He seeks to fill the void, but nothing does the trick, and so he abandons the icebox and tries again."

She handed over the latest piece of evidence: the forensic log from her Tahoe. She'd read it three times already and, by now, the tedious entries were starting to blend. She knew each of the cataloged items, and the sheet also noted trace fibers, saliva, and hair. Each was a dead end, as the trace fibers came back to standard clothing, and the saliva and hair belonged to the missing girl, Marissa Marley.

Callow sifted through the paperwork to the tab created for Marissa. Her picture was attached to the left side of the folder, with a worksheet containing her personal information on the right. Locals had already interviewed her immediate family and friends.

Something was off about the report. Callow raised an eyebrow.

"See something?" Marcus asked.

"Marissa is twenty-four. Not in college, but didn't live at home. Her residence is listed as an apartment building a few blocks from the Herman Free Library."

Marcus came around and looked over her shoulder.

"And?"

"She's twenty-four, living on her own, but there isn't a job listed here. Her last day at work, a boutique downtown, was two weeks ago."

"Is there any significance to her having a job, then quitting?"

Callow nodded, a flare of excitement budding in her stomach—not quite butterflies, but similar.

"Why didn't the locals know about the new job?"

She held up a hastily filled out job application in scrawling pink handwriting. "I'm guessing because she hadn't started yet. I'm willing to bet she was taken just before she was supposed to start," Callow stated, hopping to her feet. She stuffed her phone into her pocket. "She didn't have time to tell anyone she was quitting, except for her previous employer. Locals wrote it off because she turned her notice in weeks before she went missing, but I bet she showed up to work every day until she was taken. We need to interview the manager she never got to work for. The one who interviewed her."

CHAPTER NINETEEN

Callow and Marcus cleared the table but left the pile of evidence like unfinished laundry; something they knew they'd have to revisit, no matter how long they put it off. Callow held a hastily torn coffee-stained piece of paper on which Marcus had scrawled an address. She wore jeans and a t-shirt, and a dusty purse tucked under her arm held her pistol and badge. Near the door, she straightened Marcus's tie, but his shirt was wrinkled beyond recovery.

"What about the plan? About being bait?" he asked.

Callow had already given some thought to how their behavior might look to the Icebox Killer if he was watching. There was a lot of hope riding on their plan, but at that very moment, he could have been torturing Marissa Marley, and it was with this thought that Callow justified deviation from the plan—which amounted to doing nothing at all.

She shrugged the bag. "We're going on a date," she said, dropping her department cell phone next to her laptop on the table. "If he calls, I won't answer. If he drops me an email, I won't see it. This is as good as ignoring him. There is inherent risk he will be watching to see if we're following up on leads. That might give us away, but I think it's worth the risk."

"It seems risky. He could give away his position in his messages."

"Forensics are monitoring my email, and we don't know if he'll even call. We won't be gone longer than thirty minutes. Marissa was supposed to start working at a place called Sapphire Tavern, a bar in downtown Colleyville. I called ahead while you were getting dressed; confirmed the manager is there."

"Did you tell him who we were?"

"No. Tight lips and all." She made a motion like she was sealing off her mouth for good.

Callow looked past Marcus at the clock on the wall. 11:00 A.M. The numbers might as well have been written in blood. A pang of terrible angst threatened to upchuck her breakfast and the two cups of coffee that gurgled away in the corner of her gut.

Marcus grimaced. "I don't like it, but I don't like the original plan any better. Did you let Jedediah know what we're up to?"

She nodded, handing him his keys off a rack on the wall, where they'd mysteriously made their home next to her own. "He said as long as we aren't running around drawing too much attention to ourselves, or having a uniform trail us, we should be fine. He agreed we needed to be quick but said we did right by finding a thread to tug on."

Nothing more was said as they left the house. The news crew across the street sat inside their matte blue panel van, the door open, talking amongst themselves. If she squinted, Callow could make out the red recording light of the camera set up inside the van, peering at her like the watchful eye of a mechanical cyclops. She had half a mind to flip the camera the bird, but the crew wasn't the target of her disdain. No, her disgust was toward the Icebox Killer, the voyeur with his dick in his hands, watching his puppets dance while he held Marissa in a place God only knew. Acknowledging this with her contempt would only make her feel worse and fuel whatever sick desires their unsub was hoping to kindle.

Instead, she nonchalantly dropped into the passenger seat of Marcus's Crown Victoria, angled the air vents toward her face, and peered out the window. Outside the tinted glass, the world was so much more than the sum of the afternoon sun, the modest winter chill that was abating just enough to warrant a t-shirt and the poignant remains of humidified air from melting ice. All that was left was mud, clear skies, and a sun that was bright yet offered an insubstantial amount of heat. The day was much like any other, but as Callow looked away from the sky and toward the ground, herein lay the truth, for her eyes settled on a snow pile, now a thick icicle, stained with clumps of dirt and shit and hunks of grass from where a snowplow had cut a hasty corner.

The pile of ice leaked soiled water into a drain, and in the drain was the matted, moldering remains of a brown tabby cat. Its head was nearly in the drain, its body flat. Callow remembered seeing the cat over the previous weeks. It was often staring at her inquisitively from the stoop of the large house across the street with red shutters. Whether the cat belonged to the people who lived there, she didn't know, but it didn't matter in the end; what mattered was how quickly she remembered the cat for how it was versus how she saw it now. The sun and sky were not at all reflective of the murky underbelly where the dirty water goes, the place where the sewer runs and the body of the cat would eventually slip into the tunnel and forever remain there.

How simple the world was that only saw the sun and the sky, when what lay beneath their feet was so much more.

Sapphire Tavern was a respite for carved beer mugs, stout wooden tables with glossy finishes, and a bearskin rug at the foot of the fire. As expected for the mid-morning hours, the bar was empty when the heavy steel-strapped oak door swung back to allow them inside. A waitress, dressed in the garb of a billowy dress and exposed bust, yawned into her phone near the register in the middle of the room, clearly bored. Marcus hovered over Callow's shoulder, both apprehensive about whether they were to be approached or if they should cross the expanse to the waitress. She didn't look up.

"Anna! I heard the bell! Say the line!"

Anna peered up from her phone with an exaggerated eye roll, angled her face toward the kitchen, and said disinterestedly, "Welcome, all, to Sapphire Tavern, where travelers find peace in the bottom of a pint."

Marcus beamed boyishly, but Callow felt herself yearning to roll her eyes, too. It was clear who the Tavern's clientele was. The half-doors to the kitchen swung open and an eccentric man—not at all portly, as Callow had expected—came through. He was no taller than the top of the doors, skinny almost to the point of emaciation. He wore a feathered hat, a lanky shirt with billowing sleeves, and blue jeans, and apparently, he didn't expect to be seen from the waist up. Callow wouldn't have guessed him to be more than twenty, and certainly not old enough to have an established business. He exited the kitchen with a confident smile, one which, Callow noticed, was made up of unusually sharp little teeth. As if to complete the boyish ensemble, his teeth hadn't formed beyond rudimentary canines crossed with a child's first set of molars.

Hand extended, he crossed the room. "Welcome to Sapphire Tavern. My name is Hodge. Edwin Hodge. But everyone just calls me Hodge."

Callow took his hand and shook it. It felt small in hers, like a child's, warm and breakable. But his voice was mystically deep, challenging even Marcus's for bass and clarity. She enjoyed listening to it.

"I'm Callow. This is Oakley." She flashed her badge. "We'd like to chat with you for a few minutes, assuming you're the manager?"

He nodded strangely. "I am. You've picked quite a day. We've just opened, but as you can see, day shift on a Wednesday is not ideal for a bar." He gestured around the room. "These things take time. We cater to a younger crowd. I'm sure Anna has the place under control."

Hodge beckoned toward an unmarked door ringed with taxidermied animal heads. A snarling cougar, a bison with black marbled eyes, and a mountain goat with white-ringed horns all glared at Callow and Marcus as they followed him inside, leaving the crackling fire and the waitress behind. The office was surprisingly spacious, with a six-person plastic table loaded with receipts and order forms and a laptop buried amongst them.

Hodge unfolded two metal chairs and offered two water bottles from a mini fridge. The two FBI agents politely took them and set them on the table.

Hodge sat stiffly in his chair. "To what pleasure do I owe the FBI?"

"We'd like to ask you a few questions about Marissa Marley. She was supposed to start working here."

Hodge stared blankly for a moment before breaking into a knowing smile and a rapid nod. "Yes, she was, but she was a no-show about two days ago."

"Are you aware she's currently missing?"

"What? No! I just thought she'd changed her mind. Can't trust her generation until they show up, and it's the same for every shift after that."

"How old are you, exactly?" Marcus chimed in.

Callow calmed him with a placating hand on his leg. "You seem young, that's all," she interjected.

"I'm thirty-four. Call it genetics. I come from a small family, and this isn't the first time I've been carded. I had a restaurant before, but let's just say, they aren't so easy to start up when the bank managers think you're twelve. I tried again this year with a solid plan and some seed money. Bar first, then restaurant. We have all the workings and a menu, but we aren't advertising the food until I can get some decent staff."

The man talked quickly, and Callow quickly began to see how his quirks might hinder business dealings.

"Thank you, Hodge. What can you tell me about Marissa? I assume you interviewed her?"

Hodge settled in his chair, his shoulders shrinking, no longer tense—which was good. Callow needed to keep him talking with surety. As of now, she felt the man was being honest.

"She grabbed an application, and I asked her to fill it out on the spot. We chatted about her availability, which seemed open. She said she wasn't in college, so I didn't have to worry about her running off before I could get some decent hours out of her."

"I take it you hire a lot of young servers and have experienced something similar in your industry?" Callow asked. She wanted to follow that thread, as his tone toward his employees shifted immensely, like talking about them left a sour taste on his tongue.

He chuckled heartily, and his chair squeaked when he leaned back. "They always leave me after a few weeks. I used to think it was me, but I asked around to few of other small business owners, especially those in retail and restaurants, and they all experienced the same thing. Pay is low, margins are thin, customers are pinching pennies … Personally, I think it's work ethic. There's almost nothing I haven't set my mind on that I haven't succeeded. *Almost*. And if I had left at the first sign of discomfort … well, I wouldn't be standing here today."

"It seems as though you've done well for yourself," Callow said, feeding the man's ego.

"As have you! Special Agent! I can't imagine how exhilarating your lives must be."

"It can be. Can you tell me more about Marissa? Did she come in with anybody? Mention anything about her life that might strike you as odd?"

Hodge scratched his smooth chin, then ran his hand through his crew cut hair. It was an odd gesture, forced and out of place, as if he couldn't decide which to do first.

"Her roommate drove her—waited in the car. But she seemed in a rush. We didn't chat long. She was shy. And working for me is pretty straightforward."

Anna yelled the greeting, sounding suspiciously like she'd leaned into the door to the manager's office for extra emphasis.

"It seems today might not be a bust after all! Do you have any other questions, agents?" Hodge bounced his gaze between them.

"Can we call you if we do? Also, may we take a copy of Marissa's original application?"

Hodge stood up suddenly and sifted through one of many piles of paperwork on the table. "Of course. I'd encourage it." He grinned his sharp, predatory grin.

Callow felt off, as though she was looking into a wolf's smile. She stood, took the card and application, and offered Hodge her hand. The bar owner took it and then shook Marcus's.

The two agents saw themselves out with Hodge in tow, who locked the door to the office behind them. They walked in silence to the car, and once they were in, both Callow and Marcus seemed to release a deep breath.

"I don't like him," Callow commented.

"I don't, either," Marcus agreed. "His voice doesn't match his body. And his demeanor … Was it confidence? Arrogance? It made me queasy. Anything you saw we could follow up on?"

"No. I felt he was honest. Maybe *too* honest; too willing to help. And that smile. I couldn't help but think we were talking to a piranha."

Marcus drove the car to the lights and stopped, even though it was green. It didn't matter; there wasn't a car behind them. To the left, they could head back to the house, empty-handed, no better off than the place they were now. To the right, they could hit the freeway and, only a few blocks from there, the restaurant where Rebecca worked.

"I don't want to go home. Not yet," she said.

"Okay. Where to, then?" Marcus was typing Hodge's name, number, and business address into his phone, sending an email, most likely for the office to run his information.

"The roommate." Callow sighed. "Might be nothing, but let's follow up with them, then we can close this thread, too. Don't bother calling her. She's close."

The clock read 12:04 P.M.

CHAPTER TWENTY

Their destination was only two miles from the Sapphire Tavern, in an industrialized section of Colleyville slowly being overrun, absorbed through its cell wall by the swanky, cosmopolitan part of town. It was a battle Callow could watch in real time through the car window as impoverished, dilapidated buildings underwent sales and remodels, later to sell trinkets and handmade soaps. Sapphire Tavern didn't seem out of place in the area, and she could see the appeal.

Just two miles away, tucked behind the new roofs and colorful storefronts, was a gloomy graveyard of empty smokestacks, piles of rusted rebar, and the skeletons of many incomplete industrial buildings. Two organisms, and only one could survive as time ferried jobs overseas.

"These old buildings make great apartment complexes," Marcus observed at the lights.

Callow could tell he wanted to break the silence. The radio wasn't an option; the speakers were blown, and now they'd only scream.

"Do you remember El Paso?" she replied, giving in. "It was like this, but without the little shops, though."

"You're thinking about El Paso?"

"Kind of hard not to. This place isn't much different from the warehouses behind the motel we stayed at. Things move differently here, of course, with the buying up, remodeling, and new business. Can you imagine the problems these people must have? Taxes, working with builders, spreadsheets, rowdy customers … It all seems so mundane."

"It seems boring, you mean," Marcus stated.

"No. Not really. To them, it's probably not boring. Maybe our interpretation of 'exhilarating' changes with how we live our lives. Right now, my heart only races when we're working. Or when I'm with you. But I imagine if I owned a shop, then that would change."

Oakley turned onto Pine Street. The GPS on his phone showed a red flag a half mile away. "You'd own a shop? What could you sell?"

"Does it matter? I'm just thinking. If I really left the Bureau behind, what would I be leaving it behind for, and what would be waiting for me?"

"I'll open a Sapphire Tavern with you," Marcus jeered.

Callow snorted as the Crown Victoria crested a large speed bump. They turned right into the back lot behind a tall brick building. A fire escape hung from its left side like the discarded rail of a child's braces, and there was a loading dock on the right, at the end of a steep hill now used as a parking area. The application in Callow's lap said Marissa Marley lived on the third floor.

Outside the car, the scent of warm trash wove its way into her nostrils, spurring her into a hurried run toward the back door. A glance through the window confirmed it led into the lobby. The hallway, narrow even for Callow, was a challenge for Marcus, who ducked and grunted as his elbows clipped the doorframe. Yellow aged tile, like old bone, was marred with long black streaks where things had been dragged across it. In the lobby, the mailboxes were tagged with the shadow of graffiti, unable to be fully scrubbed off. There was no call button so the agents stepped into the elevator.

On the third floor, they exited onto a shortened hallway of the same drab coloring as the lobby. At one end was a maintenance closet; on the other, a large bay window overlooking more of the industrialized world that went on for miles. The door to the room marked "3", however, was crafted with stained glass and dark mahogany wood. The handle was plated silver, and there wasn't a peephole.

Through the obscuring glass, Callow could see a shadow inside. She knocked twice.

"Who is it?" a young woman called through the door. She sounded apprehensive.

Callow and Marcus shared a glance.

"Special Agents Callow and Oakley, FBI. Can we talk?"

"Badges ..."

They withdrew their badges and held them against the glass.

"Look up."

Callow did so, and saw a pin-sized hole with a reflective glass surface recessed in the wood and a cable that blended with the trim. It disappeared inside through a rubber gasket. They held up their badges to the camera. Two locks clicked, and the woman inside opened the door.

"Are you Marissa's roommate?"

"Katie," the woman replied. Her brown eyes were puffy and red. Her cheeks were flushed, and a single teardrop hung from her pointed chin. Her dark hair did little to hide her face, no matter how desperately she wished to stay behind it like a curtain.

"May we come in?"

Katie didn't answer; instead, she slowly opened the door and stepped back.

The apartment was more of the same shock to the cultural senses: tastefully decorated with misfit yet logical abstract paintings, and the occasional shock of red lampshades or pillows atop all white furniture. The apartment was a picturesque reflection of modern living.

Katie pressed the door shut firmly behind her and made for the couches, which looked no more than fifteen minutes post plastic wrap—immaculate, like the rest of the apartment. Marcus, in his crinkled shirt, looked wholly out of place. Katie hugged a pillow on the love seat, facing the sliding glass doors to a short balcony. Callow and Marcus sat on the matching love seat to its right.

"My name is Callow. This is my partner, Marcus. We'd like to ask you some questions about Marissa."

Katie stared at a blank television, eventually whispering, "I just saw the news. The photo. She was in your car, wasn't she?"

Callow tried to set her face to "compassionate." The girl was shaking, nearly suffocating herself with the pillow while fresh tears soaked the fabric.

"Yes. But I can …"

"Is she dead?"

"I'm sorry?"

"I asked, is Marissa dead?" Katie spat, her eyes clear with rage and staring through Callow.

"We don't think so. I don't know what the media got right or wrong, so I'll set the record straight. We think Marissa was abducted by the murderer known as the Icebox Killer. He has a timeline we think he holds to, meaning we don't have a lot of time to find your friend. We could really use your help."

Callow could feel the hurt radiating from her. Who wouldn't be torn up knowing the fate of their friend, if history was any predictor, was grim? When she'd first joined the Academy, Callow had imagined herself consoling victims such as Katie. The crimes monsters and men—and those that are both— send a ripple through families and communities alike. This was their goal, to shake the tree at its base and watch more and more fruit fall and rot until the tree bore no more fruit and its roots dislodged from the earth. Then, the tree would die—only by then, the monster had already moved on to another.

Callow realized jumping into this girl's life and asking her to recount details of her friendship wouldn't work—not in the state she was in, in this apartment, alone, watching the news and waiting for the next report to confirm her every worst fear in vivid color. What Katie needed wasn't a shoulder to cry on, but a sword with which to fight back.

"You aren't helpless, you know? That's not why we're here," Callow said.

Katie perked up, her shoulders firming. She swallowed hard and looked at Callow—really looked at her, for the first time.

"You feel as if you've lost control," Callow continued. "I feel like that sometimes, too. Especially with cases that are particularly difficult, when I've got people relying on me and I feel as though I'm suffocating."

"What do you do, then? To stop feeling like that?" Katie asked.

"I try and try again. And if I fail, I forgive myself." The hint of hypocrisy in her words wasn't lost on Callow, but she needed Katie to see a way through her hurt. "If you're blaming yourself for Marissa's disappearance, *don't*. I don't blame you, and neither will anybody else. Once you're able to see it wasn't your fault, then you can take the reins and *try*."

Katie's lip quivered. "It's hard."

Callow nodded. "And it's going to be. There are groups—survivors' groups—therapy for people who really understand. You can talk, or you can listen. Either way, I empower you to join one. I'll get you the information for one in the area. It's normally for police officers and servicemen, but I don't think they'd mind if you came."

Katie drew in a breath. "I think I'd like that."

For the next few minutes, they waited in silence. Marcus didn't reach for his phone, but he did move over to the window, his hands jammed in his pockets. When the silence built to a head, Katie finally spoke, surprising everyone.

"I knew something was wrong when she stopped answering my texts. We left off in the middle of a conversation. Tedious stuff—food in the refrigerator, classes starting up again soon, that sort of thing. She graduated, but she always helped me with my work. I'm not much for math. My dad used to help me with it while he was receiving cancer treatment. He'd only use one hand because the other had an IV and it burned him."

Marcus returned to his chair.

"What else were you two talking about? Did Marissa mention anything odd that day? Or maybe the day before?" Callow asked.

"She asked me to take her to get an application at a new bar in town. I took her, and she took a phone call in the parking lot outside—you know, by the trashcan. It stunk over there. I don't know how she could handle it."

Callow nodded along.

"Well, she never came back home. I assumed she had a boy pick her up or something. I'm sure there were a few she could have called, so don't ask me to recall any specifics. She never had anyone here at the apartment, though, and she wasn't exclusive."

"You said you two went to college together? Was there perhaps somebody she knew from there? Someone controlling or obsessive? Perhaps a secret admirer? We believe our suspect is a white male, mid-thirties."

Katie shook her head, her hair swishing across her face. "No, not that I know of. Marissa was always with her family if she wasn't here. We bonded over sick parents. Her dad and my dad received treatment at the same facility."

"Do you recall anybody at the facility ...?"

"No. Everyone was really kind."

"What about here? In the complex?"

"The other apartments aren't rented yet. The other cars belong to the owner and his wife, who stay on the top floor."

"Thank you, Katie. Can we take a look at Marissa's room?"

Katie got up silently and presented Marissa's room, one of two along the hall off the living room. It, too, was decorated in the abysmal white furniture. Her bed was neatly made. The vanity had a ring of lights around the mirror. It was hard to tell someone lived there except for one end table that held a picture, a half glass of water, and a crumpled business card.

Callow wandered through the room, checking every corner in a clockwise pattern, then she retraced her steps back the way she came. Each time, the business card stood out.

Callow picked it up from the nightstand. "Picard's Meats? Is this where Marissa worked before?"

Katie hugged herself near the door, refusing to come in. "No. One of those *'once you see how it's made'* situations. She made it halfway through the interview. Mentioned the smell, mostly. She came home smelling of blood."

"Thank you, Katie. For everything." Callow drew a notebook and pen from her purse and wrote the address and time for the survivor's meeting at the Herman Library. Katie took it, then ushered them to the front door.

"Will you call me if you find her?" she asked pensively.

Callow nodded.

Katie wrote her number in Callow's notebook and then offered a weak smile. "You're different than most other cops, Special Agent Callow."

"I try. We'll be in touch. Marissa could use your prayers right now. It's okay to pray."

Katie nodded and pressed the door shut.

CHAPTER TWENTY-ONE

"What are we doing, Marcus?" Callow asked, resting her head against the warm glass of the unmarked cruiser. She gazed out over a stretch of more brick and corrugated metal buildings, each one indistinguishable from the last, that created a narrow passage for the agents to drive through. A seemingly endless two-way street, representative of their overall case.

Callow didn't dare look at the clock. Each glance would only remind her of time she didn't have.

You're chasing your tail, Callow. Icebox wants it this way. You've been bested.

Negativity crept over the tempo of her heartbeat, which was strangely calm under the circumstances. A girl's life was on the line, and here she was, prancing around, chasing dead ends.

"Our jobs," Marcus said firmly. "The old plan was to sit around and wait for contact. How long would that have lasted? An hour? Two? *Twelve?* What happens when the timer ticks down while we're playing cat and mouse and we find another ice chest on the side of the road? And then another girl gets taken, and another? Do we sit and wait, then?"

He swore, beat his fist once against the steering wheel, and continued west.

"I'd rather say I did something. Chasing leads is something. So far, we've got more than Wainwright and Kennedy, too. They didn't know to go after the girl's job or roommate. Now, we've got a business card for another place she applied to, and someone might have seen her ..."

Callow turned the maroon and yellow card over in her hand. There was a crease on one side she'd worked the last ten minutes to get out. No matter how straight she tried to make it, the white line defacing the card remained, like a scar.

She felt too close to the card, the personification disturbing. She could bend, unfold, straighten herself out ... and still the scar would remain. That's what the job did to you: it bent you, and you tried desperately not to break, all the while carrying the creases ...

"This is what happened in El Paso. The trail ran cold," Callow said, trying to edge the conversation along without dwelling on the bout of frustration she knew would surely come if this lead dried up, too.

"Yeah, but you tracked Carson down to an area. Then, with a few interviews and a stroke of luck, you had him, and I turned you away. I didn't trust you." Marcus settled back in his seat, teasing his lips nervously with his fingers. "I didn't trust your gut, and we almost paid the price for it. I won't do that again. I say we listen to your intuition. Let's see what turns up."

The car came to a stop in front of a bodega wedged between two buildings. A maroon and yellow umbrella matching the card cast shade over the bodega's single glass door. A collage of different cuts of meat and their prices created an obscure piece of artwork that blocked the view inside. The images were visceral, sparing no expense in the level of detail they incorporated, including pools of animal blood beneath stacks of prime cuts and a bowl of chicken feet.

Callow wasn't particularly queasy, having developed an iron stomach over the years from a multitude of gruesome crime scenes, but something about the casual nature of the images was unnerving. The depictions felt somehow too real.

She pulled on the glass door. It didn't budge. She checked the listing on the wall nearby, which showed that Picard's Meats was open seven days a week between the hours of ten and six. Besides holidays, Picard's delivered once during the morning and once in the evening. It was long before six, and there were lights on inside the bodega.

"I'll call the number," Marcus offered, diving into his coat pocket for his phone.

Callow put up a hand. "There's someone coming."

In the small gap between the cuts of meat and the metal, Callow met the eyes of a grim-looking man in a white shirt, blue jeans that barely covered his rear, and suspenders working their hardest to prop up the sagging jeans. A waist-high apron speckled with blood completed the look. His face was round and haggard. His hair reminded her of the coarse curly hairs on a hog.

Callow aimed her eyes at the lock. The butcher stared back at her. Callow rolled her eyes and tapped her badge on the window. The man dragged his eyes from her to the badge, then back to her again. He held that look, and for a moment, she thought he would turn away. Instead, she watched his chest rise and fall in a heavy sigh as he unlocked the door. He stepped back as the two agents entered the bodega.

Instantly, Callow was staggered by the thick, musky scent of iron, warm meat, and beer—*stale* beer that wafted out of the pores of those who drank heavily while they worked. An image conjured in her mind, engrained there by the very smell she was engulfed in now: beer, a scathing letter stained with circles of the sweaty bottles, and then the smell, wrought from humid summer days and high temperatures, of putrid rot.

That was how Callow had found her father, beer still spilling out his pores. Pills and drink and stink and rot.

"What do you want?" the butcher growled. He was a callous man, top heavy and troll-like. Wild hairs curled out from under his sleeves like barbed wire. He wrung a towel and tossed it into a bloody pile on the floor behind the glass partition. A cutting board, three feet wide and six feet long, filled half the room.

Callow watched the butcher scrape at the board with his fingernails, not a glove in sight. She cleared her throat, donning a no-nonsense face despite the sweat that had begun to collect under her armpits and her desperate desire for fresh air.

"I'm Callow and this is Oakley. We're Special Agents with the FBI. Did you know a girl by the name of Marissa Marley? Blonde. Pretty. Young."

The butcher reached for a cleaver that hung on the wall, eyed the holstered pistols on the agents' waistbands, and seemed to think twice.

"She came in for an interview. Couldn't hack it fifteen minutes in—the smell, ya know? Comes with the job. We're straight from the farm, and we process a lot of meat."

Callow eyed the small building, corner to corner. It was likely "a lot of meat" was highly subjective.

"We process and deliver meat locally. You need to be quick. Precise. We only deal with prime cuts and occasionally chickens."

Callow raised a questioning eyebrow.

The man rolled his eyes. "She had one interview. Stayed for fifteen minutes, then bugged out. As you can imagine, not many young women find this type of work appealing, even though we pay above minimum wage. Then there are the perks."

"Perks?" Marcus asked, intrigued.

"Sure. Occasionally, a customer over-orders. We end up

with leftover cuts. Since we don't retail, I can either keep it or throw it away."

"The pictures on the door show prices."

The butcher nodded. "Per cut, per pound, in bulk. We deliver. Chilled, using reefer trucks. I take pride in my work, so none of my meat is frozen. My customers notice. *Their* customers notice. I get paid very well."

"I'm sorry, but I didn't ask your name." Callow watched to see if the man raised a hand to shake. He didn't, and she was glad; his fingers looked like grubby sausages.

"Ronson Picard. Richard Picard was my father. He owned this business until I took over."

"Have you always wanted to be in the meat business, Ronson?"

Ronson shifted into a bleak smile, rested his hands on his expansive gut, and roared with laughter. The sound bounced eerily off the walls.

"My father said I should be a doctor, but I told him no, I'd love to work as a butcher, slinging dead animals over my shoulder rather than eating them. I can't even afford my own cuts. So, no, I haven't always wanted to be in the meat business. But that's life, isn't it? You end up doing a lot of shit you don't wanna do. Now, if you don't have a warrant or any pertinent questions, would you kindly fuck off? I've got six orders out back to process before sundown, and then I've got to deliver them."

"Why sundown?" Marcus probed, craning his neck to see around the countertop.

Ronson stepped forward, blocking Marcus's view with his gut. "Reefer works a little too good. Insulated. Adds a frost to the meat. Need a bit of outside heat to keep the balance." He opened his mouth, presumably to ask them to leave again, but Callow fired off a question.

"Marissa Marley has been kidnapped and will likely be

killed soon. Given you've seen her, and she was taken not too far from here, is there anything you'd like to tell us?"

"Are you accusing me …?"

"Perhaps the Food Safety and Inspection Service would love to know about the cleanliness of your establishment? Not to mention the local cops, who'd love a DWI right about now …"

Marcus turned to her. "Jenny …"

Ronson's face turned to stone, his fists balled and his shoulders shrugging up toward his round head. A vein throbbed angrily on his sweaty neck. "No warrant. No charges. Get fucked."

But Callow was already out the door, with Marcus only one step behind.

CHAPTER TWENTY-TWO

Callow took three steps across the sidewalk from the stuffy shop and into the car. She didn't notice the slight dip of the sun signaling more precious time had slipped by. She also didn't notice the change in the air, now filled with the smell of hot asphalt and engine oil, nor did she notice the workers barking commands as they loaded a truck with a forklift across the street. The short walk served to test her mettle, for she wanted to hit something. She wanted to hit Ronson, but she couldn't figure out why. Something about him made her stomach churn, perhaps because he reminded her of her alcoholic father, a vile clone, like he hadn't died and instead the worst part of him had infected someone else.

As she climbed into the car, Marcus clambered into the driver's seat.

He put the car in drive without saying anything and turned the car around in a sharp U-turn. Cool air blasted her face while her thumb searched for the soft spot between her opposite thumb and pointer finger. She scraped at the skin like a pockmark she was trying to clear but only managed to rub it until it was red and angry. The pain was real and fought hard against the emotional pangs.

Ronson. That smell. The beer. He might as well have been her father incarnate.

"Do you want to talk about what that was?" Marcus asked, his voice timid, like a child inching toward a dog they worried might bite them.

"That guy, *Ronson*," she hissed. "It's him. And he knows we know."

Marcus was stone-faced. "That's an assumption, Jen, and you know it. There's something else there. From the moment you looked at him, I could see it in your eyes—seething hatred. You didn't look like a woman who'd just solved the puzzle, but one hell-bent on destruction. Tell me what that was, and if you really think it's him, we can run the profile."

Marcus was right, and she hated it. She was emotional, triggered by the rank smell of beer and body odor. As the smell left her clothes, she felt her anger subsiding, deflating. Marcus could read her; he knew Ronson was probably a dead end. He also knew she was talking out her ass when she'd jumped to the conclusion that Ronson was Icebox. He'd answered all their questions—truthfully, too, as far as she could tell. Even if he was an asshole.

She sent a text message to Kennedy, asking him to meet. He replied a moment later, and when the phone screen defaulted to timeout, she still stared at it like it represented a portal to the past. "We're meeting Kennedy and Wainwright at Colleyville PD."

"Why?" Marcus asked.

Callow was silently thankful he hadn't asked more about why Ronson had affected her in that way, able to assault the protective walls of her mental castle with nothing more than a snide attitude and a few short statements. Ronson hadn't been working alone, however. Her memories had double-teamed her, attacking from within while Ronson had faced her head-on. Callow was willing to bet it would be enough for even the strongest walls to bow a little.

"We need to regroup," she replied. "Weeks ago, back in El Paso, Jedediah told us we pulled a partial print from some glasses. I want to follow up on that, but if Forensics have run it through our system and haven't gotten back to us already, then it's a dead-end for now. Wainwright has probably looked over the case file, too, and I want to hear his opinion on it, even if he is a snide little shit. We can also share what we've found regarding Marissa's employers. Maybe somebody can make damn sense of it."

Marcus turned west, back toward City Hall and Colleyville Police Department. Callow dared not look up to see where the sun was overhead. She knew it was creeping, and right now, it was still at her back. She imagined its gaze like a narrow beam that crawled up her neck, to the back of her head, and then around to face her, staring, setting, as the clock drew closer to zero.

"That's a good plan, Jenny."

"Are you sure it's a good plan? Or are you just saying that because you have to?"

"I don't have to say *anything*. That's the beauty of not being a supervisor. I can fall back on taking orders. Besides, do you really think I'd do that to you? Never. I'd never leave you that alone; to bear the weight of Marissa and the others on your shoulders. It's nearly crushing all of us working *together*. I can't imagine putting it all on you."

Callow's heart thumped twice outside its normal rhythm. She filled her lungs and exhaled forcefully between pursed lips. Marcus had done it again; he'd breached her defenses—not in the way Ronson had, but as a warrior carrying a standard and an army of horses at his back, ready to turn and defend once they were safely within what remained of the castle walls. He was her reinforcements.

"My father died of an overdose," she said solemnly. "He had a letter written, just in case. He knew I'd find him and the letter. It condemned me for my choice of career. He blamed himself, declaring himself a failure as a father, and he downed beer and pills until his body had no choice but to shut down. He died alone, knowing I'd be the one to find him the next day."

"*Jesus*, Jenny. You never told me that."

"I haven't told anyone except Jedediah. He called the locals, and they agreed to keep it quiet. His death was hard enough, but harder still, in his stupor, he'd planned to write more in that letter. I could see where the pen slid off the page. He and I never got along; he hated me for choosing to stay with my mother. Joining the FBI only made him hate me more."

"Why? Why wouldn't he be proud?"

Callow shrugged. "I've tried to work it out myself in the time since—to try and make sense of it. Maybe the reveal was in the rest of the letter. Maybe he was a crook and hated cops. I don't know much about him, but I remember his anger—and I remember that smell. The smell of body odor, dirt, and alcohol. I visited him days before he died, and he smelled like that then. And when I found him, it was all I could smell. And so, when some asshole reeks, hates cops, and even vaguely *looks* a bit like my father ... Well, you can imagine, objective opinion goes out the window."

Marcus flipped the blinker at the stoplight. A black metal gate barred their way to a government gray building with a line of police cruisers out front. A keypad waited on the driver's side, mounted on a sign covered in warnings.

"It could still be Ronson," Marcus offered in a conciliatory tone. "It would be poetic if it was."

Callow nodded, her eyes seeing the gate opening, but not really seeing. "It could be. Or it could be that odd little fellow from the Tavern, or any asshole from this city. We need a bone, Marcus. A bone—otherwise Icebox is going to give us a *body*."

• • •

Colleyville Police Department hummed with the same energy the LED lights buzzed with overhead. Officers hugged the right side of the narrow hallway as Callow and Marcus walked by, handwritten stickers labeling them as visitors on their lapel. The shining FBI badges hung around their necks spoke louder.

Every officer they passed bore the same look: defeat. At the start of this investigation, Jedediah had said Colleyville PD had wanted to spearhead it. They *were* capable ... to a point. And the energy held within the station house walls reflected that. The officer guiding them—a rookie, judging by his spotless boots, pressed uniform, and uplifting, chipper nature—turned right into the patrol room. Inside, the room was dark, the shades drawn and the air still. Coffee percolated within.

A handful of people sat around a large oval conference table, their faces illuminated by the electronic blue glow of their laptops. Some were typing while others clicked through maps or documents of what had to be the Icebox Killer's case file. Callow saw the screen of the man sitting directly in front of her. He cycled through documents until her face popped up, then her Tahoe, and finally an image of Marissa.

Their guide took a step forward, touched his partner on the shoulder, and cleared his throat gently. The officer stood and closed his laptop at the same time. He followed as the rookie guided them out and across the hall, to a cramped break room where the coffee smell emanated from. Two industrial coffee makers ran in tandem. A young woman in a collared shirt and blue jeans, her hair pulled up tight to work, wiped at the stains on the counter. As soon as they approached, she scooted out of the room with her head down. The rookie led Callow, Marcus, and the officer from the patrol room inside.

The newcomer stood eye to eye with Marcus. Tall and lanky, Callow could see now that his hair, styled neatly to one side, was graying to the point of almost being white. His face was dominated by a salt-and-pepper mustache, trimmed just above his lip. He didn't wear a uniform, but a badge, a compact pistol, and blue jeans. Despite his modest attire, the man carried a fierce air about him. Callow couldn't tell if it was derived from arrogance, confidence, or experience.

The officer held out a hand. "My name is Gordon Welch." Marcus took it, then Callow. His hand was warm, his fingers bony. "I'm the lieutenant over our Criminal Investigation Division. Please excuse my attire. I've been living out of the station for about a week. Rook, you can go."

Callow caught the young officer's eye before he turned. He looked spirited, full of hope. He was slender and fit, which made him look boyish. It was clear he was meant to be out on patrol, but this duty had been assigned to him as a last-ditch stopgap. Callow saw something else in him, too: determination.

"Wait," Callow said. "Can he stay?"

The rookie stopped. Welch raised a bushy white eyebrow. "I don't see why not. Good training on interagency cooperation. Fair enough. Garcia, grab us an extra chair, and close the door on your way in."

The rookie, Garcia, returned a moment later with a metal folding chair. He closed the door behind him and pulled a notebook from his breast pocket. He hovered in the corner, and Callow caught his eye. There it was again—determination. Thanks, too.

And hope.

CHAPTER TWENTY-THREE

With the door shut, Garcia helped himself to the coffee that was largely ignored by the others. Nobody took seats, either, which raised an odd tension in the room, reminiscent of the quiet that overcame a battlefield before the initial orders were given to charge.

"I wanted to get a moment with you, Callow. You too, Oakley. Yes, I know who you are, and I also know you're not primary on this case," Welch said stiffly. He spoke in a way that suggested he rarely spoke, and that when he did, he expected others to listen. He held confidence in his shoulders, too, which led Callow to wonder if he'd served in the military.

"Your partners, Kennedy and Wainwright, are in the other room. I'll have Garcia bring them here so you have a place to meet when we're through. Until then, I need you to know two things, the first of which is, I don't think we're going to catch this guy. At least, not by the time your gal's ticket is punched. Secondly, I need y'all to catch him. On my desk are three other homicides not designated by your illustrious FB-of-I as the work of a serial killer. For whatever reason, that makes them less of a problem than your case, and so all my resources are tapped to help you."

He sniffed hard. "Kennedy is floundering under the pressure. Wainwright is quiet and useless. You, on the other hand, Callow, cannot stop yourself from getting into shit. I've followed your career closely. You aren't too far away in the mirror-windowed fortress of Quantico, and I've been doing this a long time. You've got something the others don't. I expect you to use it."

"And what might that be?" Callow snapped. She'd been waiting to get a word in after what felt like an ass-chewing.

Welch leaned in just a hair. "The wherewithal to do what must be done. I saw what you did in El Paso, and I applaud you. That's what we need: *grit*. The same callous grit this asshole has whenever he's cutting up women. You have my department's resources. Do what you will with them—but do it quickly. Time is running out, but I'm sure you don't need me to remind you of that."

She didn't. Callow could practically feel the arms of the clock spinning, each minute a tremor, each hour a life-altering earthquake. Welch turned toward the door.

"What is this supposed to be, then? A warning? A pep talk?" Callow asked.

"Does it feel like either of those to you? Don't fuck this up, Callow. Kennedy might be labeled as primary, but I know who will fall hardest if you fail. I've seen good officers suck-start their pistols for less. Garcia, when you're done scribbling useless notes, go grab the other suits and bring them here."

"Yes, sir," Garcia said quickly, hurrying out the door. Welch nodded curtly, turning up his upper lip so his mustache arched, then quickly shut the door on his way out.

When she was sure he was out of earshot, Callow said, "What the fuck's up with all these threats?"

Marcus nodded. "Welch said you'd be the one to fall hardest. He knows you're personally connected to the case. That was a personal warning, not political or whatever. He's worried about you."

"Worried about what? That I'll 'suck-start my pistol' if I don't make the case?" Callow hissed. Her blood boiled at how easily Welch had talked of officer suicide. She couldn't imagine ...

"He means well," Garcia said, reappearing suddenly. He tucked his notebook away. "Lieutenant Welch."

Callow turned to the rookie. "In his own way, I'm guessing?"

Garcia nodded. "He's the head of CID, and from what I've been told, he's built this department up from where it was thirty years ago. He was chief for a long time, then went back to Investigations. He's also the head of our Partners Program. It's a buddy system for officers after a critical incident. He established it after his partner shot himself."

Callow's perception of Welch changed in an instant. Where she had previously soured from the man's nuances and comments, she now felt her heart swell, fighting back the bitter truth behind his words. The lieutenant might well be callous, but he was *human*.

"What's your story, Garcia?"

"Edwardo. My wife calls me Eddie; my friends, Gordo. To be honest, I served, too. I'm just about getting used to being called Edwardo again."

Callow smiled. "Jenny to my friends, Callow to most. Tell me, Edwardo, before you go, what do you make of this case?"

"You care what I think? I don't know anything about investigations like you or the LT does. I'm fresh out of the academy."

Callow smiled. "Which makes your insight unique, unclouded by years of bad habits and patterns forming in your head. I was recruited to the FBI Behavioral Analysis Unit from Analytics because of the fresh angle I provided on a case. Don't let anyone think your experience is the only determinant of value."

Garcia brightened, then pressed his head down, tucking his chin into his vest. His brow came together in concentration.

"At the academy, they teach us about patrol tactics, like random or grid. One says follow our heart; the other says follow a pattern, tracing grid lines through the city. What if the killer is doing the same?"

"Keep going," Marcus prompted.

"What if you're focusing on the girls he's taken instead of the bigger picture? I've seen the case file. Hell, most of the *department* has. We're all on edge. Everyone who makes a stop is taking twice as long to interview them on the side of the road. But I've been thinking, what if the pattern is not in the type of girls? What if it's broader than that?"

"Where does this rabbit hole lead, Edwardo?" Callow asked.

He shrugged "I don't know. I'm still working through it."

She grinned. "Good. You're honest. Keep that. Some would lie and cough up a half-assed guess that wouldn't do any of us any good. Follow the rabbit hole, Edwardo. Here's my card. Let me know if you find something at the bottom."

Callow slipped him a business card. The young officer didn't beam with admiration, instead mirroring Gordon Welch's upturned lip-nod, and saw himself out.

"What're your thoughts?" Callow asked Marcus. She hoped he'd have something to say, gleaned from his outsider's look at not only the conversation with Garcia, but the interaction with Lieutenant Welch as well. Marcus sipped coffee and made a face that said it was clearly burnt. He set it aside, disappointed.

"He's prior service, for sure. Probably seen some shit, based on the way he talks."

Callow rolled her eyes. "*We've* seen things, too. It's irrelevant. I mean, what do you make of what he said? What about Edwardo? Or even just the uniforms we passed in the hallway?"

"We all want the same thing, Jenny. All for different reasons. I want justice for Carmen, just like you do. Welch wants his section back under his control, given that the FBI has pretty much commandeered all his resources. Edwardo wants to prove himself. We've all got our place."

There was a subtle knock at the door. Kennedy and Wainwright joined them.

Callow surveyed the two agents. *Have they been crying?* Their eyes were red-lined and puffy, their lips chapped. Their suits had been abandoned for polo shirts with an embroidered badge and baseball caps. Kennedy carried an overstuffed backpack spewing files as if it was his personal anchor ball. The blond hairs in his scraggly, patchy beard were overgrown.

Wainwright, despite his eyes, appeared as he always had: neutral, noncommittal, and lacking compassion. His steely nature was what troubled her about him, regardless of the little heart-to-heart they'd had.

Callow understood Kennedy's appearance. He was primary on the case, and that meant he had to bear the brunt of the pressure. Pressure was working at his nerves, dipping into his sleep and testing his resolve. The red eyes indicated that what meager rest he'd had was rough. She felt a hint of compassion for him then, wondering if the pressure he was under came from himself or from those bearing down on him, expecting results.

"Kennedy. Wainwright," Marcus acknowledged them both in turn. They nodded. "Coffee is stale, but you both look like you could use it. You look like hell."

Kennedy shifted the bag off his shoulder and into an empty chair. He shrugged off a knot. "Been dragging the case file around with me while we canvased the neighborhoods.

It's been useless, of course. If we're canvassing, it means we've hit a dead end. Tell me you've got something, Callow. Jedediah said you were chasing down a lead?"

"I was. Marissa Marley was job hunting at the time of her abduction. The first job, she never took, working for some asshole in the industrial sector a few miles from her apartment. Picard's Meats, a distributor for expensive cuts in the area. The owner's name is Ronson Picard. He's a tool; clammed up quickly. The second place she applied was some hip new bar downtown called Sapphire Tavern."

"I've seen it," Wainwright added, handing Kennedy a cup of coffee. He drank from it without a fuss.

"Marissa was a no-show on her first day at Sapphire," Callow continued. "We only knew about the job because the locals never put the pieces together that she was twenty-four and living with a friend, but had no means of income. The roommate they interviewed gave us the info for Picard's. The owner of Sapphire Tavern is one Edwin Hodge. He's weird, but seems legit."

Kennedy leaned his head against the wall, lifting it and dropping it with a hollow *thud*.

"What're you thinking?" Kennedy asked, eyes closed. "This hurry-up-and-wait bullshit isn't working. Jed gave us thirty minutes before we're out canvassing again. We stand out like a hooker in church."

"I don't think that's the expression …" Marcus ventured.

"Whatever. Point is, we're getting railed if Callow doesn't have something."

"I might," Callow said. "A new direction, at least. Do you remember a while back when we got that partial print from one of the Icebox victims' glasses?"

Kennedy snorted, rifled through the bag, and tossed a wrinkled sheet of paper on the table. "Yeah. It was the victim's fingerprint. Forensics confirmed it was postmortem, meaning Icebox was messing with us. He pressed her finger on the glasses after he killed her just to lead us down a wild goose hole."

"Wild goose *chase*," Marcus said softly.

"What about you, Wainwright? Anything new?" Callow asked. She wanted to be sure their loose ends were tied up before she presented her own. Hope was fickle; it could lead you off "down a wild goose hole," as Kennedy would say, causing you to miss what was important. Hope was for the desperate—but Callow saw no sense in denying it. They sure were desperate right now.

Then, something began to nag at her, like a missing song lyric or the last note of a catchy jingle. It tugged and poked and prodded at her thoughts. Callow had long since learned to chase that feeling, for it was normally her intuition throwing her a bone, seeing something she hadn't.

It came in the form of Garcia's voice. *"What if the pattern is not in the type of girls? What if it's broader than that?"*

CHAPTER TWENTY-FOUR

Callow took a position at what would have been the front of a classroom. Marcus and Wainwright sat around the table while Kennedy used the lull in the conversation for a bathroom break. Callow glanced nervously out the small rectangular window next to the door into the hallway, imagining Jedediah might burst through the door at any moment like a white knight with a location and a photo of their suspect. No such miracle happened, and Callow was left wringing her hands. A whiteboard stood erect, tucked against the wall, a black marker on a shelf below it.

Rather than pacing, she wheeled the whiteboard so that it was at her back, there if she needed it but not certain whether she'd actually use it. What would she write that couldn't already be found in the conference room across the hall? What dots could she connect? Callow didn't have all the answers, only a fool's hope that talking through what they knew might result in closing more gaps in their knowledge and, hopefully, fashion enough pieces to put together a profile. Hope upon hope.

Kennedy opened the door, squeezing through what small space the whiteboard allowed. He didn't question it; he simply settled into his seat and looked ready to pass out, his eyes glazed over and halfway closed.

Callow cleared her voice. She made no move for the marker. "Let's run the loose facts. Whatever you've got, spit it out, no order—only what you find most important about what you know," she said.

She felt like an underprepared schoolteacher, asking the class to help decide what they wanted to learn that day. There were no nerves about quieting them; they'd been through enough together that formalities and nervousness were long gone. Even Wainwright looked like he was in his element. He spoke up first.

"Three girls. Colleyville downtown. All between the ages of twenty and thirty. The method was the same for the first two vics—timeline, too, suggesting the pattern was important."

Callow signaled her agreement with silence. Marcus sat up a little. "There's symbology in the way Icebox works. What he does represents how he feels about his victims. He most likely has some surgical expertise or knowledge of the human body. Victims are found near where they were taken."

She took up the marker and wrote "LOCATION" on the board. It seemed important, in her mind: the point of abduction, and the dump site for the body. "Marcus, pull up the map from the case file—the one showing all important locations. Kennedy, go."

"The victims were taken in broad daylight. They had normal jobs, meaning he isn't chasing hookers. He also has a hard-on for Callow."

Callow had expected that detail to come through—her connection to the Icebox Killer. Her thoughts on that were already settled, though. It was a connection by chance rather than necessity. Icebox had been planning to dump the second victim near Rebecca's work, no matter what; it had been sheer luck that she was the one to find the victim, and that she and Callow were related.

Callow wrote her name on the board. This wasn't the time to argue about the validity or importance of the facts. She waited to write until Marcus handed her the map. She drew a compass, then a crosshair to indicate the division of the city of Colleyville.

"Carmen, found at Cooley and Smith, Chicken Empire, south." She marked a cross on the south side of the crosshairs. "Gwen Hammond, Second and Broadway." She marked another cross to the northeast. Marissa was taken in the south as well." She marked the third location as if they'd already found a body there.

Wainwright rubbed his chin. "What about the other abduction sites? Or at least the victims' last known locations? Can you mark those, too?"

Callow marked more spots on the makeshift map. It only cluttered the appearance, making the board look as if it'd been hit with buckshot. There was no rhyme or reason. It all seemed so random …

Callow stared at the board until the marks ran together and the room grew warm and fragrant with sweat. No amount of perseverance with so little knowledge would draw water from the well; it all came down to cold, hard facts. Callow wasn't ready to give up. Carmen wouldn't have. One time, she'd watched Carmen suck down five burritos for a dare, only to vomit, then eat the sixth because that was what the bet had called for. Carmen had forced Callow to finish college when she'd wanted to drop out to be with some guy who'd promised her the world, but turned out to be a wash … and married. Carmen had also been the first to encourage her to apply for the FBI Analytics Unit. No, Carmen wasn't a quitter, and so Callow felt it only right to give the same kind of effort her friend would have. She needed to swallow that last burrito, no matter how badly she'd vomit.

"Forensics. What have we got? Kennedy, toxicology?"

He was nodding off. Kennedy lurched himself awake, removed a red-labeled manila folder from his bag, flipped it open on the table, and thumbed through it lazily. "Alcohol. Nicotine. THC. Probably not important; weed is legal here. Everyone smokes it."

Callow nodded and wrote "ALCOHOL" on the board. "It is, which means it's probably unimportant. The alcohol is what's interesting. Alcohol can remain detectable in the blood for up to ten hours. It was present in both victims' blood. Gwen was taken on a Wednesday—she had a job. Carmen was taken on a Friday morning. She was also employed."

Kennedy didn't seem half asleep anymore, and Callow's writing was becoming sloppier the faster she wrote. She was onto something, something she prayed would come to a head, otherwise the letdown at the end would be soul-crushing ...

"Marissa has a job—or was supposed to," Marcus said. He looked anxiously to Wainwright and Kennedy, who had equal eyes of excitement.

"We are left to close this loop, then, gentlemen. Someone, talk."

The marker hovered over the whiteboard as nervous glances were exchanged. Kennedy resorted to flipping through the case file, but based on the half-cocked look in his eyes, the dreary laziness of his eyelids, and the weight of the dark bags under them, he wasn't really seeing anything.

After a while, an inevitable groan escaped Callow's lips. Her head pounded, wholly believing they were on the cusp of making a connection, a discovery—something they'd missed. Recounting what they knew on the board was intended to bring forth new ideas by displaying old ones and letting their minds do the rest.

A grave stillness swept over the room as an officer with heavy footfalls and keys jingling on his belt passed by. All looked to Callow, who looked to the board, then back to her team.

What if there's nothing more? What if there's no stone left to turn? No path left to take? What if it takes finding Marissa's body to complete the circuit?

Callow could read that idea forming on their faces as clearly as she could read the case file in front of her. It was a fact none of them wished to say out loud, but it resonated quite clearly in her own head.

The Icebox Killer has outsmarted you.

The thought made her stomach churn. This game of cat and mouse had never seemed so dire.

YOU'RE BOTH SO ALONE.

Misplaced anger toward herself, her team, the world, was hard to ignore. It came like a tide, creeping until all the sand was wet, but even when the sand was dry from the sun, a shadow of where the tide had reached remained. Callow felt much the same way, having driven back the tide of anger until only the shadow remained.

"We can do this," she said timidly. "We can beat him. We've cut all the others off at the pass. What makes *him* any different?"

Kennedy peeled pieces off his cup and deposited them inside. "Time. We're out of time, Callow. The details came too late. Colleyville PD took forever to handoff ..."

"We can't blame Colleyville," Marcus snapped. "Since when has assigning blame got us anywhere?"

"They held onto the case and you know it! I met their lieutenant; he's washed up. Rode hard and put up wet. He's retired on duty, and I can tell by the look on your face you thought the same when you met him." Kennedy crossed his arms defensively.

"It doesn't matter if Welch held the case," Marcus retorted. "Who cares if he flopped and delayed? Do you think I give a shit about his bitching? It means nothing. We're here, and we have a job to do."

Kennedy snorted. "You have to say that, since you and her have been …"

Marcus shoved his chair back and reached over the table, crunching Kennedy's shirt into a fist and twisting it. "Finish that sentence."

Kennedy smirked. "You hit me, you're done."

"Then I'll have no reason to stop. No reason to toe the line," Marcus growled.

Callow was barely listening to the drama unfolding. It had faded like a television blaring in the background. White noise. Marcus had said something that rang a distant bell in her head, so much so she'd turned her back on them all to face the whiteboard with all her notes and markings like it was a treasure map unfolding before her.

"Toe the line …" she muttered under her breath. "*Line* … Guys? Hey, guys! Put your dicks away."

The room fell silent.

"I think I found something."

CHAPTER TWENTY-FIVE

In minutes, Callow had the whiteboard erased and the room confused. What was once a basic map with a cross section of Colleyville was now a detailed array of city streets and notable locations, including the locations of each victim's place of residence, employment, their last known location, assumed abduction sites, and the dump sites where their bodies were found. In essence, it was a mess that had left Callow sweating, exhausted, and her hand in cramps. She sat in an empty seat and admired her work.

"What do you see, gentlemen?" she asked inquisitively. The question wasn't rhetorical; she wanted someone to counter her theory. She could see it clear as day, the facts having sparked a theory that fit as the missing piece in her investigation. With this final detail, if someone else could corroborate it besides her, she had faith that her profile would be spot-on.

Not just spot-on. Objective.

"A mess," Wainwright grumbled. "It's so busy. Why not erase a few things so we can read it?"

Callow pushed herself to her feet. "Okay. Looking at this, what's *not* useful?"

Wainwright was thinking clearly, almost callously. He opened his mouth, then rubbed his chin. "Get rid of the buildings first, and ..." He peered over a map on the table. "Draw a radius from the north end of Main to the south, as that marks the city's center."

Callow did as he said, using a paper towel to erase the buildings. "Icebox is a sociopath. He thinks he's beaten us, and so he's playing. That's why he took that photo of Marissa in my Tahoe. He thinks he's outsmarted us."

"Get rid of the locations where he dropped off the bodies," Marcus said.

Callow erased them.

"He tried to muddy the waters, to misdirect us ..." Callow continued.

"And get rid of the street names," Kennedy added.

Callow was left with the victim's residences on a north parallel and their places of business on a middle parallel. The connecting lines created the four points of a square, spanning the western side of the map.

"How does this help us?" Wainwright asked unenthusiastically, deflated.

Callow smiled. "He's cheeky. He thinks we wouldn't figure it out. But we did."

She erased the victims' assumed abduction sites and added two more dots on the map to create a third parallel. What was left resembled a six-point dominos piece. Callow stepped out of the way.

Everyone sat up in their chairs.

"What are those two new dots?" Kennedy asked.

"Those, my friend, are the locations where Icebox will dump Marissa and where he'll grab another girl. It's just a pattern, left to right," Callow explained. "You don't believe me. I can tell by the look on your faces."

"It's just so ... *simple*," Kennedy said glumly.

"And that's why I think we missed it. We know him to be

an intellectual, highly educated, so it's not unusual to suggest his game is 'dumbed down' for the other players. I think I'm ready to run the profile, unless anyone objects?"

She met each member of her team by eye, one after the other. Most shook their head. Marcus nodded. *I'm ready.*

Callow took a deep breath and stared at the whiteboard. Her vision blurred instantly, and she began seeing, but not really seeing, all that lay before her. Her memory became an encyclopedia, ready to reference all the information she knew about the case in an instant. Criminal profiling was a technique taught to members of the BAU at the Academy. It was a ritualistic analysis performed hundreds of times in practice to see the collective body of the facts and look for holes, or to help an agent look for missing information based on the details they already had.

"Unsub," Marcus prompted.

Callow drew from her memory first. "Serial killers blend in well; chameleons to their environment and social circles. They are mostly males between the ages of thirty and fifty. We believe our unsub has medical training due to the surgical precision with which he removes the victim's tongue, eyes, and teeth while they're alive."

"Unsub ..."

"Assuming his medical experience follows traditional pathways, he most likely has ten to twelve years of school to his name. If he followed the medical route directly out of high school, this plants him in our age bracket."

"Victims ..." Marcus said.

"Women. Young. Pretty. Age isn't a factor, as Marissa is in her early twenties and Carmen was in her thirties. Nothing of significance about their appearances."

"Victims ..."

Callow pictured Gwen, Carmen, and Marissa, putting their headshots in a photo lineup in her mind. Nothing came to her. When she didn't answer Marcus's prompt, he moved on.

"Toxicology ..."

"Alcohol was found in both Gwen and Carmen's blood. This is odd, given the half-life of alcohol, and the fact that both victims had jobs and were taken during normal business hours."

"Chameleon ..." Marcus said ominously. His use of the word was intended to cue her thoughts on how the unsub could get close enough to his victims to abduct them.

"He must travel inconspicuously. The dump sites are nowhere near the abduction sites, suggesting the method of transport was a vehicle. He'd have to move quickly, since they were taken during the daytime. A van or truck is most likely."

Callow imagined herself walking the city streets near Marissa's apartment, the industrial buildings watchful eyes on her back. She imagined a truck driving toward her, a man getting out menacingly. *How did he take them?* It had to be inconspicuous. Accessible. Convenient.

"Struggle..."

Callow returned to the present. "They didn't struggle—no need to when they are sedated."

"Sex ..."

"No signs of sexual abuse. Sex is about power, but sometimes serial killers display their perceived power by other means."

"Power ..."

"He takes them in plain daylight. Taunts authority. He believes he's won and will continue to win."

Callow's mind fed her the image of Marissa in the Tahoe, terrified, eyes wide and pleading. She could almost hear the girl's muffled cries through the photograph ...

"Power ..."

"He relies on craftiness, deception, and a strong sedative

rather than brute force to overpower the women. None of the victims were notably petite."

A final image came to mind: Carmen's bracelet, a single red drop of blood staining the sterling silver. Callow naturally reached for the space on her own wrist where the bracelet's twin should be. She couldn't get herself to wear it.

"I think that's it," Callow concluded, turning to face her team. It wasn't her most confident profile, but it felt complete. When she'd run the profile on the Red Mud River Killer, the key identifying details had manifested themselves in the profile. Jedediah called it her "trance." Her suppositions had led her and her team to narrow down the facts and predict where the killer would be next. In this profile, she hadn't discovered anything new, instead only confirming her previous assumptions—but the outcome was just as valuable.

"What now, Callow?" Wainwright asked.

Before she could answer with *"I wish I knew,"* the door to the stuffy break room burst open. Garcia looked out of breath, as if he'd just run the length of the hallway.

"Agents, another call just came out through Dispatch," the young officer said. "A possible kidnapping. Welch wasn't going to tell you because he doesn't think y'all know what you're doing, but I do. An eyewitness heard something from halfway across the park."

"A potential kidnapping isn't normally our thing ..." Marcus said.

"Detectives are with the witness now."

"This doesn't sound like our guy. Could be nothing, but we should check it out," Callow said.

While a plain sight kidnapping was always something terrible, it was a job for the local police. Where things got complicated was when kidnappings bled into murder and body after body started piling up, or when the homicides crossed state lines. Plus, the kidnapping was way outside the timeline of events for their unsub; they still had time before the window was open for Marissa's body to show up.

"Where's the park?"

"Off Third Street. Welch won't be there to say no if you show up." Garcia looked down the hallway and waved politely as a pair of uniforms breezed by, then ducked his head back inside. "I'm going out. I've got a cruiser, and my job was to escort you around here, not play babysitter."

"Thanks, Garcia. We'll head over there. Wainwright, Kennedy, stay here and see if we can drum anything else up. Consult with PD and give Jedediah a call, just to keep him in the loop."

Wainwright got up, and Kennedy wearily followed him out the room.

"Callow?" Garcia asked.

"Garcia."

"I've got a gut feeling."

"Chase it down," she said definitively. "That feeling is your mind putting the pieces together. Never let that go."

With that, Garcia shut the door, leaving Marcus and Callow alone together. She turned to him.

Marcus smiled knowingly. "You didn't have a next move, did you?"

"Of course I did," she lied. "But as this is happening now, it takes immediate priority. PD can benefit from our insight. Come on."

CHAPTER TWENTY-SIX

Callow and Oakley arrived at Hanklin Memorial Park right as the ancient behemothic cathedral bell struck 1:00 P.M. Within hours, Icebox's window would commence, where he'd drive whatever nondescript vehicle into the suburbs and somehow, *someway*, arrange Marissa's body in a terrible effigy on the ground for all to see. The first few to find it would ignore it, their minds unable to comprehend reality's cool touch. But then somebody would scream, and a circle of gawkers would surround the scene, and eventually, sometime, Callow's phone would ring.

Marcus took the car around the entire park once, past the dull clang of the bell and beyond a playground that looked more like excess drill pipe than a plaything meant for children. It was the color of deep rust and had only one swing. It was still, and there was nobody playing on the slide.

Past the playground, along a winding cement running path, was a park bench partially blocked by the backs of two men in matching suits. Finding a parking spot on the street, the FBI agents climbed out and headed toward the suits now walking in their direction.

They met in moments. The suits bore gold badges, prominent on their distended guts, and pistols that sagged their pants, which were already well beyond a size large. One detective looked retired on duty, ancient and wrinkled like a vegetable left too long in the sun, and he limped as he walked, a notebook tucked under his arm. The other was clearly his replacement. Chunky and fresh-faced, he walked with his shoulders poised, his haircut—a bad Tom Cruise rendition—styled to the side. He held out a hand to shake. Callow took it, then Marcus. His hands were soft, unworked.

"I'm Detective Switch. This is Willoughby. You must be the agents in charge of the Icebox case. Garcia told us you'd be swinging by."

"We are. I'm Callow. This is Oakley. First thoughts? What do you think this was?"

Switch shrugged, pursing his plump pink lips. "Looks like bullshit. Eyewitness didn't see a damn thing; only heard a scream. We've got uniforms checking for camera footage, but let's be honest, there's a hundred reasons why someone might scream in a park. Probably just kids."

"What makes you think it *isn't* Icebox?"

Callow wanted to assume it wasn't him. Taking her mind off the case, if only for a few minutes, might help her to think clearly; to rejuvenate her senses, in a way.

"He's still got a body on tap. Why would he grab another? Especially now? Here?" Switch said, waving his arms around to indicate the little square of shops, restaurants, and the park at the center of it all.

"Who's the witness?"

The older detective ripped a piece of his notebook paper, scribbled on it, and handed it to Callow. "Come on. Nothing we can do here. Time to eat."

Willoughby wandered past Callow and Marcus, nearly sulking, slouching as he walked.

"Boss's orders." Switch gave another annoying shrug. Callow sensed arrogance and found it hard to believe he was so relaxed given the circumstances. It made him seem careless.

"Before you go, detectives, do you mind sharing your interview notes? Just in case the witness revealed more to you than she will to us."

"*He*," Switch corrected. "And you'll have an official report from us with all the processed notes when it's posted. The evidence technicians will file their own reports, which you can request as well, *if* there's anything to report. Good day, *agents*."

Callow was ready to blow her lid. This was the type of behavior that got girls killed: a wannabe, dick-swinging contest. She was no stranger to it, but she'd hoped for better. It wasn't unusual for locals to squabble with the Feds over jurisdiction. But this? This type of behavior was tolerated from the top down.

Suddenly, Garcia's message made all too much sense. Colleyville PD had held onto the Icebox investigation from the beginning and hadn't made any headway; the lieutenant had seen to that. All for what? Pride? Glory? It was impossible to imagine that in a world where the clock was literally ticking down on a person's life, the minds of those supposed to protect them went to plaques on the wall and pats on the back. Callow's plaques were reminders that she could do the job, not that *only* she could do the job, for there were many people, a squad of the best profilers the FBI had to offer, and an army of local police all hunting the same person.

Sure, she could threaten to call supervisors and the detectives' day would get wrapped up in bureaucratic red tape. Phone calls would be made, but nothing would come of it. Instead, she let them go, and as they did, she didn't give them the grace of her time, starting a hurried step toward the park bench where a man rested his head in his palms, swaying. Marcus was at her back, and she could feel him seething. That was like him, though. He wouldn't make phone calls; he'd just make the detectives feel so small, they would give up the information, *if* he gave them the chance.

"Hi there," Callow said. She had a sense of familiarity about the man. Recognition. Her suspicions were confirmed when the man lifted his head.

"Oh, hello, Agent Callow. Hello, Oakley."

"Hodge? What're you doing here?" Callow recognized the odd little fellow from the Sapphire Tavern. He'd changed out of his unusual attire and was wearing respectable jeans and a simple t-shirt. He appeared downtrodden, like he'd just lost something near and dear to him.

"Why aren't you at the bar?" Marcus asked.

Hodge sat back against the metal bench and crossed his arms defensively. "Well, about half an hour after you left, FSIS came in for an inspection. Apparently, I'd missed my last one. I vaguely remember sending an email ... Oh, well. I wasn't wholly prepared, but I keep my establishment in top order, so the only hiccup came from not being able to get the loading dock door open."

He rubbed his pencil-thin arms as if he'd just felt the bitter cold. Callow could make out the goose flesh sprouting across his skin, pushing the little blond hairs to attention.

"Anyway, the door was stuck, and the inspector declared it a safety violation. They shut me down for a week, so I came here to clear my mind. I sit at this park sometimes, to watch the birds by the big fountain. I'm already on a shoestring budget. Running a restaurant isn't cheap. Running a *closed* restaurant will bury you."

Marcus nodded along. "My mother had a dream of starting a little Italian place, but when we looked at the numbers, they were cutting it close at best. I'm sorry that happened."

"Yeah, well, I'm glad it did, right?" Hodge separated his palms in a gesture encompassing the whole park. "Seems I've become somewhat important."

"I'm sorry, too, Hodge," Callow added. "And I have to agree with you there—I think it was perhaps fate that allowed you to be here. I'm sorry this burden is on you, though. Do you think you're in a place to talk? The detectives are running an investigation and ... well, I would love to hear what you have to say."

Hodge snorted. It was forced; intended to hide what he was really thinking. Callow caught the microexpression—a fraction of an emotion nearly impossible for the body to hide. *Malice.* Yet he had attempted to show amusement.

The average person only passively recognized microexpressions, leading to a feeling or a hunch about a particular person. Witnesses in the Ted Bundy case, for instance, said the man was charming, but also that something "didn't quite feel right" about him. Those witnesses couldn't see what Callow had just seen. She'd been trained to detect liars and those masking what they truly felt.

But before Hodge could answer, Callow's phone chimed. She ignored the message.

Hodge met her gaze. "For you, I'm an open book. You treated me like a human. Those detectives looked down on me. Perhaps it was my size; my appearance, maybe. Conversely, I think it was just how they chose to do business. *Assholes.*"

This was a lucky break. Witnesses often couldn't be relied on to relay their recollection of an incident twice due to stress and depending on the emotional impact of the crime. The more tragic an incident, the less likely they were to be coherent. Hodge seemed calm and willing to talk, and Callow wasn't about to pass on that opportunity, especially when they had nothing and the Colleyville PD detectives had *something ...*

"We'd like that, Hodge. Do you think we can take you somewhere quieter to chat?" Callow asked, looking around as if an appropriate meeting place would spring up out of the ground.

"Where do you have in mind?"

Callow hunted for a secluded area of the park, settling on a patch of oaks a few yards away. From the shadows of the ancient trees, they could talk with sincerity and still see all around them. The trees were a coveted spot at the park, as not many existed there, and these ones shot from the ground with thick leaves and branches that quarreled with each other in the sky like adolescent brothers.

She pointed. "Over there should work."

Hodge was already on his feet. "Lead the way."

CHAPTER TWENTY-SEVEN

Sitting cross-legged on the grass, Callow felt awkward, but standing didn't feel right. Hodge had sat down, childlike, to play with a blade of grass, and she knew he was unlikely to feel comfortable enough to open up with her towering over him. The bar owner looked down at the blade of grass between his fingers, only looking up to squint longingly at the sun. Marcus was nearby, behind them, pacing up and down while on his phone.

Sometimes, the job was more than you bargained for. Sometimes, it required you to sit like a child at recess while the ants climb your pants and into your crack and you scuff your favorite shoes or wrinkle a newly pressed suit. Sometimes, the job required leveling yourself with your victims or witnesses so that they might see you as a safe space to confide intricate details, sometimes vile details, in a useful order.

Callow was self-aware enough to recognize what the job demanded from her. This—changing her approach, allowing him to perceive her patience—was what it took to connect with Hodge, and it was something she was sure the Colleyville detectives certainly hadn't done. For that reason, she wondered if Hodge had more stashed in his brain than the detectives had been able to find. It was on Hodge to want to talk first, and so Callow waited.

Despite the modest temperature, Callow was growing warm around her collar. Perhaps it was the tension; the ticking clock that drove her heart up into her throat. Perhaps it was her nerves, or the very human part of her that was desperate for an answer she hoped Hodge might have to reveal.

Finally, to her relief, he asked, "Do you feel like you're winning, Callow? You know—all this?"

He was testing her, to see if she'd commiserate. It was a self-conscious maneuver, she was sure of it, in the same way strangers turn toward or away from someone depending on how they feel about their first impression. This was Hodge's way of turning toward Callow. She just needed to match his body language.

"Nobody wins in this, Hodge. It's all a loss—because if I'm involved, it means there's a lot of loss."

"That's a morbid way to think."

"It's a morbid job."

Callow's phone buzzed time and time again. Hodge met her gaze with his beetle-like eyes, waiting to see if she'd pick up. She reached into her pocket and blindly handed the phone to Marcus. He took it and stepped away.

"How do you deal with everything you see? Don't you harbor anger?" Hodge asked.

"I harbor a lot of feelings, but mostly I try to maintain control—and that puts a lot of pressure on me."

"What's one flaw about yourself you wish you could change?"

She thought for a moment. "I wish I knew when to ask for help."

"I've seen you in the paper, you know. I reckon you were pretty angry to do what you did to the last person who crossed you," Hodge said dryly. He'd dropped the blade of grass and stared off toward the far end of the park as he said it, his voice grim and foreboding.

An image flashed briefly of the damage she'd inflicted, and her mind spared her no details of the gore. Could she admit she was angry then and not just doing the job?

Absolutely.

"I was angry then," she admitted.

"And it felt good?"

"Yes."

"Then what makes you different from the man you're hunting now? Ignore the obvious. Drill down to the emotional core. Part of why I wanted to open a bar was to hear about the woes of men who'd downed a little too much booze, whisking away their filters and inhibitions. I live for those unfiltered stories, so please, indulge me."

Callow thought about her actions that day, writhing in the muck and the sludge of the Red Mud River. In the end, she wasn't sure she had acted with much purpose. It seemed so obvious: good versus evil, righteous versus unholy. But the true extent of who she was, she supposed, was displayed in those desperate moments fighting for her life in the mud.

"There's a line. A line I won't cross. A line between us and them. And that's all there is to it."

Hodge picked up his blade of grass again, finding it blindly with his fingers amongst the many beneath his legs. He sighed heavily.

"I went to that bench to watch the birds. A homeless man fed them for a year until he died, I think, but the birds kept coming. Anyone who sits on that bench can enjoy their company for a while, at least until they realize you don't have any food for them. I went there to clear my mind about the restaurant, and within minutes of sitting down, I heard a scream."

Callow waved Marcus over. He opened his phone and gave a signal that he had started the audio recording.

"Did you *see* anyone struggling? Any commotion?"

"No. Just heard a scream. I didn't see a specific vehicle that stood out, if that's what you're wondering—just a few in the area. That seemed to be all the detectives cared about. I was halfway across the park, and they judged me when I told them I didn't move once I heard the scream. There were people ... and traffic. This is a hub of activity. I reckon if this really was the killer you've been looking for, whoever took that woman knew her."

"What makes you say that?"

"If he was able to take her in broad daylight, she obviously wasn't scared. He must have had her trust."

"Did you see a girl?"

"No."

"Is there anything else you'd like to tell me?"

"No, but I will tell you something I haven't told the detectives."

Callow held her tongue.

"*Good luck.* The detectives can go fuck themselves. They looked down on me, and they didn't listen. I told them what I knew, but they don't know how to talk to people. Not like you."

"One last question. How did you notify the police?"

"I called 911 on my cell phone. Would you like the number? It's different from the one on my card."

"Sure."

Hodge swiveled around on his backside until he was facing her, then gave out his number. Callow wrote it on a piece of paper from her purse. When she looked up, she saw that Marcus was waving at her, signaling frantically that he needed to talk. Regardless of the information essentially being the same as what he'd provided to the detectives, Hodge's interview was a stone turned over, a thread chased, and one she could close out.

"Thank you for your time, Hodge. Can I call you if I have any more questions?"

"Of course, Agent Callow. And may I call you if I remember anything else?"

"Of course."

They exchanged pleasantries, and Marcus shook his hand warmly. Hodge bowed politely and strode off toward a statue of a man and his German Shepherd, and from there, he turned east away from the park.

A flurry of movement caught Callow's eye. A dark blue blur was hustling across the park—a police officer, given his awkward gait, heavy footfalls, and unmistakable uniform. As he came closer, she was elated to see it was Officer Garcia. He didn't seem to share the same sentiment, though, as his face was twisted in concentration as he sprinted across the park in full uniform.

Hodge was leaving in one direction, and Garcia was running at breakneck speed from the other. While Garcia ran, Callow and Marcus began walking toward him.

"What do you think that's about?" Marcus asked, eyebrows raised.

"What? Hodge or Garcia?"

"*Both*. Normally when cops run toward something, it means something bad is going down. Hodge, too. He seemed to want to talk, but he actually didn't have much to say."

Callow didn't comment. "Who was on the phone?"

"Jedediah the first time. I told him about Colleyville PD's bullshit and explained what we're doing and what they didn't do. He was livid. Probably dialing the chief over there as we speak."

"And the second call?"

Marcus stopped midstep and held her phone out before him as if to say, *"See for yourself."* She took it quickly and browsed through the call log. There was nothing out of the ordinary other than a missed call from Garcia.

"The messages," Marcus stated.

Callow tapped the icon. At first, she didn't recognize anything out of the ordinary, her eyes moving quickly through messages from Kennedy, Wainwright, Jedediah, and Marcus. There was also a message from Shannon asking about milk and another from Rebecca with a link to a newspaper article.

Then she saw what had made Marcus's face scrunch up as though he'd tasted something sour: a blank message, no sender, at the bottom of the list.

She tapped it and nearly dropped the phone. The message consisted of three words that carried the same weight as a linebacker in full tilt. The message was eerie, and she wasn't sure whose voice she heard saying it in her mind as she read the words:

TICK TOCK, JENNY.

It might as well have said *"SEE YOU SOON,"* the same message she'd received while in the hospital.

Callow's breath came in ragged, short, quivering bursts as she tried to control her body's response to the words. Every sense seemed to be telling her to run, scream, and never turn back. She wanted to be away from the torment—the taunting, the cold trails, and the hunt. She wondered in that moment if she'd made a mistake by returning to duty so soon. Perhaps Jedediah was right—and Marcus, too. Perhaps she should have taken time off to recover, so those three simple words weren't able to tear down whatever wall she'd built in her mind to protect herself.

TICK TOCK, JENNY.

The Icebox Killer had her number. He had it, and he was taunting her, knowing the feeling that would grasp her heart. If he couldn't get her to cave, he could get her to cower.

She glanced around fervently, as if the killer would be standing alone beneath a spotlight, cell phone in hand, smiling and waving. *Here I am, Jenny. Come get me.*

She wasn't that lucky. In the end, as her heart pumped fast against her ribcage, all Callow was left with was the feeling of being watched—a deep-seated unease and the sense of impending dread.

SEE YOU SOON. TICK TOCK, JENNY.

A hand gripped her shoulder and she spun, yelping and smacking it out of the way—

CHAPTER TWENTY-EIGHT

— Only to come face-to-face with Garcia, drenched in sweat, looking both surprised and exhausted.

The young officer rested his hands on his knees, panting profusely. His uniform shirt was untucked, and one of his boots was unzipped.

Callow waited anxiously for him to regain his composure. He had not only tracked her down, but he had run to meet her, too. When it seemed he might be able to answer, she asked, "Is everything all right, Edwardo?"

Garcia shook his head. Callow's stomach flipped over. The worst thoughts clouded her mind.

He's taken another girl. He's killed Marissa and taken another.

After a career like hers, Callow had come to realize nothing good came from a cop sprinting across an open field.

"Why didn't you call?" she asked, resting a hand on his shoulder. He took two deep breaths, coughed once and stood up, arching his back in a stretch.

"I did," he said between breaths. "You didn't answer."

Callow raised an eyebrow as she recalled her call log.

"Sorry, I was caught up interviewing. What's going on?"

"I did what you said—I followed a hunch. When the

patrol room cleared, I had about an hour to look over the case file. I've seen too many cop shows not to know the smallest details can be the most important, and so I went to where I could find those kind of details: the trace evidence packet."

Garcia was referring to the packet of papers from the crime lab that analyzed everything from found hair follicles to mineral compounds found in the dirt on a victim's shoes. It could reveal a lot about a crime scene, or reveal similarities that were otherwise unseen by the naked eye. The only problem was, Callow had already looked over the trace evidence and found nothing of note, as had Marcus.

"I looked over the packet and I think I found something. I wanted to be sure and so I brought a copy of it with me." He dug into a hidden pocket on the front of his uniform and withdrew a thick wad of paper folded into a square. The outside layers were warm and damp with sweat. Callow took it and glanced at her watch. 3:05 P.M.

It was hard to concentrate on the minute handwriting and the row upon row of neatly printed lettering detailing the forensic technician's findings. Callow was tempted to skim through it and wait for Garcia to hit her with his big revelation, but that was the lazy way of doing things—just waiting for the answer instead of seeking it out yourself. Garcia also had a decent point, one built on a lesson from the Academy about objective analysis. The idea was, if two agents came to the same conclusion from one packet of evidence and their information hadn't been shared, and if all had gone right in training, the agents *should* come to the same conclusion. If any agent felt something different, then that outlier needed to be explored.

Right now, Callow felt like the outlier. Rather than wasting more time, she indulged the officer, flipping through page after page, nearly twenty of them, all detailing the same information.

Iron. Manganese. Copper. Iodine. Zinc. Cobalt ... Nothing

unusual there. Callow was about to skim the page when she saw a handwritten note at the bottom that read *"HDPE."* They already knew about the HDPE based on what Kennedy had told them, but the handwritten note was curious. Why was the presence of HDPE of particular interest to the forensic tech?

Callow flipped the page, skimmed the trace elements, and then found another note about the presence of HDPE found on the heels of the victims' shoes *and* fingernails. "Transfers," they were called. She skimmed the evidence from the search of her Tahoe, now excited, her heart racing as much as Garcia's must have been on his sprint across the field. She saw it again: right hand column, halfway down.

HDPE.

Callow was hit with a feeling of déjà vu so strong, she nearly fainted. It was as if a past self was reaching through time to choke her, to shake her and wake her up to what was clearly an important fact, something she wouldn't dare to ignore. Kennedy's mention of HDPE hadn't triggered her back at Quantico, but something about seeing it written in black and white and listed multiple times sparked a reaction. She wracked her brain for the importance, the relevance of HDPE, and her thoughts returned to her father. Normally, he had no place in her business, but now, with things this dire, there was no time for past grudges. Callow allowed herself to revisit her memories unimpeded.

She remembered working in the garage behind an A-frame house set in a thicket. They were happy there, Callow and her parents, until poverty had driven them from their mountain abode into the city and her father had begun to drink away all their money. At that time, her mother had been too terrified to leave the house through fear of suffering her husband's wrath.

Callow saw herself in the corner of the living room while her father ordered car parts from the TV. The image was fuzzy, the signal weak. Her mother would often have had to get up and smack the side of it or twist the antennas around to get a better signal. Most of the time, it had only made things worse.

Callow remembered the thick carpet, shit brown in color and shaggy like a curly-haired dog. She remembered the wood-paneled home and the popcorn ceiling and how she used to lay on her back and count the kernels while her parents screamed about money in the kitchen. Then, for whatever reason, she remembered that bloody TV again, and the never-ending supply of beer cans that seemed to appear in her father's hand as soon as the last one was empty.

The TV changed to show a new type of interior paint for Chevrolet cars. Her father had owned a 1969 Chevette in those days. Callow remembered him dialing the number on the TV for a car part he didn't need, placing the order with money they didn't have, and slurring every second of the call. Just before the memory faded, Callow read the disclaimer on the TV: the new car parts weren't made of metal or fiberglass.

They were made of HDPE.

"What's HDPE?" Callow remembered asking her father.

"What? What the hell are you talking about, kid?" her father had growled.

"What is HDPE? It says on the TV that the part is now made from HDPE."

"Get me a beer and I'll tell you."

Callow watched like a guest in her own past life as a much younger Genevieve Callow went to the kitchen and innocently fetched another beer from the refrigerator. She placed it into her father's open hand, which had seemed to be permanently cupped in the shape of a beer can, as if when one was removed, the hand would maintain its shape until another can replaced it. She waited patiently by her father's side until he suddenly jumped.

"You're still here?"

"You said you'd tell me what HDPE is."

"Oh, right." He popped the tab, took a massive swig, and set it down with expert precision in the cupholder of the recliner. *"HDPE stands for high-density polyethylene. Plastic. It means plastic."*

"Plastic? Like in my dolls? Or Mom's favorite cutting board?"

Callow's father groaned and rolled his eyes. *"Exactly. Exactly like Mom's cutting board. Now, why don't you go find your own HDPE to play with?"*

Callow fell hard from her memory, her knees almost buckling. She felt hot, and she was panting. Marcus was looking over the case file, and Garcia had been waiting patiently. The two of them looked over at her.

"HDPE. It's present on all three," she said definitively, handing the papers back to the officer. "It stands out."

Garcia smiled.

"How so?" Marcus asked.

"It's plastic. HDPE is plastic, and the trace elements of HDPE have the same density as a number two plastic. We found HDPE on all the victims. Number two is the type of plastic used to make cutting boards."

Garcia's eyes and smile settled into a look of relief. Callow was sure he was relieved to have affirmation; to know he wasn't chasing his tail. She had recognized the same thing he had, something the evidence technicians had failed to annotate, the parts of the equation they hadn't added together.

"Does this mean anything to you, Jenny? What is the relevance of plastic and the victims?"

Callow turned to Marcus. "It means they were placed on a cutting board. When was the last time you scratched a cutting board with your fingernails or touched one except to clean it? These women scraped at the board so much, trace plastic was found under their nails. We wrote it off as simple *transference* from the coolers Icebox uses when he transports and stages the bodies postmortem. We didn't make the connection that it could be *antemortem* evidence."

Marcus ran his hand through his hair, then tiredly down his face. He took a step back. "*Jesus*. Okay. What next? Plastic manufacturers? Department stores? What're we doing?"

Callow desperately wanted to answer Marcus's question with a definitive answer and a plan of action, some way to launch from their still position into a sprint like a horse in the Preakness, rushing toward the finish line where this nightmare would finally come to an end. But she was left scratching her head, the odd moment of warmth from the day causing her scalp to itch and sweat under her dark hair. They were on the cusp of the answer, she could feel it, the minute details singing a song for her to hear, translate, and act upon—but they weren't there yet. She could hear the melody, the rhythm …

All that was left to discover were the words.

CHAPTER TWENTY-NINE

Callow, Marcus, and Garcia walked westward across the park, leaving the patch of shade trees to their back and a bit of their hope with it. There was a massive puzzle laid out before them, with no instructions and no image by which to create the larger picture. The tension was insufferable, and Callow had even caught Marcus checking his watch on the sly every few minutes, which wasn't helping.

"The cutting board would have to be huge," Callow commented, the words sounding strange, as if the idea itself refused to be spoken aloud. "Marcus, you mentioned plastic manufacturers. What if the unsub had the cutting board custom-made?"

Marcus shook his head as he walked. "Sounds like a dead end. Every large business from sandwich shops to pharmacies use them for one application or another."

The trio arrived at Marcus's Crown Victoria. Garcia's patrol car was parked behind it. The road ahead faced the setting sun, which seemed to glean, struggling to hold itself aloft.

Callow sighed. They were too close to give up, but the situation was dire, and their case kept hitting dead ends.

Remembering an old instructor's wisdom, she heard him say in her head, *"You didn't figure out what worked; you found all the things that* didn't *work. Eventually, there will only be one path forward."*

The only problem was, waiting for those wise words to once again come true was costing Callow time she didn't have.

Callow absentmindedly messaged Rebecca to let her know she was all right, and Shannon, too. She plugged away at the message on autopilot, not wanting to get in the car where she would be expected to answer the question, *"What now?"* She didn't have an answer. No path forward. No task to complete.

She received a reply almost instantly, and for no other reason other than to delay getting in the car, she turned to Garcia. The young officer looked at her with hopeful eyes while he adjusted his uniform shirt. He opened the car door, retrieved a circular can of chewing tobacco, and pressed a wad into his lip.

"Terrible habit," he said offhandedly.

"We've all got them," Marcus said. He glanced at Callow, sensing she wasn't yet ready to fire off directions. "What's the plan now, Officer? Back to the beat? Or do you have something else you'd like to look into?"

Please say you have something else …

"There are calls pending. I have to take them. I had to drop a petty theft and called in a favor with a few others to be here. Now, I've got to make good on my promises."

He spat.

Here it comes.

"What about you guys?" he asked. "Where will you go now?"

The question shot a spike of angst through Callow's heart. Marcus had no further delays to offer, and what kind of person would she be if she lied to the young officer after he'd made a point of seeking her out to help with the investigation? He'd surely see through her lie, anyway. Finally, her mind gave her the answer, and like her text message, it came from autopilot.

"I don't know. I need time. Time to think about what we've got. Time to consider and run through scenarios, profiles, and all the luxuries that time allows."

She waited, watching the young officer's face to see if his demeanor would change; to see if he'd suddenly become hostile with disappointment, frustration, or disbelief. Those feelings would be reasonable now, and Callow would understand if he felt that way.

He spat. "Fair enough," he said simply. "Well, agents, you have my number. Call me if you need anything."

"You aren't upset?" Callow asked suddenly.

Garcia froze, his hand on the car door. "Of course I am, but not with you."

"Why?"

"Because while this is your job, it's not your *fault*. If there's one thing I've learned so far, it's that I can't carry the weight of the world's decisions on my shoulders. On my first night on the job, I was too late to a burglary in progress, and a woman lost her life's savings. A month later, her car was towed, and a day after that, she hung herself. Was that my fault? Or was it just another case of bad things happening to good people?"

"I'm sorry."

"I am, too, but not for myself. I'm sorry for *her*. I'm sorry for her loss and pain. But I can't blame myself for things out of my control. I did my job. I responded as fast as I could. I took the report, and I even followed up with her after the case had been forwarded to a detective. Nothing changed, nothing got better, and life moves on. And I know I did my best. Do *your* best, Agent Callow. That's all anyone can ask of you."

"And what happens when my best isn't enough? What if I fail?"

"Then at least you can live with yourself in wake of the destruction … Goodbye, agents. Be safe."

A car drove by and honked twice. Garcia waved in a friendly manner before getting in his patrol car. He pulled away slowly, waving goodbye, and merged with the oncoming evening traffic building around the square.

"He's a good cop. He'll make a good supervisor one day," Marcus said as he watched the patrol car disappear from view. "Let's get off the street, Jenny."

He opened the car door for her and she slipped in. By the time Marcus got in the driver's seat, a tremor had overtaken her hands—a tremor born from frustration, exhaustion, and a hint of sadness.

"It's a game, Jenny. A really, really shitty game," he said.

"And if we lose?"

"People die. You know this. The cards are stacked against us, but we persevere, we endure, we keep fighting, never showing our backside and never faltering."

Callow wasn't really thinking, but rather mentally sifting through page after page of the case file without any real detail. She couldn't remember the specifics, like the dates, times, and addresses, but she could remember the major moving parts. She looked away from Marcus, out the windshield.

"He's out there. Watching. He's got Marissa right now, and if she isn't dead, she will be soon."

"Yes."

Callow's heart began to race with an idea that quickly flared like a fire fed a burst of oxygen. "What if the reason we keep losing is that we're playing *his* game?"

"Go on …"

"We're being reactive, chasing whatever trail he left us and hoping there's a clue left behind. We're following him around like a lost puppy, and he's gladly letting us."

"So, what do you propose?"

Callow saw the empty park bench, a flood of pigeons now patrolling the area in the hope of being fed. They all looked the same, not one standing out with an extra ring around their necks or a spot on their wings. Only one, the largest of them all, walked with a limp, and Callow watched the bird until it melded with the flock, forever invisible until the next passerby dropped a kernel and the frenzy began.

The smoldering fire in her mind flung sparks into the air. It flared with growing strength, an idea that burned hope for fuel and spat out elation and energy. She was becoming more invigorated by the moment.

"We need to get a step ahead. And I have a crazy idea on how to do it."

Marcus shifted in his seat toward her. "I like crazy. I'm all ears."

"Call your trooper friend; the one who pulled me over. Ask him for a favor and let him know it's urgent. Tell him we can't wait for him to consider. We just need him to forward a message on to the survivors' group en masse."

"What survivors' group?"

"I went to talk to them about survivor's guilt. You see, I realized something: Icebox taunted me at my weakest, sensing that I was reaching out for help. He managed to corner me and leave me thinking I was alone. But I'm *not* alone: I have you, and we have each other, and we have so many others like us who may have taken off the uniform but never really quit. Call your friend and drive. We're running out of time."

Marcus put the car in gear. "Okay. Where to?"

Callow looked at the road ahead, the trail of brake lights, the endless line of cars, and a sun that was a giant Bat Signal screaming for help when nobody would come.

"Back to where this all started. We need to cover our bases for what we're about to do, and we'll need all the help we can get to do it."

Marcus frowned, the car still idling. "What about the team? Do you want to put in a call? And what about the locals?"

She shook her head. "They obviously don't trust me—Welch made sure of that—so we can't rely on them right now. We'd be better off with Kennedy and Wainwright, but I doubt Jedediah is going to authorize them running off with me on a hunch. We're on our own—but we aren't *alone*, Marcus. Let's call in the troops."

Callow filled Marcus in on her plan as he drove.

CHAPTER THIRTY

Disappointment.

Callow, once enlivened with the light of hope, was suddenly brought down from her mountain when she heard from Marcus that no help would be coming.

Her stalwart plan to storm the metaphorical beaches of the city with cops was instantly deflated when she heard she wouldn't be joined by the full ranks of the survivors' group. The ones present at the meeting plus the rest of the roster made about a dozen or so in its entirety. But only those from the meeting had come out.

Marcus pulled the Crown Victoria into the parking lot for the Herman Free Library and must have sensed her dismay pouring from her skin. There were three cars in the parking lot, while a fourth pulled in behind them.

"That's Wainwright and Kennedy," Marcus observed as the two men in suits exited a black Malibu. One lit a cigarette.

Callow felt a pit hollow out in her stomach. "That's it?" she wondered out loud as the three other vehicles emptied, their drivers approaching the car. "We can't cover nearly enough ground with the full crew, let alone six of us."

Marcus ran his hand through his hair—not in the seductive way Callow liked, but out of worry. He, too, was feeling the pressure, and for it to have broken his otherwise tough yet carefree exterior, it meant she wasn't wrong about her assessment of their current dire straits.

"A logical guess is all I have," she said, her voice wavering on "unconfident."

"A logical guess, but a solid *plan*. We've been chasing our tails. I think once you hear what the others think about your idea, you'll know you're on the right track," Marcus replied.

"And what if I'm wrong? What if this flops? I'm putting *everything* on the line, including Marissa's life." She trailed off, looking out the window as Kennedy and Wainwright shook hands with the newcomers like old friends.

Marcus was undeterred. "When you told me you'd found our unsub back in El Paso, I didn't listen and it almost got you killed. You felt so strongly in your heart that it had to be him. No other possibilities." He turned toward her, but she couldn't bear to face him. "And you saved that girl's life at the risk of your own. I should have been there to back you. *I* should have been in the mud there with you, not that beat cop."

Callow's heart thumped wildly in her chest. Was it nerves? A boiling angst at what she was about to do, which felt all too familiar to the events in El Paso? Or was it the feelings she had for Marcus Oakley, choosing a terrible time, as always, to surface?

This was what Marcus did, though; he brought others up around him. And when she was faltering, as she was so close to doing now, he was there to pick her up.

"You believe in this? In what we're about to do?"

Who am I asking—him or me?

Wainwright approached the driver's side door, prompting Marcus to put his hand on it. "I believe in *you*," he said before stepping out into the cold.

Wainwright and Marcus engaged in a muffled discussion.

Her eyes filled with tears—not of sadness or sorrow, but the culmination of massive amounts of pressure weighing her down, grounding her in this reality. This was *her* show, and it was time to call the shots. At its core, her plan comprised taking control back from the Icebox Killer and putting it back in her court.

For Marissa. For Gwen. For Carmen.

Callow got out of the car to meet the men waiting for her near the hood: Wainwright, Kennedy, Marcus, Officer Edwardo Garcia, and Trooper Tony Mackeras. The weather had grown cold quickly, the temperature dropping far enough for their breath to form in clouds and their peacoats and puffy winter jackets to no longer be optional.

Tony wore a beanie that said "STATE POLICE" across the front. The headlights of a vehicle turning onto the street nearby illuminated the badge and gun on his hip.

They each looked to Callow. She was about to ask a lot of them, though they didn't know that ahead of time. If they were on edge, they were doing a great job of hiding it. How could she come to expect less from those in the service of others? The men gathered around her were all committed to answering the call when a fellow officer or agent needed help with a life-or-death situation, and the same could be said of so many in law enforcement. Duty was a powerful motivator. Callow had put out the call, and those who could answer were here. For that, she would be eternally grateful. If only now she could put that sentiment into words.

"I'm out of options and nearly out of hope," she said glumly. Honesty had to be the best policy here; trying to lie her way into the hearts of these men to convince them to help her would never work. She had to be clear about what she wanted; the risks she was expecting them to take. She paused, and the streetlamps came on overhead. One showered her in yellow light—a stage light.

"And I've got one idea. One plan to flush out Icebox. And

if anyone can think of a better one, please let me know when I get done because I could really use a lifeline."

More deafening silence. Kennedy puffed on his cigarette, his face illuminated by the glow.

"He's outsmarted us and kept us chasing our tails for months. That ends tonight."

Callow turned her back to them, suddenly compelled to look toward the last dregs of sunlight as the sun dipped below the horizon, casting great shadows from the multitude of buildings that made up the circuit board of the city of Colleyville. Somewhere in the dark, the Icebox Killer was waiting …

A van with dark lettering—a news van—turned into the parking lot. She addressed the men again.

"Icebox is going to murder Marissa and dump her body in the next few hours. I want to disrupt his process. I want to turn this entire city into a fucking microscope and put him under it so he feels watched everywhere he goes—and then we're going to be waiting. I've thought about this a lot, and what I know about this killer is that he loves his process. He loves to repeat it, *perfect* it, and do it again. We're going to mess with that."

"Callow, why are the media here?" Wainwright asked, concern in his voice. "What are you about to do?"

She spoke very quickly. "If you want to leave now, Wainwright, I understand. You too, Kennedy. In fact, if you all want to leave, I won't blame you. But I'm going to get in front of that camera, and I'm going to put this entire city on watch so the Icebox Killer can't possibly complete his process without anybody seeing him."

"What about Marissa?" Wainwright asked, shifting his weight from side to side nervously.

Marcus stepped into the circle. "We're going to call Icebox out into the open, warning the entire city to be vigilant. It probably won't amount to much, to that end, but I'm hoping *something* will come through. Most likely, Icebox will try to test his boundaries and reach out to Callow."

"Play to his ego," Wainwright observed.

"Yes," Callow replied. "We think we've established a pattern of where he'll dump the body," she said, speaking mostly to Tony at this point. "Worst case, we catch him there, but before that happens, I want to run the details by you all. You come from many backgrounds and experiences, and that is too valuable not to try and use. I'm going to bring you up to speed, then I'm getting in front of that camera and I'm going to call him out. He'll be too tempted not to make a move for me."

Her rousing pep talk—if that was what it was—came from the heart, the words flowing quickly from mind to mouth without much stoppage in between. Her course of action felt right, even though she'd certainly be fired for an unsanctioned press briefing. But what else was she to do? How could she forgive herself for not trying every possible route to get justice for Carmen?

Callow didn't care about some damn plaques on the wall—this was about a promise to a friend.

"I won't judge you if you walk away," she said finally.

The news crew had a tripod and floodlights set up. She eyed each member in the circle one more time, and not a soul budged. She couldn't sense hesitancy from them, nor fear; only the raw determination that came from knowing that what they were doing was right. She felt it, too, and that warmed her heart.

"Local PD can't help? Sheriffs? Detectives?" Wainwright asked, one final check he probably knew the answer to.

"We're shorthanded as is, and the higher-ups won't spare the manpower for a guess-and-check. Same thing with County," Garcia added. "We're on our own."

Wainwright nodded briefly. "I'm in."

Callow spun around and pulled a sheet of paper from a

notebook in the back seat. On it, she scribbled the locations of where the victims had been taken, where they had been dumped, and where she thought the killer might land next.

"You've seen this before," she said as Marcus held a flashlight over the crude drawing. "Those who haven't, these are abduction and dump sites. *This* is where we think he'll drop Marissa." She pointed to the most southeastern point. "He knows what Marcus looks like, and me. He knows how to spot locals, but he doesn't know anything about the rest of you. You are going to be my eyes."

"What're you going to do, Callow?" Kennedy asked.

She ignored him. "The Icebox Killer took my friend, Carmen, from me. He sent me his calling card while I was in the hospital. He took a picture of Marissa after he dumped her in the back seat of my fucking Tahoe, and he sent me a message today, taunting me." She looked up and around. "Now, I'm going to call *him* out. I'm going to be bait."

"No damn way," Kennedy said. "That's *crazy*."

"It's necessary."

"It's a suicide mission! If this doesn't work, your career is done for." Wainwright spat toward the media van, indicating he knew exactly how severe a policy breach her proposal was.

"And we could still miss the shot. This is a terrible idea, Callow," Tony said solemnly.

"I'm doing it regardless. I have to do something! If there's another way, please suggest it to me. Do you think I *want* to do this? I want to go home. I want all this to stop; to wake up, and for all of this to have been a nightmare. But every time I close my eyes, I see Carmen's severed head …"

"You can't let her do this, Oakley," Wainwright said softly.

Marcus sighed. "Nice try, kid, but I agree with her. I'll be nearby. We need you all out in the streets, eyes and ears." He put a supportive hand on Callow's shoulder, and she could feel the warmth through his touch. "It's happening—and we'd rather do it with you than without you."

Callow reached up and gripped Marcus's hand. His touch warmed her clammy fingers.

Wainwright groaned. "We're all getting fired, possibly prosecuted—you know that right?"

Callow shook her head. "I'll take the fall. It was my idea. I'm Senior Special Agent, and I ordered the three of you into it. Then I lied to Tony and Garcia about what we were actually doing."

"You believe in this plan that much?" Kennedy asked, lighting another cigarette with the cherry of the previous.

"Yes," she replied. Her mouth had run dry.

He blew out a cloud of smoke and looked around at the others before his eyes settled back on Callow. "Fuck it. I don't have a better idea. Give us the details."

CHAPTER THIRTY-ONE

The reporter from Channel 7 feigned composure, but even with the sun now gone and the parking lot lights casting shadows upon their faces, Callow could see the lines cut into her brow. Callow was tired, too, but that wasn't their only similarity. As the reporter held her notebook and pen, poised to take down Callow's every word as if it were a confession, it was all too obvious that the job, with its after-hours callouts and the occasional, unprompted, and—most importantly—unsanctioned press release from the FBI, was putting her through her paces.

A technician flitted around Callow, attaching a microphone to the collar of her shirt and then pointing out how to connect the battery pack to her belt. She did as instructed, but it was in slow motion, as if her body was acting without her mind's permission. She might as well have been watching her own body from above. At some point, the technician drifted away, and Callow was left alone to face the high-vis lights behind the camera and the reporter.

Her team didn't stand with her. They were behind the camera, safe. If they stood with her, she would appear to have their support, willing accomplices who had put their careers and safety on the line for her—great for the headlines, but not so great for their employment status. That wasn't part of the plan visible to the public, to her superiors, or to Jedediah. Behind the camera, she could protect them from what was to come.

The reporter waited patiently, received the okay from the technician, and counted down on her fingers. As she, too, faded into the background, Callow was left staring at a blinking red light, and the rest of the world watching. She contorted her face into a mask she believed conveyed confidence.

She had no notes to look down at; no lines written on her hands or on a prompter to read from. This wasn't prepared. It was a leap of faith, born out of necessity and brought to life out of desperation. Their trail had run cold. There were no more answers, nothing left to speculate over. Callow needed an edge; to charge forward until she was one step ahead of the killer.

"My name is Senior Special Agent Genevieve Callow of the FBI's Behavioral Analysis Unit, and I am speaking directly to the people of Colleyville and all those who will listen."

She paused. The introduction was easy—it was the known, the part she could recite like a well-practiced hymnal. What came next would have to come from her heart for it to be convincing, and that was no easy feat.

"For months, I have been tasked with identifying and tracking the Icebox Killer. We've made progress, but we're out of time. Some of you may have seen something; heard something. Some of you could have been watching. I know I have. Every night, I double-check the locks on my doors and draw my shades, and I wake up thinking about the women he's taken, and those he might take next. I'm sure I can't be alone in this worry."

Callow's hands started to shake, so she balled her fists to hide it. She looked past the camera and saw Marcus press a phone to his ear, wandering off behind the news van. *Too late to stop now.*

"We need help. From you. A million eyes and ears. I'm sure you've all seen the recent reports about the latest missing woman. Help us bring Marissa Marley home, and help us bring justice for Gwen Hammond and my friend, Carmen Watts …"

She drew in a deep breath. "The Icebox Killer is weak. He needs to hide and crawl on his belly like a snake. He preys on women he can surprise and overpower with chemical agents. He is driving a van or a truck—something where noise is dampened. He is likely a male between the ages of thirty and fifty, well educated, and possibly has some medical training. He is technologically savvy, and likely has trouble maintaining relationships with others."

Callow's eyes refused to focus; she could only look at the bigger picture of the world beyond the camera lens—the cars fading into the distance, their taillights blurring in the dark.

"He is a coward. He hides amongst you, hoping you're afraid. You should be. I am. But I'm not here to instill fear—I speak to you tonight to *empower* you. Be vigilant. Be wary. If you see something, *say* something. The FBI has a hotline set up for tips. Flood it. Look alive, Colleyville. I will not sleep until you can rest easy."

She focused on the red light blinking just beneath the massive lens, drawing from the depths of her heart the determined glare she thought a lioness might adopt when challenging a pack of hyenas threatening her cubs.

Come get me, you bastard. I'm afraid, but I'm not alone. I am strong, and you are weak.

The recording light turned off, and Callow felt her shoulders slump, the tension releasing from her upper back. She walked away from her makeshift stage, leaving the reporter clambering after her, asking questions to the wind, all of which were ignored.

Tony ran ahead to unlock the door to the library, and everyone filtered inside. Last to arrive in the lobby was Marcus, who carried an armful of handheld radios. Tony locked the door behind him and stood blocking the view.

The reporter, looking quite flummoxed, stormed off toward the van.

Marcus wandered around the group, handing out the radios. "Closed channel. Just us so we won't be clogged by local traffic. Also, Icebox won't be able to pick it up on a scanner if he's listening. These are the same model as those used by the state river cops in Texas. They use cell phone towers, so you should have service—if you believe the brochure. Honestly, they don't work nearly as well as they claim."

Callow took one from him. He paused an extra moment in front of her and gave her a supportive nod. "*Well done,*" he said with his eyes.

"Ol' Jedediah is blowing up your phone, Callow," Kennedy said. "Mine, too. I told him I'm on the shitter and hung up, but I'm not sure how long we'll be able to stall him."

"No pun intended," Marcus joked.

"He's probably calling to fire me," Callow said, rolling her eyes. "There will be time for that later—*after* this works. Check yourselves while you listen. I'm going to hand out stations and the plan."

Marcus, Kennedy, and Wainwright ran their hands over their weapons without drawing them from their holsters. They tightened their belts, checked handcuffs, and otherwise situated themselves. Tony thumbed a wad of brown tobacco from a tin into his mouth and offered it to Garcia. Garcia tucked a wad into his lip, pulled down on a ballistic vest under his shirt and proceeded to check the pouches on his duty belt.

"Here's the plan. We're going to surround the next dump

site." Callow indicated the presumed next point in the pattern by prodding the map, then she set about pointing out each station. "I'll be *here* with Marcus. Wainwright and Kennedy, you'll be *here* and *here*, two blocks away. Garcia, you'll be *here*. Stay in your cars, and stay out of traffic. We're looking for a vehicle. A van or a truck."

"That's it? 'A van or a truck?' That's one in a million, Callow ..." Kennedy chimed in.

She shook her head. "One in a million becomes one in a *hundred* if we stick to our locations. We went too broad in our searches before." She glanced at Garcia, for it was he who had given her the idea. "I'm putting everything on black that he's following this pattern. I think he'll go there again tonight, furious or emboldened in response to me calling him out. He needs to appear strong after I called him weak. I'm hoping he'll scout the area to dump Marissa, then find me waiting instead."

"Okay. I'm in," Tony declared. "We see the van—then what? Call it in?"

"When we've got eyes on, we'll converge before he has a chance to grab me. I'm going to La Sturgeon. It's a restaurant at the corner of my station. It has large glass windows and barely any customers. I'm going to give him the opportunity he can't ignore."

"What makes you so sure he'll come that way?" Wainwright asked. "He could go down any number of streets in that area."

Callow stretched her back. "Bruce McArthur was a mall Santa. Fred West drove an ice cream truck. Dennis Rader installed alarms. These killers thrive on blending in. At this point, it's my hope the press release has made every back alley and side road impassable—a massive red flag for every nervous eye in town to see."

"Not bad," Wainwright said, his fingers thoughtfully

rubbing his chin. "Are there any other details you think we might need?"

Callow wracked her brain, filtering through endless pages of reports, crime scene photographs, interviews with the victims' families, and more. Only one thing stood out: the newest, most underdeveloped detail.

"HDPE. The trace evidence reports we pulled from all the victims showed a high level of HDPE." She trained her eyes on Kennedy. "We think he cuts them up on a large cutting board."

"Manufacturers? Do you think he might have had a custom one made to fit a body?" Kennedy asked.

Callow shook her head again. "We already discounted that. Large sheets of HDPE have plenty of industrial uses. They're everywhere."

"Fair enough." Kennedy rolled a cigarette between his fingers. "And your profile? Has it changed?"

She recalled her miasmic moment with Marcus and the others, spewing fact after fact, delving into the mind of a serial killer, feeling as if a fine grit was laid upon her psyche. This was the price she paid to think like they think, and it felt *disgusting*. Not only did she have to consider *why* they did what they did, but Callow had to be able to justify it in her mind; the same way a detective might try to commiserate and find "reason" with a rapist—because then, and only then, would those sickos divulge their secrets, much in the way she hoped the Icebox Killer would divulge his tonight. She had stepped into his mind and found his reason—power—and now she was about to test him.

"It hasn't changed. He's tested us plenty. Now, it's time for *us* to test him."

"Uh, Callow?" Wainwright said, looking through the glass door of the library. "We have a problem."

She could sense the apprehension in his voice. Whatever

was shaking Wainwright's calculated exterior certainly didn't bode well for the rest of them.

She met him at the glass doors in time to see the hulking figure of Jedediah Gold himself, talking flippantly with the Channel 7 reporter, who was shrinking by the second into her van. Jedediah wore basketball shorts, tennis shoes, and a plain t-shirt that said "FBI" in yellow across the front. He had clearly been at home and had rushed out the door the moment he'd seen his protégé's face on the TV. The reporter pointed toward the library, and he stormed in their direction.

Callow seized up like a child, caught with her hand in the cookie jar. What would the fallout be? How much would Jed disrupt the plans she had in motion, knowing what was at stake? Or would Jedediah finally learn to trust her decisions? He had never put her as primary on the case—only as a consultant—and she had regularly overstepped. Now was her chance to lay out her thoughts in full. Being objective didn't work. Waiting and canvassing didn't work—in fact, another girl had been taken while the FBI's most elite team stood by and did nothing. This time, she felt a swell of confidence steady her hands and slow her heart.

Instead of waiting for the ASAC's fury to catch up with her, Callow nodded to Wainwright to unlock the door, and she walked through to meet Jedediah head-on.

CHAPTER THIRTY-TWO

Jedediah Gold wasn't a violent man on the surface; in fact, he was icy calm, collected, when all others might rage and scream and destroy things around them. Callow reckoned this uncanny ability of his came to him at about the same time he received the large half-moon scar that adorned his head—sort of a memento of times gone by, times long since forgotten.

And so, when Jedediah picked up the camera and its tripod and launched it across the parking lot, Callow knew she was in the shit.

For a moment, the man was the culmination of years of rage suppressed beneath his comforting Southern shell, and when the expensive equipment was nothing more than a mangled pile of expensive plastic and glass, lit from above by a streetlamp, Callow watched Jedediah slip back into his old shell. He walked calmly past her with a slight incline of his head, and she turned on her heels to follow him inside the library. Wainwright locked the door behind him.

"Is there coffee?" Jedediah asked, turning left at the hallway intersection and heading into the kitchen.

"There's a one cup machine. Let me get it for you, sir ..." Wainwright started to say.

"No, I'll get my own damn coffee, rookie," Jedediah growled, disappearing into the kitchen. Harsh fluorescent lights came on overhead, and a minute later, the one cup machine was gurgling with boiling water.

"Someone speak!" Jedediah barked as Callow and Marcus exchanged nervous glances. She was relieved to see Kennedy and Wainwright were doing the same, while Garcia, who probably had yet to comprehend the severity of what was going on, stood stoically off to one side.

"The PD officer can leave," Jedediah yelled as mugs clinked in his wake.

Garcia took a timid half step toward the door, but Callow cut him off. "*Wait,*" she mouthed.

Jedediah returned to the hallway a minute later, brandishing a generic white coffee mug as if it was a judge's gavel. It was steaming with black coffee. He seemed to appreciate the warmth in his hand rather than the taste and smell, which were substandard at best.

"One of you is the mastermind behind this ... this *shit show*, and the damage is done, so somebody better damn speak because I'm sure you're on a timeline for whatever fugazi plan you've concocted."

Jedediah leaned against a half table in the hallway, a framed picture of Mary Magdalene dangerously close to his hand. One twitch and the photo would topple over, falling and crashing to the ground.

Marcus took a step forward as Jedediah dipped his face into the cup. The ASAC shook his head. "No, I know it wasn't you, Oakley, but nice try. It was either Callow or Kennedy, I know that for a fact—Kennedy, because I told him to take this case, and this so-called *plan* sounds exactly like the type of backwards shit he might pull, or Callow, because she can't seem to follow a single damn order she hasn't handed out herself, and she's not beyond trying this kind of backwards shit, either. I will say this—I'm disappointed, but then again, I should have expected it. It was *our* idea to bring the media into this in the first place."

Callow immediately cleared her throat, stepping into the semicircle that had naturally formed around Jedediah. Even in such a ridiculous outfit, he was imposing in size, stature, and demeanor, appearing much older and wiser than most people would expect.

His lip upturned. "Of course it was you," he said. "It *always* has to be the great Genevieve Callow."

"The profile is solid, Jed. The plan, too, if you'd only listen…" Callow pleaded, but Jedediah pushed off from the half table, standing to his full height, menacing and casting shadows from the light in the kitchen.

Jedediah lowered his head to look at the floor. "There is *no* plan! You're done! And the damage is done, too. You crossed the line, Genevieve, and I can't protect you from this!" he boomed.

But Callow didn't hang her head, and she didn't flinch. She didn't even blink. She had been through too much, risked it all, to be told no without having her voice heard on something she was supposed to be an expert on. This was *her* show—by proxy, courtesy of Icebox. If only Jedediah would hear her out for just a minute …

She turned to her side and unclasped her holster and badge from her belt. Silently, and without emotion, she set them on the table next to Jedediah and made for the door.

"Where are you going?" he asked, his customary fatherly tone back in his voice but his eyes still fixed to the floor by his feet.

"To finish what I started. I don't need the job to do it. I don't need the badge or the gun. And I don't need *you*."

"I could have you arrested."

"Do what you will."

"What would Rebecca think?"

"I know she'd support me, which is what you should be doing, Jed. But like you said, the damage is done. Why not let this play out, and then when it's over, you can handcuff me yourself."

"*Jesus*, Genevieve! You can't keep running off on your own, dragging your team behind you and leaving us to pick up the pieces," he said to her back.

She turned, fists balled out of bubbling rage. Was that really what Jedediah thought she was doing? Going rogue and guessing, and *occasionally* getting lucky? That wasn't what she'd been trained to do. That wasn't the direction her instincts sent her, and it definitely wasn't how she showed Jedediah how much she respected him. She wasn't an adolescent child looking for a few thrills, only to come home with her tail between her legs when the world spat her out, covered in the scars of her mistakes.

"She's not alone, Jedediah," Marcus said in his bold, smooth voice. "It's a good plan. We all agree with her. You should hear it out."

The ASAC expelled his breath through pursed lips. "What about you, Wainwright? You already expressed to me you thought Callow was unfit to lead the investigation. What was it you said? '*Compromised*?'"

Wainwright nodded. "She *is* compromised, sir, but nobody else has managed to get as far as she has."

"And you, Kennedy? You've told me more than once that you're making headway on this case. You told me you were on the cusp of breaking it, of finally identifying the killer."

Kennedy looked slyly at Callow, then trained his gaze on Jedediah. "Did I? I don't recall. I was probably just parroting what Callow was already saying. I get so confused sometimes. It's great having a Senior Special Agent to refer to for a consult."

Officer Garcia stepped forward. "I've known Callow for many...."

Jedediah raised a hand. "Don't lie ..."

Garcia shirked away, embarrassed, like as though been caught with his fly down.

"You could always say you didn't know about it, Jed. Deniability," Callow attempted.

But one thing Callow herself couldn't deny was the overwhelming sense of pride she felt pushing away all the doubt and darkness in her heart. These men, some of whom she barely knew—her co-conspirators, if she indulged herself a moment of theatrics—hadn't stood by when she'd thrown herself on the pyre. Instead, they had accepted their part in things, lifting her up and raising her beyond the flames, carrying her and the weight of her decisions. She wanted to hug her team, or maybe cry, or perhaps whoop in triumph, for she could see Jedediah was conflicted about what was occurring, and it was tearing at his fibers. His heart had to be telling him to stop, pause, and listen to what Callow had to say, to let her explain herself and the plan, while his brain was yelling at him to chase her out of the library and later refer her for prosecution for whatever they might call tonight.

If anything, his features softened as his flaring temper came down to a more reasonable level. Jedediah stood up tall, his chest expanding, then resting.

"You fucked up tonight, Genevieve, but I know you don't do anything without good cause. And somehow, you've managed to convince the rest of the team that this plan of yours has got legs. Who am I not to at least hear it out? Go on. Explain."

It took Callow a few extra seconds to comprehend exactly what Jedediah was saying. It wasn't until Kennedy broke free from the pack, slipping a cigarette into his mouth and stepping out the front door, that her mind caught up with her body.

Smiling at Jedediah's acceptance, Callow went through the profile again, identifying all the major known features about their unsub, including the presumed medical experience, the cutting board theory based on the HDPE traces, and the unsub's usage of a van or truck. She immediately followed up with all the actions taken by local police and the BAU team and found there wasn't a single rabbit hole to chase. All that remained was the plan.

"Bait? You plan to be *bait*?"

"Yes, just as you used me as bait. And up until five minutes ago, I planned to be *armed* bait. I know Icebox will strike along this street next, canvassing the area for a weak target. He will perceive me as an opportunity he can't ignore, and when he makes his move, the others will be waiting. We'll know far in advance when he's in the area even if we haven't identified which specific vehicle is his. My announcement should have driven everyone inside and given them cause to be more vigilant than before. Everyone is looking for a show, and the Icebox Killer intends to give the people what they want."

"How can you be sure he'll show up? How do you know he won't just stay with Marissa?

Callow clasped her hands thoughtfully behind her back, hoping to avoid Jedediah seeing the tremor in them.

"He *has* to respond, since I responded. Up until now, he's only taunted me, attempting to force me to interact. Now, the conversation's started, and his ego won't let me have the last word. I wonder now if dropping Gwen's body in the parking lot of my sister's workplace was deliberate, just like the text message and photograph and portion of Carmen's locket was on purpose."

"He texted you?"

She nodded solemnly. "He wants me to play, but I don't think he *expected* me to play, and certainly not to change the game. I've upped the ante—I've put the city on notice, made it harder for him, testing him. And now he will have no choice but to play. It's in his psyche. Swells his ego."

She pointed to the spot on the map again. "He's struck here, dumped here, consistently. The known points are to make it easy for him to remember where he's dropped a body before, kind of how Jeffrey Dahmer returned to the dump site of his victims for weeks on end, even while they decomposed."

Jedediah was on his feet, pacing, one long, beefy finger tapping his lips to the beat of his footsteps. His coffee now sat abandoned on the table.

"Everyone stages at regular intervals, looking for the vehicle out of sight, and you stage in plain sight as an easy target, with backup readily available to swoop in at the first sign of distress. We find him, we find the girl. Do I have that right?"

All eyes fell on Callow, and for once, she didn't feel unbridled pressure as she had in the meeting room surrounded by senior leadership as they'd issued their grave warnings. She felt better than before, more righteous, as if she'd been lost in the woods and had suddenly found the right path her instincts said would lead her to safety. She felt ready to take on the Icebox Killer, whereas before, when the wound was still fresh and Carmen's crime scene photos still haunted her dreams, she only prayed for a reprieve as she fell into lockstep with the puzzle. Then, she had been controlled by the game. Now, she was a contender.

"That's right," she said with finality. "He's going to strike again, Jedediah—I can feel it. He's going to strike, and he's going to mess up. And then it's game over."

CHAPTER THIRTY-THREE

When the dust settled, Jedediah was left in the shadow of the library's overhang, the lights inside shut off, and Callow's plan endorsed without him explicitly giving the word.

Trailed by her team, Callow stopped in the middle of the parking lot once more. With the news crew gone, they were alone.

"Keep your radios on channel two. Plain speak; no codes."

Jedediah eventually joined the circle. "I'd like to be of use. There's no way the higher-ups are going to believe I didn't know about this."

Garcia moved to turn over his radio.

"No," Callow said, stopping him. "Jed, can you go back to Colleyville PD and see what assets they can provide? I have no pull over there—that much, Lieutenant Welch made clear. But the more boots on the ground we can get, the better."

"Will do," Jedediah agreed. "I'll see what plain-clothes detectives I can round up. We don't want to spook the unsub with a massive police presence."

"Agreed. Garcia is the only one of us meant to be seen, and only if we need to push the unsub somewhere we want him to go." Callow looked the others over. "This isn't about pride, or jealousy, or payback. This is about *justice*. This is the job. When you're out there, keep your eyes open and your ears pricked. I wish I had more in the way of a pep talk, people, but we don't have the time. Good luck, everyone.

Callow made for Marcus's car, Wainwright and Kennedy to theirs. Garcia waited in his patrol car. Jedediah loaded into his pickup and immediately began babbling into his phone. Whoever was on the line was guaranteed not to agree with what was about to go down, assuming Jedediah wasn't just running interference. Callow knew she had inadvertently put her mentor in a bind: support her and risk his job, or worse, the lives of the victims now depending on their judgement.

She briefly reflected on how tangled the web had become, and how quickly. All that was left was to face the spider. She had a team, and they were ready.

She sent a text to Marcus. "That's your location. Drop me off down the hill, and I'll walk to the restaurant," she instructed.

He put the car in gear. No air-conditioning was needed; no music to cloud her thoughts. He drove in silence.

Halfway there, Callow performed a radio check. Everyone answered in kind.

Her phone buzzed, and for a heart-stopping moment, she hesitated to open her messages for fear she'd find a picture of Marissa. She glanced at the phone and saw the sender wasn't blank: it was Jedediah.

Good luck.

It was so simple a message, and it surprised Callow how much sway was held in those two words. The sense the plan could still go either way fought for resurgence, but Callow damped it down. *Showtime.*

Marcus stopped at a red light. A light drizzle coated the Crown Victoria's windshield, and the interior fogged up. He turned on the air conditioner, resulting in a blast of harsh air that smelled like rain. On a normal day, the rain would have excited her; she could sleep deep during a rainstorm, or read a book and never turn an eye to the TV until the clock ticked down. The rain could still her nerves. But for reasons unknown, it was failing to do so now, and all Callow could see were the puddles forming on black asphalt and the cars reflected in them.

The evening dark consumed them. Now came the real test of her theory. Any moment now, they risked a call about a woman's dismembered head being found in a cooler. If that was what she were to find tonight, Callow pleaded with God that one of her agents would be staged just right to catch the man responsible.

"In position," Wainwright said over the radio. The others soon followed suit.

The light turned green, and Marcus drove through traffic around a bend until the warm, inviting lights of La Sturgeon flooded the street corner at the top of the hill. The large windows offered ample view of inside the restaurant and advantageous overwatch of the streets below. There was one exit at the front, and one, from the kitchen, out the back, which spilled into a gloomy alley. From her current position, Callow could see anyone who sat by the window, and anyone who left out the back. She pointed to a parking spot between two cars facing the restaurant. Marcus moved over and put the unmarked cruiser in park.

Callow pulled on a plain grey sweater from the back seat and moved to get out as Marcus grabbed her wrist gingerly. She met his eyes and saw a sadness there despite the smile. She knew it was forced. His face bore worry lines across his brow, and his lips were dry and cracked. She could feel his hand was clammy—unusual for him, as she was used to the rough but warm comfort of them. She held his eyes, but no words came. What *could* she say at a time like this? Was there anything appropriate?

Marcus didn't speak, and when she turned away, he

gripped her hand in both of his and kissed the top of it sweetly. Her heart fluttered, and Callow blinked rapidly. Suddenly, all logical thoughts were shoved aside and, in that moment, she wanted to leave with him; to hold his hand and just walk away from all of this. An obscure thought, really—if she walked away, her freedom would come at too high a price.

Marcus understood her without a word. She lifted her hand and pressed it to his cheek, exchanging the same silent message. *Come back. Come back to me*—just as he had whispered to her only months ago, right before El Paso.

The radio in Callow's hand squawked. Her face shifted into mission-focused seriousness, and with a final glance, she stepped out into the light drizzle.

She dragged an earpiece from her pocket, connected it to the radio, and stuffed the rubber mold into her ear.

"Callow's moving," Marcus said in her ear. "I've got eyes on."

"All clear," Kennedy said. "No trucks."

"Look for vans, too. Box trucks. Removal trucks. Could even be a goddamn Amazon truck," Callow mumbled into the microphone attachment along the earpiece cable.

She made it to the restaurant, nearly skipping up the curb past a young woman and her husband pushing a stroller covered by a blanket. A blue and white Budget truck came to the intersection.

"Check the truck to your left, Jenny."

"I see it. BBM3436. Run it, Garcia." Callow studied the driver. An older Asian woman looked back at her.

"Comes back to an Andrea Chan out of Maryland," Garcia advised. "How do we know the unsub isn't a mid-forties Asian woman?"

"Trust. The. Profile," Callow said lowly, tugging on the restaurant's door handle and seeing herself inside.

La Sturgeon was a bad representation of an Italian-style

villa, with crudely painted murals of a city divided by a river and a village that overlooked the sea, but instead the colors ran and blended together. Dishes clanked together from the kitchen while something sizzled on the grill. A young woman, no more than twenty, escorted Callow to a table.

"I'd prefer a booth, please. By the window."

The young girl nodded and offered the middle seat of three at the large bay window.

"Coffee, too," Callow said.

The girl nodded gracefully and made for the kitchen.

Callow kept her back to the kitchen, eyes fixed on the double doors. What was she expecting? For the unsub to just waltz inside and sit down at the table with her? Perhaps Icebox would be that bold. Perhaps this was the game they were destined to play. She remembered old video tapes she'd been shown in training of an officer interviewing Jeffrey Dahmer in prison. The conversation had been casual, like something one might have over dinner with an old friend. She remembered thinking, *"That's it?"* as if Dahmer or Gacy or any number of the serial killers in recent memory had two heads and bulbous eyes, or spoke in tongues about the Devil, or were invincible to pain.

"Red truck with a camper cover. Long bed. Does that count?" Kennedy asked, bringing Callow back from her reverie.

"Use your judgement," Callow hissed into the mic hidden up and around the hood of her sweater.

"Hi, just one?" a waiter asked, holding a brown plastic-coated menu and her coffee.

"Hopefully not."

The waiter set the cup down in front of her and passed her the menu. Callow didn't touch either. Instead, she stared out the window, where the rain cooled the air. She saw the front headlights of Marcus's Crown Victoria shut off, and then Garcia's patrol car roll through the intersection a block over.

Callow looked at the same cream-colored coffee cup, the one with the fat walls and matching saucer, the same at every restaurant, as her phone buzzed in her pocket. No lurch of her heart this time. Jedediah had sent her another text. She opened it.

Got this out of the detectives: Marissa's roommate called PD. She found a letter to her friend, Alexandra Corbel, written the day Marissa was taken. 301–829–3434.

Callow decided to give Alexandra a call in a few minutes as a way of passing the time, to occupy her mind whilst sitting like a staked goat. That, and she needed to at least appear as if she was ordering something to eat.

But not a single part of her wanted to engage in the simple act of eating. It seemed too mundane for the situation, like a shock of neon on an otherwise black façade. Eating was so … *normal*.

The waiter returned, resting his notebook on his distended belly. With the man standing before her, Callow had to admit it looked weird not to be ordering anything, and so she asked for the house steak, medium rare. Marcus would have scolded her for ordering it cooked any other way; said it ruined the flavor, just like most spices besides salt and pepper. She ordered a side of asparagus and rice, but it didn't really matter—she was more indulging the waiter than her stomach. The waiter walked away neutrally.

While she waited for the food, Callow cradled her coffee with one hand, punched Alexandra's number into her phone with the other, and waited for the call to connect.

Alexandra Corbel picked up on the first ring.

"Hello?" she asked weakly. Callow could hear the waver in her voice. She had clearly been crying.

"Hello, Alexandra?"

"This is she."

"Alexandra, my name is Special Agent Callow, FBI. I'm

calling about your friend, Marissa. Is this a good time to talk?"

At the first crackle of the transmission in her other ear, Callow held the phone away as Wainwright said, "Red Panel Van. Carpeting company. They're unloading down the street ... Nope, not turning your way, Callow."

Callow returned her attention to her cell as Alexandra replied, "I guess. I've already talked to the detectives, though. They told me ... They told me I didn't have anything useful for them to go on, and to call them when I did."

Callow scowled. Not only was it wrong to dismiss a witness in that way, but it also showed a lack of respect for a person who was clearly in distress. From what she'd seen of Switch and Willoughby in Hanklin Memorial Park, the PD's half-assed efforts didn't surprise her. She only hoped Alexandra wasn't too upset with them to talk to her now.

"I'm so sorry for the way they treated you. I think anything you have to share is valuable, and I'm willing to listen if you'll tell me what you know. I think we're close to finding Marissa, Alexandra, and you can help us close that gap even further."

Alexandra hiccupped, then sniffled. Callow looked up, but she wasn't really seeing anything. She imagined sitting next to Alexandra, consoling her, rubbing her back and handing her tissues.

"Marissa was my best friend. My *only* friend, really. Are you sure it was him? The Icebox Killer?"

What was she to tell this poor woman? If Callow said she was sure, she'd be devastated. If she said the opposite, the woman might lose hope. But she had to lean in one direction or the other; getting stuck in the middle wasn't any good for anyone. The middle led to inaction, and if she stayed there and allowed history to repeat itself as she failed to act, Callow would have to speak with countless distraught friends like Alexandra and have this same conversation again and again. Remembering the case and all she and her team had uncovered up to this point, there was no way this wasn't the Icebox Killer. She would have to tell the truth, imagining that Alexandra would prefer the courtesy of not being lied to and being hurt twice over.

"It's him."

Alexandra sniffed again, then forced a cough after a whimper escaped her lips. "Okay, Agent Callow. At least you're real with me ... Let's talk."

CHAPTER THIRTY-FOUR

"Where were you born, Alexandra?"

"Baltimore, Maryland."

"I was born in New York. My parents moved my sister and me to Frederick when my father got a transfer. Frederick isn't too far off from Baltimore, is it?"

Callow was trying to scale Alexandra's defensive walls, the ones she'd built to protect her from emotional hurt. In training, the technique was called building rapport—essentially, building *trust*. And once that trust was given, the Academy wasn't shy about ensuring cadets understood just how valuable that trust was. Those Callow hunted often used the same techniques, but to a different end: earning the trust of those around them, only to abuse it in the worst of ways. The moment the victim realized their mistake, the moment that *knowing* became embedded in their minds—*that* was what a killer craved. That one moment when reality set in.

"Guess not," Alexandra offered meekly.

"Looks as though we're both a long way from Maryland. What brings you here?"

"I came to Colleyville for college—an internship. There

aren't many jobs in this area, though, so I probably won't stay."

"I don't imagine you will. Downtown is swanky, but the pay probably isn't very good, and the outskirts are all industrialized. What are you studying in college?"

"Criminology."

"Well, you still have time to change your mind and pursue a career that doesn't hit so close to home."

Alexandra chuckled, sniffed, and coughed. Callow had unexpectedly made her laugh; laugh, when all she wanted to do was give in to the darkness, cry, and think the worst thoughts. A little levity could help transform paralyzing fear into stalwart clarity. Clarity led to action.

"Marissa walked in the park almost every day. It's not far from the apartment, and she likes the trees, and the quiet."

Callow didn't speak. Now, it was Alexandra's turn.

Outside, the clouds had darkened the skies enough that Callow wondered if it'd ever be light again. Rain fell on the window, obscuring her reflection. She tried not to see herself, but her eyes kept focus. She looked tired—and *afraid*. She imagined Alexandra on the other side of the glass, looking all too much like she did.

More headlights appeared down the street as they crested a hill, blooming out from the dark and blasting the window, their intensity causing Callow to look away. She rubbed her tired eyes. A crash of falling plates came from the kitchen, then muffled yells.

"It's loud, Agent Callow. Are you trying to eat? I can let you go, and we can talk later?"

Quiet. Quiet.

The word resounded in her head like a mantra she couldn't dispel. Callow heard more yelling from the kitchen—a woman, probably the waitress, voicing her displeasure with the kitchen staff.

She went there for the quiet.

"Agent Callow?"

An idea bloomed in her mind, the proverbial lightbulb illuminating in a steady flash of images and random thoughts. The park. A girl. A man. Walking. A truck. A van? A truck. The cold. Iceboxes. Cold. A cold truck? A *reefer* truck?

He likes the cold …

"He wanted her quiet …" Callow whispered. She shook her head, finally returning to the present. Alexandra was still on the line. "Alexandra, I need to go. I think you've given me something I can work with."

"I have …? I didn't say much of anything."

"You said everything—those detectives just didn't listen. I'll call you back tomorrow with more details, but I need to go now. Thank you."

"Thank you, Agent Callow. Be safe."

Callow hung up, then spoke into the microphone on her lapel. "Reefer truck, gentlemen. We're looking for *reefer* trucks, not vans or pickups. They're insulated, inside and out. It's all metaphors. The cold, the isolation, the iceboxes. He's showing us through his victims how he feels on the inside. He separates his victims from the world, then he separates their heart and organs from their bodies. He puts them in the ice chests so they can feel what he feels. It fits his M.O., the cold—all of it."

Various acknowledgments came over the radio. Callow's heart was pounding, and she found herself looking out the window again, peering over her shoulder and craning her neck at odd angles as if a bloody reefer was about to drive right past the restaurant. She soon gave up when she'd drawn the attention of an elderly couple sitting at a table to her right.

Callow settled back in her seat, mindlessly stirring the coffee. The instant rush of adrenaline and subsequent crash deflated her back into her body, a very human body that hadn't eaten much that day, so when the waiter returned with a steaming plate, her stomach growled. Perhaps food would settle her nerves.

"Apologies. I would have had this out sooner, but we had to remake it."

"I probably would have eaten it off the floor," she said, smiling weakly as she unwrapped the utensils and sat the napkin in her lap. The waiter walked away.

She ate in minutes, what started off as small, polite bites becoming a torrent of forkfuls to satiate her knotted stomach. It soon stopped growling, cramped, and she gulped down the cold coffee while she allowed her indigestion to settle.

When she was done, Callow checked her watch. Nearly thirty minutes had passed since she'd parted with the group, and beyond the occasional transmission regarding license plates and average check-ins, radio chatter had been minimal. It was as if their excitement, like Callow's rush of adrenaline, had deflated, and they were now left to ponder the what-ifs. When energy was high, Callow felt united with the others across the city landscape, all eyes looking out for one another. When energy was low, she was just one person, alone in a restaurant and staring out the window, waiting for something terrible to happen. That was where her mind stayed for the next hour, bouncing between the various facts of the case and the terrible what-ifs:

White male. Thirty to fifty. Medical training.

What if you don't catch him? What if he slaughters Marissa?

Reefer truck.

He gains their trust. How does he gain their trust?

What if he's just waiting until you leave? He could be there, in the rain, waiting…

The restaurant was nearly empty by the time her waiter returned. Callow realized her plate was gone, the coffee, too, and the noise about the establishment had completely died down. The smell of cleaning solution was in the air as each table was systematically wiped down. She realized she'd sunk low in her seat. When she sat up, her rear was numb.

She rifled through her wallet, tossed a few bills to cover the check onto the table, then got up to leave.

"Miss?" An eager-looking woman caught her attention.

"Hi. Yes?"

The woman wore a proper suit and carried a black planner in her hand. Her hair was pulled back into a neat bun, and her face had hard, sharp angles. She carried herself like management.

"May I ask how you enjoyed the food? Nothing formal—just your thoughts. My name is Lydia. La Sturgeon is my restaurant, and if ever I get a chance, I like to ask for feedback. If your meal was unsatisfactory, I'm happy to refund your money, so please don't feel pressure to talk me up."

The owner had a pleasant smile, genuine, and Callow appreciated that. She had no doubt she wasn't willing or capable of doing what she said.

"The food was excellent. Perfect for a rainy night. Coffee was a bit burnt, but nothing I'm not used to."

The woman beamed. "I suppose you'd know your coffee."

"How so?"

The woman leaned to one side, eyeing her ear. "Only two people use earpieces like those: cops and restaurant staff. And since you don't work here ..."

Callow's mouth upturned in a brief smile. "You're observant."

Lydia shrugged. "I have to be. Details count. Our vegetables are checked for freshness. Cooked foods are thrown out at the end of the night. People can taste the difference, and we make it up with efficiency. Simpler meals that cook faster so we don't have to reheat everything."

"How do you manage to pack a punch with flavor, though, if your meals are so simple?" Callow asked, enjoying the temporary distraction.

"Our meats. Local. Always fresh, never frozen. Meat is at the center of every dish. Some argue the cheese, the garlic, the pasta are what make us true Italian cuisine, but those are only ingredients. Meat's the only thing that can hold its own on the plate. Thank you for visiting, and for chatting. We always appreciate our local law enforcement. Flash your badge and your next meal is on us."

Lydia dipped her head, then made for the register, hopping into a conversation with a waiter. Lydia handed the waiter a kitchen timer from a nearby drawer, and she set it next to the coffee maker.

Attention to detail indeed, Lydia.

Near the front doors, Callow paused, the implications of what she was about to say finally settling in. Their plan hadn't worked. What was supposed to be a leg up, an opportunity to turn the tide, had only ended up being a waste of time. Had she gained anything from Alexandra other than another corner piece to the puzzle? She hadn't gained any time; only crumbs and insight into Icebox's mind, none of which helped her team in the immediate. Walking outside, into the dark and drizzle, was almost shameful; to have to step out in front of all the watchful eyes of her people, who had all placed their faith in her, only to see that same tired, defeated Callow she saw in her reflection. The closing restaurant made facing her colleagues unavoidable no longer.

"I'm coming out. I'm going to regroup with Marcus and we'll wait a bit longer," she said into the mic, trying to mask the worry in her voice.

She stepped outside. Into the dark. Into the rain. Into the cold.

Her light sweatshirt barely protected her from the cut of the wind. It wound between the fibers, finding her skin and sending shivers up her spine. She jammed her hands into her pockets.

As she stepped into the roadway, a set of headlights came on among a line of cars a block away. *Marcus.*

As she took another step, compiling her thoughts and staving off a series of yawns, another car approached the intersection, engine screaming, and blew through the stop sign. Callow saw the oncoming headlights, two bright eyes of the Devil come to take her. She froze, and the world moved in slow motion.

She saw the faded yellow bowtie of the Chevrolet Impala; the various pockmarks on the hood from rocks flung up along the highway; the spidering cracks along the windshield; and a terrified young woman—blonde, pretty, and familiar—at the wheel …

Callow couldn't move out of the car's path; her muscles wouldn't react the way her brain commanded them to. What should have been a leap backwards translated into a backward fall-and-twist, the world turning sideways.

She closed her eyes, expecting the shock and pain of rubber rolling over her boots or the dull *thud* of the bumper on her soft body and the delayed onset of pain. The world rushed back in a roar as the car barreled down the street, away from the restaurant.

Callow's elbow stung, and something hard and plastic dug into her thigh. She picked herself up out of the gutter and did a once-over. She'd jarred her elbow, which was already swelling, but nothing felt broken. Her pants were damp from lying in the gutter, and minor scrapes littered her hands.

She looked at the ground and saw that she'd landed on her radio. The screen was cracked and dull. She picked it up and keyed it once.

"Radio check."

No answer.

She tried again, watching the Impala meander forward, wondering what could cause someone to be so terrified that they'd nearly run her over without hesitation and then keep going. "This is Callow. Can anybody hear me?"

Absentmindedly, she followed the car, its brake lights coming on, then dulling again as the Impala stopped at the next intersection and turned into an alley.

Suddenly, the noir alley was soaked in a red sheen, reflecting off puddles and off the tiny rivers wrapping around gutters and into the earth. Through the Impala's rear window, Callow had an eye on the back of the driver's head, and the girl didn't appear to be moving much—shell-shocked, terrified. Callow felt a need to check on her, a duty, just to know she was all right. Whatever could cause that amount of fear in someone, the kind that could blot out pedestrians from her focus, ought to be investigated.

What jarred her the most was *who* Callow had seen.

Marissa? Impossible.

Instinctively, Callow pressed the butt of her service pistol beneath her sweater, feeling the rough polymer of the grip. It was still there, and that gave her the last bit of confidence she needed to keep moving.

CHAPTER THIRTY-FIVE

Callow approached the vehicle as she would any other traffic stop: she walked cautiously, each step purposeful, each follow-up step readily planned, her body bladed, keeping her right hip angled away and her elbow resting on the butt of her pistol beneath her sweater.

She tried the lapel mic again. "Oakley? Wainwright? This is Callow."

The radio crackled in her ear.

She couldn't afford to wait. Something about the vehicle sparked something in her mind, similar to the feeling of a memory resurfacing. Though she wasn't able to get a good look at the driver, she could have sworn, when the lighting was just right, she'd seen Marissa.

Her mind was playing on her hopes.

She approached the side of the unremarkable faded blue Impala.

The license plate didn't raise the hackles on her neck, either. She had a feeling of hesitancy when first approaching it, but the feeling quickly faded. The woman at the wheel needed her help.

Callow touched the cool metal of the trunk as she

approached the driver's side window. The windows were up and covered in droplets of water. Light from the brake lights continued to bathe the alleyway. She considered her placement if the driver decided to remove her foot from the brake pedal, and Callow took a step out and away from the vehicle before taking a furtive glance to the left and into the driver's seat window.

Callow caught a glimpse of a woman in a black leather jacket, a mop of frizzled blonde hair obscuring her face. Her head was lolling on her neck, and her arms were wrapped over the steering wheel. Callow realized she wasn't wearing anything else.

Just some drunk coed.

It wasn't unusual. Just another DUI.

Ready to call it in for what it was, just some poor girl who'd had a bit too much to drink, Callow tapped her knuckles on the window—to no avail. She removed her cell phone, preparing to dial 911, when she saw that her phone screen was cracked from the fall. It made sense now why things were quiet on the home front—why Jedediah hadn't called in to check on things or even texted, or why Rebecca also hadn't done the same. Callow stuffed it back in her pocket.

Unsure of the state of the girl in the car, Callow decided to check on her condition. Upon opening the door, she was instantly hit with the smell of alcohol. It came in a humid wave, and there was the hint of urine in the air as well.

Callow saw that the girl's hands and feet bore red, chafed rings around the wrists and ankles. Her stomach seized up.

This girl wasn't some drunk. She was a *victim.*

Callow reached over, tilted the girl's head back, and gasped. *"Marissa!"*

Instantly, Callow flipped modes from investigator to rendering aid, checking the girl's pulse on her neck and shaking her by the shoulders. She didn't care how Marissa had come to be here now; she was safe, and that was all that mattered.

"Marissa! *Marissa!* Look at me!" Callow cried.

She mumbled something under her breath that sounded like, "... Let me go."

"Shh. Shh. It's okay. I've got you. You're safe," Callow comforted her.

The pulse in her neck was weak, and her skin felt clammy to the touch. The girl's face was sallow, muted, and pale, her piercing green eyes drooped in a lazy, drug-induced haze.

Callow stretched across the girl's body and removed the keys from the ignition.

Callow tried the radio again. "Marcus? Wainwright? Get EMS down here! Hello?"

Craning her neck down the alleyway, she prayed just one driver, just *one*, would turn the corner. It became too much to wait, and Callow paced. Marissa was breathing, so CPR wasn't necessary, and she lacked any apparent injury beyond the marks on her wrists and ankles and her loss of consciousness.

She's been tied up.

Suddenly, the alleyway was just a little bit darker than before.

Callow softly sifted through the girl's hair, which was matted and unkempt. She tilted the girl's head to the side, trying to get her to open her eyes, and when that failed, gently, with one finger, Callow lifted one of the girl's eyelids. The pupil was evenly sized.

Callow's heart took off in her chest like a starting pistol.

If Marissa is here ... that means Icebox was ...

The thought hit her at full force, driving the air from her lungs and causing immediate dizziness. Callow stumbled backward, tripping over the car, and fell onto her hands, jarring her wrists. Then she saw something else as her eyes adjusted to the stars coursing across them, the byproduct of landing hard.

One faintly raised bump, just below the girl's left ear, like a mosquito bite, and a tiny pinprick of blood.

It all fit together now: the drooping eyes; the erratic, inattentive driving followed by a lolling head; unresponsive to stimuli; and, finally, the mark on her neck.

She had been drugged.

With what, Callow didn't know, but that meant the girl could be overdosing at that very moment. Callow sped around the front of the car and opened the passenger's side door. In the footwell, she found the girl's wallet, ID card, and cell phone. Underneath that was a small empty vial labeled Xylazine.

For animal use only. Property of McClung Animal Hospital.

Realizing the implications of Marissa's condition and how quickly the medication—a tranquilizer—worked, Callow drew her weapon and hung it by her side.

She didn't feel any safer. Every shadow could be a sanctuary for Icebox to hide in. He had to be close. The injection site was fresh, as was the girl's medicated demeanor, the drugs having only just taken hold.

The red marks around the girl's hands and ankles suggested she'd put up a fight, escaped her bonds, and made it to the car before the medication had taken full effect. *Smart kid.*

Callow peered into every corner, then, remembering the girl's phone, picked it up to dial 911. *Send the cavalry.*

Her hands, shaking with adrenaline, could barely press the buttons on the side of the phone, her fine motor functions less than viable. Then it dawned on Callow that the buttons *were* working—the phone was simply out of battery. She tossed it into the back seat, then checked Marissa's pulse again. Still faint, but alive.

"Just hold on," she whispered. Then louder, *"Help! Somebody!"*

Whether she was speaking to herself or the girl, Callow didn't know. Any second now, Oakley, Wainwright, or Garcia would crest the hill and see her at the bottom of the alleyway. They'd see the car with its brake lights on, nearly touching the corner of one of the buildings after running up on the sidewalk. Somebody would see, and then Marissa would be safe, and she'd give them everything they needed to track down the Icebox Killer.

She'd been right. Icebox *did* mess up. Marissa Marley was the one who got away.

Callow's mind immediately summoned the counterpoints. With Marissa having escaped, Callow thought it highly likely that Icebox would devolve into an emotional cataclysm, unable to control himself, forcing him to direct that maelstrom at someone else. Had Callow just opened up Pandora's box?

She turned her back to the car and looked up toward the restaurant. A dog's bark echoed off the walls of the alley. A few blocks away, a driver honked his displeasure, and a man screamed obscenities. Even further than that, a patrol car's sirens wailed.

How desperately she needed to hear those sirens getting closer! Callow couldn't leave the girl, and she couldn't call for help. She was stuck in the middle, and it was the wait that was tearing at her heart. The wait, and knowing that there were people counting on her, Marissa included, and she had no other choice but to stand by.

The ambient city noises slowed to a crawl until all that remained were Callow's pulsing heart and the slow rattle of Marissa's labored breathing. Remembering the girl only wore a leather jacket, Callow ducked back into the car to look for a blanket or something else to cover her up with.

Finding nothing suitable in the back, she checked the

trunk, using the key fob to pop it open. Inside was an apron and a pair of clear plastic gloves—and nothing else. Callow brought the apron to the front seat and covered up the girl's legs. She then used the seat control to lower the back of the seat until the girl was lying flat.

Marissa now appeared to be sleeping peacefully, and Callow felt an immense weight lifting from her shoulders. For the first time in a while, she tried to focus on the positives. Marissa would live, they would talk, and that conversation would offer them the final piece of the puzzle. Finding Marissa here meant that her suspicions of where the Icebox Killer would dump the next body were correct, and that made her feel better, too.

Callow tried to formulate which questions she would ask first.

How did you escape? What did he look like? Do you have a name or a location of where you were held?

A loud crash from behind, like a metal dumpster lid closing, startled her out of her thoughts and caused her to reach for her Glock. Callow spun, only to see a small black cat jetting across the street.

She lowered her weapon.

She was just jumpy; nervous and anxious from the wait. Rather than standing with most of her sides exposed, she went to the driver's side of the car again. Marissa had shrugged off a sleeve of the jacket and was starting to shiver. Seeing this, Callow leaned into the car and struggled to pull it up and over with one hand.

She holstered her weapon.

Callow suddenly felt something was immensely off. A sixth sense. Intuition.

Whipping her head around, melding shadows with the subdued glow of yellow streetlamps, Callow pulled herself out of the car in time to see movement in the dark. A block down, someone hid in the shadow of an awning. She'd caught just the corner of the shadow's jacket sucking into the black, prompting a feeling of unease to sweep over her—the feeling of being watched times a thousand. The feeling, and *knowing* that someone was there, even if the eyes were deceiving.

Callow slowly backed out of the way of the car door and used her left hand to press it shut. It clicked softly. Marissa didn't stir. And still, Callow refused to look away. With her right hand, she slowly drew her weapon, raising it, pointing it at nothing but a shadow and a feeling some ten yards away.

A standoff ensued, a battle of wills. If Callow held, she knew the shadow would reveal himself and she'd have a shot. If she looked away, the beast in the dark would descend upon her, closing the distance in the same time it took her to blink, moving at inhuman speed with the intent to do inhuman things to her and Marissa.

She held strong, but the front sight of her pistol wobbled. It was growing heavier by the second, her lungs unable to draw enough air to support the muscles that screamed for relief. Even as her eyes watered, Callow held fast, because the stakes would be too dire if she didn't.

Come on. Come on. Come on!

Her eyes stung. Tears rolled down her cheeks. Then, as she felt in her heart of hearts that the countdown to the end of her trial surely had to begin, Callow lost focus. She lost sight of her surroundings as her strained eyes failed to make out the details of the world. The car beside her faded into the background, as did the individual streetlamps and windows on the sides of the nearby buildings. All that remained was the shadow and Callow.

And it was this extreme focus that caused blood to rush through her ears like the torrential waters of a dam, loud and uncontrollable.

The rush of blood was so loud, she didn't even hear the rapid footsteps approaching from behind …

CHAPTER THIRTY-SIX

Pain. Pain is nature's great equalizer. When your body is riddled with pain, even the greatest of minds must cough up the strength of will not only to overcome the pain, but to react to it.

Callow was in pain. She had been in pain before, but not like this, and there were no clear thoughts to be had. Like a gathering storm, Callow's mind flashed incoherent images—things that had never happened and things that could happen but never would.

She saw Marcus on the beach, smiling, no suit, or gun, or badge in sight. Rebecca threw him a football, and he missed it. Marcus would never miss the catch.

She saw herself in a little coffee shop, a book propped up against a window, until someone pressed a pistol to the glass and squeezed the trigger—

The image flashed again. She saw Wainwright and Kennedy standing over her own body in a dark alley, her face bathed in the amber glow of the worn taillights of a nineties Corolla.

Or perhaps that *had* happened? Perhaps that was happening right now?

The alley felt familiar, unlike the other images. Briefly, for a fleeting second, Callow felt morbid relief in the thought that her battle was over—that she'd fought the good fight, and now she'd be on her way to her next great adventure in the paradise in the sky.

But if that's true, why does paradise hurt so bad?

It was then Callow realized the pain—dull, throbbing, sometimes stabbing—was rhythmic, and centered on her head, and she was not in fact being carried to the great pie in the sky—

But being dragged by the leg.

Consciousness came quickly. Getting knocked out wasn't like in the movies; you were out for a few seconds at most, and then came confusion and pain. Now, Callow recognized her plight for what it was—confusion, and now pain, each phase more seamless than the last.

Callow took stock of what she could. Her arms were bound behind her back by firm but thin twine that cut into her skin. Her fingers skirted the road's surface as she was dragged like a half-full sack; a limp carcass.

If she didn't act soon, that revelation would soon be a reality.

The shadow had found a way around the car, as shadows do, and had somehow come at her from behind, striking her right where her spine connected with her skull. She remembered the familiar rattle some pistols had and realized she'd probably been hit with the butt of one. And now, as the shadow dragged her along, each tiny stone was a speed bump for the swollen knot on the back of her head to ride over.

Stifling a groan, she shoved her immediate desire to buck and scream down deep. It wouldn't do her any good: her bonds were tight, and the shadow had the advantage.

The "shadow?" Call him what you know he is. The Icebox Killer. He came for you. You played a battle of wits—and he won.

But he hadn't won yet. She wasn't dead—far from it. She'd experienced those same negative, self-defeating thoughts in El Paso, when the Red Mud River Killer had managed to get the drop on her—but that hadn't been the end of the story. She'd turned the tables there, and she could do so here. She refused to become one more victim claimed by the Icebox Killer. She just needed to be smart and choose her moment.

Callow opened an eye just a sliver. From what she could see, she was being taken back up the alley, but their course had veered off to the left, meaning any second now, there would be a curb.

A pigeon cooed from a hidden nest.

They stopped.

Callow heard another grunt. Someone else had been taken, too.

She opened her other eye and, with a slight twist, saw Marissa's matted hair, the girl's limp form fully overpowered by the medication injected into her body. Callow knew right away that if it came down to a needle in the neck, she wouldn't just buck and kick; she'd bite and scream, thrash and turn, like an animal trapped by the leg, ready to gnaw off her own limb if it meant not getting that injection. If she succumbed, if her strength failed her ... she knew *he'd* be able to do whatever he wanted.

A car door opened and shut, and a pair of rough, gloved hands seized her lower jaw in a vicelike grip. She clamped down instinctively.

"I know you're awake. Open your mouth so I don't have to break your teeth," her captor growled.

For the first time, Callow had heard his voice in the flesh. He was real, touchable, *human*. There was nothing distinct about his voice; nothing she recognized other than the twinge of familiarity that came when the mind tried to piece together puzzles. It was easier for her to solve the mystery of the killer's identity than to deal with her reality now—the reality of staring death in the face.

Her captor pressed his fingers into her cheeks, and she tried to open her mouth and eyes at the same time. A rag, smelling of sweat and oil, was pressed into her mouth. She gagged viciously, bucking and groaning, while the fingers forced the rag into place, depressing her tongue. The hands let her head go but still covered her mouth.

She heard a strip of tape being pulled from a roll—and then it was stretched oppressively across her lips. Callow opened her eyes fully. They were still watery from the pain, her vision blurred. She blinked a few times, quickly adjusting to the dark, and finally laid eyes on her tormentor.

He wore a ski mask, a dark coat, and leather gloves. Even in the coolest hours of the night, he had to be pouring with sweat.

How hopeful she had been that he'd just reveal himself to her now! But the Icebox Killer wasn't known for arrogance—he was known for the methodical capture and killing of women, and it had been Callow who had drawn the arrogance out of him, forcing him to confront her. She tried to fix that fact in her mind, remembering to use it to her advantage.

"There. I wish to talk, Callow—but not here, not now. Fight me and you will die now, alone, in the gutter. Be quiet and choose to live just a little while longer. Nod if you understand."

Callow nodded, short and defiant.

"Good."

He stepped away for a moment but returned before Callow could lift her head, stooping over her and tossing her over his shoulder. She groaned into the gag as his shoulder dug into her stomach and forced out the air. She saw the stars for a moment, then brick walls, and finally the metal roof of a box van, its roll top door immediately recognizable. She smelled cool metal and felt the lingering icy chill of a walk-in freezer.

In that discovery, she realized her assumption had been correct. Icebox *was* using a refrigerator truck. That realization only served to feed her inner defeatism; that she'd tempted the Devil with only a snare trap in waiting, and the Devil now called her name. You couldn't catch the Devil in a snare.

Callow heard another strip of tape being pulled, followed by the soft *thunk* of Marissa's head as it connected with the bed of the truck. She felt Marissa at her back, and there was a glimmer of hope in that simple touch. A glimmer of hope that would carry Callow through the dark as the roll top door closed and locked. A glimmer of hope that fueled her heart with fortitude and strength—the core things she would need to fight through the pain she knew was coming.

The truck started, rumbling at idle for a brief moment before backing out with a steady tonal *beep.* Then it pulled forward and made a left-hand turn. Just another late-night delivery ...

Callow began to count the turns and the seconds that passed. *Left. One. Two. Three.*

The clarity that came with realizing she really could have died in the gutter like an animal offered her a stark choice: react or renounce. If she chose the latter, if she buried her head in the sand and refused to fight back, there was no question in her mind that she would die soon after. But even in her lowest moments, Genevieve Callow's hopeful mind had the power to translate that choice into something surprising.

One more chance to live.

She pulled on the ropes around her wrists, hoping the sweat from her skin would lubricate them enough to gain space, a centimeter at a time. Simultaneously, she begged her body to produce more saliva, to soak through the gag and wet her tongue and lips. If she could wet her lips, she could work at the adhesive on the tape and eventually purge the rag from her mouth. Then her mouth and voice would be free, and she'd have a weapon and a tool.

She had her legs, too, which hadn't been bound. Closing her eyes, she came to realize there was a slight rubbery feeling on her neck and a heavy lump in the inside pocket of her jeans …

Her weapon was lost, but she still had her radio. The lapel microphone was small, discreet, and easily overlooked. The earpiece had been ripped from her ear and had settled around her collar. She understood how easily it could have been unobserved in the dark.

This thought—that she only needed to free her hands and voice to call for help—filled her with hope, even if Callow couldn't say exactly where she was. Now, the dark in the back of the truck was a little less consuming, and the Icebox Killer wasn't the Devil anymore, but human. And humans were flawed and made mistakes …

Centering her thoughts in this way helped to keep her prior pattern of defeatism, the one that could beat her into submission and make her just accept her fate as one of the fallen girls, at bay. Just like El Paso, she would have her chance to fight back. But every second she remained trapped worked tirelessly to strip away her courage, affirming this cold, lonely box as her coffin.

Marissa twisted slightly, and by some miracle, her hand touched Callow's. It was warm, despite being tied behind her back. There was sisterhood in that touch; instant recognition of someone else worth fighting for. In the dark, Marissa's hand could have been Rebecca's, Shannon's, or Marcus's … Why shouldn't she fight now the same way she would fight for them?

Her number hadn't been punched yet.

Callow began to work at the gag with her tongue, then, remembering her feet were unbound, she crunched into a fetal position and drew her arms in front of her. Despite the chill of the refrigerator truck, she broke into a sweat, the stickiness prominent beneath her armpits.

The cooling unit hummed away, a solid drone that might as well have been the call of a frozen beast with unlimited breath. With her fingers free, Callow finally managed to rip the tape from her mouth. It stung her lips, peeling away skin and trapped hair. She spat out the rag, then began to gnaw at the twine around her wrists, hope and angst drawing a tremor up through her arms. She had a chance now.

She worked on the bonds until the truck rocked left around a wide turn, slinging her across the floor. She landed with her back against something hard and plastic. The truck stopped for thirty seconds before continuing.

Left. One hundred. Left. One hundred and thirty. One hundred and fifty. One hundred and eighty. Two hundred and ten …

She gnawed and chewed and pulled at the twine, but the strands were extra thick and fashioned in several layers. It seemed her captor hadn't cut corners in tying her hands.

Remembering Marissa, Callow felt around in the dark until she found the girl's legs. They were secured with several layers of duct tape. Her wrists made a metallic jingle.

The familiar metallic jingle of handcuffs.

The most Callow could do for them both was work on her own wrists. Hands shaking more than ever, she fished around her neck for the earpiece and shoved it into her ear. She reached a hand into her pocket, ejected the battery from the radio, and reseated it by pressing it against her side, hoping … no, *praying* it would work.

Using her cheek, she pressed the button on the lapel mic against her shoulder. "Marcus?" she croaked. Despite her successful efforts to wet the gag and loosen the glue on the tape, her voice was hoarse, her tongue like sandpaper.

"Marcus, it's Jenny."

There was deafening silence, and Callow was on the verge of breaking down, having been given this massive ray of hope to stand in, only for a cloud to linger close and leave her in its shadow.

"Jenny? Jenny, is that you?" Marcus's voice sounded odd, muffled, like the signal was weak in the box truck or the radio had been damaged in all the commotion.

"It's me! It's *me*, Marcus," she said quickly, hugging the radio closer to her body as if it was a floatation device.

"Jenny, we've been looking for you. Where are you?"

She spoke quickly into the microphone. "I'm in a van. A refrigerator truck. He got me, Marcus. I messed up. He got me."

"Okay, just breathe. Take stock of what you have. Do you have your gun?"

"No. Christ, Marcus, I don't know. I've got Marissa here with me. She's alive, but he dosed her."

"Don't worry, Jenny, we found the car in the alley. Every cop in the city is looking for you right now. Keep talking to me. Do you have any idea where you might be?"

Callow looked around as if she could see street signs through the truck's thick insulated walls. "No. No, I don't think I do. But I've got the directions we took after leaving the restaurant and how many seconds have passed between turns. Umm … first left turn, south from the restaurant, then one hundred seconds. Another left, then three hundred more. *Fuck*, Marcus, I can't remember if we turned again!"

"It's all right, you're doing good," he replied soothingly. 'Listen, you need to be ready to fight until we can get to you. Uniforms are going to be pulling over every truck in sight—you just need to hold on. Give me anything you can—your first thoughts so we can find you. C'mon, Jenny. You know this!"

Marcus was placing a lot of hope in her ability to think clearly, regardless of the circumstances. Clearing her mind seemed an impossible task, but she fought through her fatigue to achieve it. Perhaps that was a skill the Academy had taught her, or perhaps it was part of who she was.

She took two deep breaths and opened her mind to everything she could remember about the case. All she had said and seen, every action she had taken, every note she had written. Some of it came in fragments, others as a complete recollection, until one solitary detail rushed to the front of the line.

CHAPTER
THIRTY-SEVEN

The birds. Callow remembered birds ... but not just any birds. *Pigeons*. A flock of pigeons formed in her mind, followed by green grass and flowing pines that still had their needles. There was a park bench, and two men in suits walking toward her.

She clamped her eyes tighter, as if to seal in this important memory.

She saw birds, and then a figure in a long coat seated at a bench, appearing distraught, his head in his hands. The details were obscured, fuzzy, like a weak TV signal. The two men in suits approached and she saw herself talk to them. She was watching her own memories play out.

Then, that figure came back to talk to her. She couldn't make out his face. He came back to talk, but he walked around the outside of the trees first. Over and over again, the figure walked from the other side of the park and then to talk to her. The more he did it, the more the pigeons seemed to congregate behind him in a circle, waiting for feed that would never come ... because the park bench was empty. The birds were hungry, and yet the figure walked by them every time to talk to her.

Why? Why is my mind showing me this?

The answer roared at her like a freight train, headlamp shining on her, horn blaring, brakes screaming like a banshee. Callow was released from her memory with the answer on the tip of her tongue—the answer to who the Icebox Killer really was, an answer that had been right in front of her the entire time …

She immediately became aware of two terrible things. The first was that the radio was only relaying garbled messages into her earpiece …

And the second, the truck had stopped.

"… Jenny! Jenny!"

The rest of Marcus's message was too distorted. Callow looked at the radio and pressed the backlight button. The screen glowed green, a blinking battery sign in the corner displaying low power.

"Jenny. Don't give up. You're … not … quitter. Weapon … Anything."

"Marcus? Marcus! No, no, *no!* Marcus! Main Street! *Main Street!* Go to *Main Street!*"

The screen powered off. Callow pressed the backlight button in vain, once, twice, and a third time before finally giving up, dropping the radio to her side.

She couldn't cry. She was too tired to cry, and the pressure built behind her nose and in her sinuses, leaving a knot in her throat.

No clear thought flowed through her mind. She was a whirlwind of them—some negative, some self-loathing, and others, painfully optimistic. The others were words of encouragement and useless platitudes like *"Pick yourself up"* and *"Never give up,"*—things she might have heard in the Academy, training that had no hope of preparing her for what she was experiencing now.

Callow knew who the Icebox Killer was—and yet she couldn't tell anyone. Immediately, she felt dumb for missing it, for being too caught up in her own ambition and her will to prove Jedediah wrong, her misguided attempts to play cat and mouse where only she had to follow the rules. She'd been blinded by ambition, consumed with rage, and disillusioned by hope, all of which had led her to this point—in the back of a reefer truck with a brick for a radio.

The truck sputtered, and suddenly she wished for the hum of the engine again. While the engine was running, the Icebox Killer was preoccupied. Now, he had nothing holding him back.

Callow shrank to the back end of the truck, then she remembered Marissa and scampered forward to drag her with her. As she held Marissa's leg, Callow collided with something stacked in the far corner. She felt around blindly, feeling the familiar corrugated plastic exteriors and gasping in shock.

Coolers. There were a dozen coolers stacked across the back of the truck, held in place by bungee cord.

Callow felt herself shiver uncontrollably, her teeth chattering.

Coolers. Are they full of body parts? Or are they still to be filled? One for me, and one for Marissa?

She was no longer able to keep her heart under control, pumping blood and endorphins through her body which pumped sweat from her pores and added elasticity to her skin. It also dulled the pain that came as she pulled at the twine around her wrists until it cut into her skin. She used her teeth to chew at the fibers, pulling each one until they slipped from her teeth and came crashing down, jarring them to where they nearly cracked.

After this panic-ridden cycle of pulling, screaming, chewing and biting, Callow felt a hint of slack around her left wrist. She leaned back, planting a foot on the knot and pressing, not caring if her wrists dislocated and broke.

She pressed and pulled, grit her teeth, and expelled her

breath, flexing every muscle, relaxing, only to do it all again until, finally, her left hand came loose. The skin around her wrist was rubbed raw, cut in places, pulled and stretched to the point of being numb, but her hands were free, and her fingers were intact. The exertion almost caused her complete collapse.

Shrinking down, Callow cradled Marissa's head, brushing her hair with timid, tremoring fingertips. Perhaps this was how it was all meant to end. She closed her eyes and imagined what it would be like to just shut out the world.

"Get up, Jenny," Marcus said. Even in her imagination, he wasn't letting her quit.

"Get up, Jenny." Oh, no, not you, too, Rebecca.

"Get up, Jenny." Even Hank Juarez was making a guest appearance in her subconscious.

Icebox wanted her to feel alone, but even in the darkness of the truck, the voices in Callow's head reminded her that she wasn't. He wanted her to feel as if death was close, but if her fate really was already sealed, why *shouldn't* she fight back?

Hearing the voices telling her not to give up reinvigorated her. She could fight because others couldn't or wouldn't. There was honor in that—and hope, too. She could inspire hope in others to fight when the chips were down—when all the odds were stacked against them, and all that remained was to go for broke. Her father, as displeasing and disgruntled as he was, would have told her to, *"Put up* until you get *put down."*

Rising to her feet, that thought warmed her again, livening her senses. It made Callow realize there was still a job to be done; someone she'd sworn to protect who depended on her; to *put up* until she got *put down.*

She looked at the radio in her hand, tossed it up, then caught it, testing its weight. The smooth plastic felt good in her hand. She threaded the radio cable through her shirt, then yanked the cable taut. She held the radio firm in her right hand, tightening the cable and weaving it between her fingers. With her other hand, she wound the receiver around her wrist.

Now, she had something—a makeshift weapon of heavy plastic and a thick rubber cable. With it, she hoped to wrap the cable around her captor's neck, or land one solid strike across his temple to knock him out.

Callow felt around, padding the cool metal floor with her hands until she found the plastic coolers. She hefted them up and over the bungee cord, walked them to the roll top door, and stacked them three-high. She did this until there was a wall of coolers between her and the door. Now, she could hide when that door opened, hopefully gaining her a moment with which to surprise her captor. It was all she had, and though they were meager defenses, she felt empowered. This empowerment also allowed her to ignore the fact that some of the coolers were heavy, while others were not at all.

Like a lioness ready to pounce, Callow tucked herself against the outer wall. She left one hand on Marissa's ankle, just wanting to feel her there, to know she was not alone. For what seemed like ages, Callow hid in wait. Her knees screamed for relief, but she didn't budge, knowing that at any moment, the lock would disengage and the door would come sliding up, and then it was a fight to the death.

Time moves differently in complete darkness. It moves even more differently when all you can hear is the soft breathing of another person a few feet away, the constant thrum of your own heart, the blood gushing through your veins, and the occasional creaking of the cool metal walls expanding to the slightly warmer temperatures outside. Callow could have been waiting for an hour or more and it would have felt the same as fifteen minutes.

When faint footsteps padded on concrete outside, Callow was once again thrust into fight-or-flight mode, zapping what little energy she had left. She tried to envision herself smashing through the coolers, wrapping the cable around her captor's throat, and squeezing until her fate changed. The plan went smoothly in her head … but if the evening had taught her anything, Callow knew better than to rely on plans.

The footsteps stopped near the back door, and a voice said, "Genevieve? Are you awake in there? I can hear you breathing."

A lie. He can't hear you. He's playing games.

"I said I wanted to talk, Genevieve, and I suppose by now you've worked that gag out of your mouth. You may scream here; it won't make a difference. I built this place for noise. I would much prefer a civil conversation, however."

She contemplated saying nothing, but the Icebox Killer was crafty, smart. He had already worked out his mistakes and probably knew she was waiting for him to open the door.

"If you don't want to talk, Genevieve, I will fill the box with smoke. I don't need to open the door, and I won't until I'm ready."

She was right; he'd worked it out. She remembered his arrogance and prepared herself to use it to her advantage, for it seemed that was all she had left.

"I figured it out, Icebox. I know who you are. I was just a little too late," she said to the door, projecting her voice.

"*Icebox,*" he hissed. "How terrible a moniker. That was not a name I chose, of course. It's so crude."

"And what would you prefer I call you?"

"I'll ask the questions today, Agent Callow. Tell me, what facts came together to complete your little puzzle? I've made it this far without a mistake, and I would like to fix my … *imperfections.*"

Callow drew in a steady breath. "Xylazine. It's the tranquilizer you used. It's for veterinary use."

"Go on …"

"And this truck—it blends in. Nobody would look twice at a reefer truck, especially in the industrial district."

"Clever girl. I can sense there's more ..."

"And the girl who was taken, Marissa. She interviewed for Picard's Meats with Ronson, just a few miles from your business. Then you talked to her, interviewed her, and got her address from her application."

"So warm, Agent Callow, though you must be so cold in there ..."

"The pattern of the streets where you took the girls and the places where you dumped them. Hard to move a reefer truck up and down one-way streets. You had to move east to west to where you could make wide turns, and that's when you discovered you could drive around the park ..."

"Good, Agent Callow! And the last of it?"

"And the part I missed, the part I should have seen." Callow lowered her voice in defeat. "You were at the park that day we met the detectives. There was no scream. No fourth victim."

"Good! Say my name, Callow. My *real* name ..."

Callow stood up, tensed her arms, willing all her inner strength into the muscles so they no longer felt like two dead branches but weapons, her tools by which she was to save herself. Now was her chance. She controlled her fate. All she had to do was speak the word.

"Go on ... Say it."

Callow waited, and waited, storing her energy.

"Say it!"

Time to fight the Devil ...

"Hodge. It's you, Hodge."

CHAPTER THIRTY-EIGHT

As soon as the name escaped her lips, each syllable a vicious poison that singed her tongue, the locks on the door disengaged and caught Callow off guard. She barely made it to her feet in time as the roll top door began to slide upward rapidly in a screech. Callow concealed herself behind the coolers just as the door rolled up to the halfway point. Hoping she'd catch Hodge off guard, she plowed through the nearest stack of coolers and into blinding light.

For a few moments, there was a cascade of plastic containers and a cacophony of grunts and cries. Of the coolers she'd knocked over, three of them were full, and the containers and their contents appeared to have landed right on Hodge.

Callow leapt from the truck, pouncing on him, completely unaware of her surroundings as her battle-focused eyes sought his—the glowing eyes of the Devil himself—through the fibers of his black ski mask. In the light, Hodge was just a man dressed in dark clothing, leather gloves, and a raincoat, laying amongst the scattered contents of the coolers—red, bloody bags of half-thawed meats.

A normal man. Not a beast or a demon. *A man.*

Callow landed knees first on Hodge's stomach. His initial reaction, the swinging of a black semi-automatic pistol—hers, she presumed, obviously taken during her capture—only managed to connect with her lower jaw, shooting stars across her eyes. She took the hit, reared back with the radio, and slammed it down on his nose, which crunched beneath the impact. Hodge grunted, bucking sideways with his hips and throwing her off.

She needed to move quickly. If he managed to align the pistol with her body, it'd be over. Callow saw blood—the blood of a man, leaking from the bottom of his mask in two veinous lines.

She ducked, catching his pistol-bearing arm with the cable of her radio and twisting upward in a pirouette movement, entrapping his twist. She drew the cable down over his head and pulled on it.

Initially, she thought she'd snapped the cable, the tension too much for it to bear, until she heard Hodge wailing. Like a goat dying in a field, he wailed, clutching his wrist, which hung at an odd angle. Unable to no longer bear the weight of the pistol, he transferred it to his other hand, and the first shot rang out.

The snap of the round and the flash of the gunpowder igniting filled Callow with confusion, but she couldn't afford to see if she'd been hit.

Clutching the radio, she reared back, leapt forward a step, and swung for his temple at an upward angle. He ducked, but not without the radio connecting with his lower jaw. Callow heard something snap; whether it was the radio's screen or Hodge's bones, she didn't know. She was about to repeat the maneuver when she saw Hodge recover quickly, close the gap between them, and uppercut her in the nose with a meaty fist. She lashed out in a vain attempt to block the hit.

Hodge, unable to hold the pistol and still fight, dropped

the gun but managed to hit her. Callow saw stars. Her world spun, and as she stumbled, her foot connected with the pistol, sending it clattering away from Hodge's searching hands. She tasted blood and fought to keep herself conscious.

He'd struck her with his weaker hand, where he was less confident in the strike, otherwise she surely would have been knocked out. They both stood poised, circling each other. Callow used the time wisely, to take a breath and quickly survey her surroundings. The radio in her hand was still intact, but her cable had snapped somewhere in the commotion. The ground was concrete, probably a loading dock. There was a door with a key lock to her back, the reefer truck ahead of her. Walled in, she had no choice but to fight.

Hodge wiped blood from his mouth with his sleeve. He sniffed, and it sounded wet, forcing him to wheeze through his mouth. Callow focused her attention on his broken wrist, which he cradled close to his chest.

Callow watched his eyes—the same predatory eyes she'd seen flashes of in the park, and before that, in the tavern. The eyes of a man who could wear a mask by day and only take it off to do unspeakable things. His face was the mask of a monster, and with the blood leaking from his concealed face, he certainly looked like one.

Callow felt herself get in sync with his steps. When he stepped left, she followed, not willing to give up ground either toward the door or the reefer truck. She watched intently as his eyes moved a hairline toward the ground, a reaction she realized he had been trying to abstain from. She followed his movement and saw the pistol, nearly ready to tilt off the dock.

Go ahead. Go for it.

This was her chance—a risky, necessary chance. She needed one good moment, one clear second when he was preoccupied, and she could make her move …

Hodge's eyes locked on hers, and right as they shifted

toward the ground again, Callow drew back her right leg, judged the distance and the timing, and watched Hodge leap in slow motion in the pistol's direction, his good arm outstretched. Callow swung her leg around on a pendulum, infusing her kick with all her anger, frustration, sorrow, and pain.

She kicked him for Marissa and Gwen. She kicked him for herself, and she kicked him for Carmen.

She felt sweet relief when her boot connected with soft tissue, and she expelled a burst of air as Hodge tensed up and collapsed onto his back, his arm still outstretched toward the gun.

His breath came in short, wheezing rattles. Callow froze for a moment, willing him to just die, praying that these were his last moments so she could finally be at peace. Was it wrong to hope for such things? Was it wrong to wish death on another, to urge their life to end? Or was it righteous when that life had committed so many atrocities that the only way this would end was right here, right now, in a pool of blood …?

Callow prayed someone would answer—that God would answer, if he was listening. She looked at the broken man in the mask, laying amongst the scattered contents of the coolers, the individual bags of half-frozen meats, offal, and blood. She felt panic needling her heart as she wondered if the contents of the bags were human … but seeing familiar cuts, she was sure they were not. Suddenly, Callow felt months of pain and questions that needed to be answered seizing control of her body. She pounced on Hodge again, grabbing him by the collar, her hands two vicelike grips.

"Why?" she screamed. "*Why!*" She slapped him, and he grunted. "Tell me! Tell me! Tell me why!" She screamed, manic, the veins in her neck bulging.

Suddenly, Hodge's body constricted and he began to thrash,

but Callow held on. She dug her feet into his inner thighs, forcing his hips down. Hodge didn't speak; he only grunted like an animal, fighting desperately to throw her off. Callow was about to hit him again with the radio when she realized it wasn't attached to her hand anymore. She looked around for it, or anything else she could use—and spotted the pistol.

It was within arm's reach for both of them, but Hodge had the advantage. He'd seen it first.

With a final buck of his hips, he managed to elongate himself enough to roll his body and seize the gun with his unbroken hand. Callow threw herself off him as the barrel came around and he pulled the trigger.

Another snap and a flash, and now her ears rung. She was at Hodge's side, and though she couldn't hear anything, Marcus's voice popped into her head. In that moment, time moved at a fraction of a second. The gun was coming around to meet her head. Her ears hummed.

Remember: one arm over the neck, grip that arm, and press. Don't forget to flex!

Callow saw the maneuver in her head, envisioned it once, and then took the chance. Each round fired from the pistol sent a shockwave through the air, like cannons going off, splitting her ears and blinding her, but each shot missed as Callow clenched Hodge's back.

One arm over the neck, grip that arm, and press. Don't forget to flex!

Remembering Marcus's little mantra, she seized Hodge in a rear-naked choke. She burrowed her face into his sweaty, bloody mask, making sure that if he managed to aim a shot at her, there was no way he wouldn't hit himself in the process. Luckily, as he flailed, and his body fought for breath and blood, his motor functions failed him, exacerbated by his use of his off hand.

Callow squeezed. And squeezed. And squeezed …

Until Hodge flailed no longer, his body deflated, and his shoulders slumped. Until his breath slowed to nothing.

Though she removed the pressure from his neck, she held that position for a long time, ready to engage it once again if he moved. But Hodge stayed limp, and she was flooded with a different feeling than before—a feeling of finality. As Hodge's arm fell away from hers, Callow saw marks where his nails had torn at her skin, something she hadn't felt in the midst of the fight. And when his hand finally sagged to the ground, grasped in it was a small bronze key.

Callow sat that way for a long time, unable or unwilling to move, for fear that Hodge would get up and come at her again. She stayed that way until Marissa began to stir. She stayed that way until she felt a vibration in Hodge's pocket and saw the electric blue glow of a cell phone.

Callow removed it and dialed 911, letting the dispatcher know they were at the Sapphire Tavern, around the back by the loading dock. Within minutes, the sweet melody of sirens filled the air, but still Callow didn't move.

Marissa stirred awake and Callow felt their shoulders touch. She groaned, and Callow draped them both in a blanket she found wadded up in a nearby milk crate while Marissa rested her head on Callow's shoulder and cried. Still, Callow didn't move. She comforted the girl like a frightened child.

And when the interior door to the tavern finally burst outward and the Colleyville SWAT team filtered in, Callow didn't let go until Marcus pried Marissa out of her arms, because to her, it was Carmen she was holding.

CHAPTER THIRTY-NINE

Three people sat in stony silence outside the boardroom on the third floor of the FBI's headquarters in Quantico. To their back was frosted glass. Inside, the muffled voices of the FBI's senior advisory team, leadership, and legal aids all took turns discussing what they thought had happened exactly one week ago.

Of the three people outside the room, Callow was the most discussed, and she quickly learned to recognize when the people within were talking about her. Tensions were higher in their voices, the inflections not so subtle—and the noise reduction glass couldn't muffle *everything.*

She hated that the top brass could deliberate and ponder for days over a handful of split-second decisions, as if she, too, had had those same days to think those decisions through, including collectively discussing with a legal advisory team.

The second person outside the room was a gloomy man who yawned as if he was two steps from retirement. His tie was looser than everyone else's, and his pants weren't dry-cleaned or pressed. Callow trusted Thomas J. Riggs, her private attorney, however. He had seen her through many critical incidents on the job—but this time was different. Never had the leadership discussed a case for a *week*. Three days was normal, four was troublesome — and a week made Callow wonder if she'd be leaving the building in handcuffs.

Riggs reached over and took up her hand. His was warm, soft, and wrinkled. He wore a flamboyant watch that ticked too loud, and Callow had been listening to it to pass the time.

"Easy, kid. I've had my hand on this case for a week, and I've never seen such a clear-cut case of self-defense and stellar investigative work."

His words rang like a dull bell, and Callow didn't look over at him. "Then why do I feel as if I'm under investigation? Why is any kind of administrative action even being considered against me?"

Callow still had the faint marks on her forearm where Hodge had peeled away her skin with his fingernails.

"Nobody batted an eye about El Paso," she mumbled, sinking further into her chair.

The third person sitting outside the room gripped her other hand. In fact, he hadn't left her side since he'd carried her out from the loading dock of the Sapphire Tavern. Jedediah had been, too—and when he'd given Marcus a crossways look for carrying Callow from the building, she watched him unclip his badge from his belt, offering it up, saying, *"If this bothers you, I'll quit."* Jedediah hadn't said a word.

Callow's head swelled and stayed that way, and that filled her with the hope Riggs was hoping to instill himself. She found hope in Marcus's warm hands that things would work out; that her actions—the risks—had all been worth it.

Jedediah had called Shannon and Rebecca the night Callow was found. It had taken a week for her to regain a semblance of her hearing, and her balance was still off. Gunshots caused concussive damage, traumatic brain injuries, and bleeding from the ears—or so the doctor who oversaw Callow's short stint in the hospital had told her. He had warned, however, that the longest lasting symptoms would not be visible, and she would have a long way to recovery. That news didn't strike her as odd. It was what the doctor had said next that she remembered most clearly:

"The man you apprehended will be here for quite some time," the doctor had said as he'd left her bedside.

"The Icebox Killer."

"In recovery and under watch. His voice may have returned by now. An impressive choke hold you had on him."

She enjoyed the memory of the chokehold she'd had on him, the feeling of his body going limp, and almost felt dirty for doing so. It wasn't right to revel in the pain of others. That made her no better than the sociopaths she hunted.

Riggs had said that if Hodge had died, the case wouldn't even be up for review. It was because he had survived that the disciplinary committee had an obligation to examine the case.

That was six days ago. Luckily, the nightmares hadn't started yet, though Callow knew they were coming. They always did.

"What do you think will happen to me?" Callow asked hopefully.

The waiting was the most brutal part. She'd been sitting outside this very room for days, unable to bring herself to eat a full meal or sleep a full night. The next day was always on her mind, quelling her stomach as she imagined hearing the verdict being read aloud, her fate decided. At first, she'd been terrified, questioning what direction her life might lead if she didn't work for the FBI anymore. Would Marcus drop off his badge as he'd suggested not too long ago? Could they really use this as a platform to dive off into a new, mundane world?

After a few days, just when the worry had nearly boiled over into panic attacks and headaches, it was gone, and all that remained was *a* verdict. An end to all this.

Callow missed her bed. She missed Rebecca and Shannon. If the FBI let her go, would it really be that bad?

The door opened, and Jedediah leaned his head out. "Genevieve? We're ready for you."

Callow got up. Marcus and Riggs stayed seated.

"Aren't you coming with me?" she asked them, wondering if now, of all times, she would have to do this alone.

"This is your meeting, Callow. I've guided you as far as I can," Riggs replied with a heartfelt smile. "What happens next is out of my hands, and whatever you say in there won't influence their decision. You'll be fine, kid."

"And they won't let me in there because they know I'll say something to get myself fired," Marcus said. "I'm banned from visiting Colleyville PD for the same reason. Go talk and let me know when we're going on vacation." He winked.

Callow didn't feel like smiling. She wanted to vomit, her stomach suddenly determined to vacate what little contents it held. After all this waiting, she was suddenly afraid of the answer again.

She looked up at Jedediah, trying to read the board's decision from his face, but there was nothing there. Then she looked to Marcus and read his expression. She saw hope—and excitement. He no longer appeared nervous for her, and that was odd. Despite her now standing and him still sitting, he still held her hand. He had been here the entire time, and now, though she would walk into that room alone, he would still be waiting for her.

Callow followed Jedediah into the conference room, the tension in her neck and shoulders releasing as her body fell into a state of acceptance, knowing that whatever came next was going to be okay.

The conference room was a muggy, glib room with a massive table and a white screen on one wall. On it was a summary of her recorded statements with the discipline committee. The panel were all seated on the far side of the table, and there was only one seat for her. Jedediah stood in the corner.

As she sat down, Callow recalled the names of the committee... Of the three people presiding, it seemed fitting that two of them were the same leadership that had attended the briefing held in Jed's office after Marissa Marley was photographed in Callow's car.

Chief of Staff Wendy Bryant. Deputy Director Samuel Goforth. Special Agent in Charge Adam Friedman.

Callow sat with her back straight and her hands resting neatly in her lap. She didn't tap her foot, nor chew her lip. She waited, calm and collected. Eventually, Wendy Bryant cleared her throat and looked to her left at the other committee members, who all nodded in turn. Callow passed the time by trying to read them. Their expressions offered nothing.

"Senior Special Agent Genevieve Callow ..."

"Yes, ma'am."

"This committee has come together many times in the past. We've taken our years of experience, corroborated by the FBI's procedures, and what the law says into account, to create a solid picture of what we think happened and why."

Callow waited for a question. Bryant continued.

"I must say, after hearing your testimony and reviewing the case file, this has to be one of the most *fucked up* investigations I've ever seen. Lone Ranger shit, disobeying directives, utilizing outside agencies without approval—and, to top it all off, an unsanctioned media appearance which inevitably led to your kidnapping and nearly your death."

This was it. The bad news. Callow could hear the fire in the woman's voice. She could see her eyes were bulging slightly, and the vein in her neck thumped rhythmically. She sat back in her chair and thumped a pen on her notebook.

"Unorthodox. Foolhardy. Reckless," Bryant said as she

looked into her lap. The other committee members didn't move.

Callow felt tears growing in her eyes. The room was suddenly sticky and hot. Jedediah shuffled from side to side uncomfortably.

"Your employment should be terminated …"

Send me home. Let me go. I'm done, anyways. I'm tired.

"… But this committee cannot ignore your accomplishments in this case, either."

Callow perked up. "Excuse me?" she asked, weakly, wondering if her ears had deceived her.

"Genevieve. This board and the agency owe you not only an apology, but a debt of gratitude. Marissa Marley is safe. Subsequent search warrants of the Sapphire Tavern premises revealed the DNA and remains of the other victims, as well as cutting boards made from HDPE —a remarkable discovery, by the way—mementos from the victims, and several stolen vials of Xylazine in a safe in the tavern's office. Additional warrants served on the suspect's residence revealed more human remains. Checks on the reefer truck confirmed it was purchased by Hodge approximately one year ago, and with the vehicle identified, we were able to cross-reference its details with existing street camera evidence from the nights of the murders. In each case, the reefer truck was seen crossing the toll road near where the bodies of Carmen Watts and Eliza Gwen Hammond were disposed."

Callow looked down at her hands, unable to focus, too shocked to speak.

"What some might call insubordination, we recognize as ingenuity in this case. We did, after all, authorize something similar be done to you by utilizing the media," Bryant continued. "We know how close you were to the case because of your personal connection to one of the deceased, Carmen Watts. And though we thought that might blind your profiling abilities, it appears a little emotional connection might be good here and there."

At the mention of Carmen's name, the tears flowed, but they were tears of relief and joy, not anguish.

"When your team saw dead ends, you enlisted the help of others and found yourself a competent surveillance team when you were shorthanded. They, too, will be personally thanked for their assistance on this case. Genevieve, we recognize that Edwin Hodge coming after you was inevitable, and so when it happened, you had systems in place. Plans go awry. The situation is fluid, and not only did you survive, but you did so without any help."

Callow sniffed. She wasn't feeling anything now. She was just present, living each second that passed by as they pulled a week's worth of grief from her shoulders and released all the tension she'd placed upon herself to bring Carmen's killer to justice.

"Genevieve, I speak for all of us when I say thank you on behalf of the FBI. We have come to summary judgement based on the facts of this case that you will be granted three weeks of paid leave, courtesy of the department, for some much needed R&R. You will be granted an additional commendation medal at a later date, and no further action or disciplinary measures will be taken against you at this time. Media silence is required as part of this deal. Do you understand?"

Callow could only nod.

"Thank you for your diligent work, Senior Special Agent. We will be excited to see you return in three weeks. Rest well."

At that, Bryant snapped her notebook shut, and someone shut off the projector. At once, all three higher-ups on the committee stood and began clapping. Jedediah opened the door to the conference room, ushering in Marcus, who squeezed her shoulder and coaxed Callow to her feet. Riggs and Jedediah clapped from the corner of the room, both showing toothy smiles, and Marcus clapped awkwardly while trying to embrace her.

The fanfare died down and the committee members filtered from the room, each taking a moment for solemn congratulations and individual handshakes. Callow indulged them, forcing smile after smile when all she wanted to do was collapse in an armchair and let the relief continue to wash over her.

Bryant leaned into Riggs and Jedediah's ears as she left and then shut the door behind her. Callow turned her head and saw both men had lost the color from their faces.

"Out with it, then," Callow snapped. "There's always another shoe to drop ..."

Jedediah wiped a nervous hand up and over his bald head, and Callow got a read on him.

Insecurity.

It was odd for him to be unsure of himself. Jedediah always knew what to say.

He let out a great sigh and said glumly, "He wants to talk to you."

"Who?" Callow asked.

"Hodge. His lawyer said he's prepared to waive his right to a speedy trial and will give a full confession, but only if he talks to you first."

Callow choked up. Never had she thought this meeting would end up with her still holding her badge, but to throw this kink in it, too—this outlandish, confusing, terrifying kink—left her unable to summon the full breaths needed to speak.

She spoke very softly as a result, as if Hodge was listening from the other room. "Is he going for an insanity plea?"

"No. He'll plead guilty. He just wants five minutes."

"No," Callow replied. "I can't."

"I hear you, Genevieve, but it's just five minutes. He said

you don't even need to talk if you don't want to. We've got him chained four ways from Sunday to a bed; his legs don't work; and there will be a uniform posted outside the door. Marcus will be on standby. I know you've already given *so* much, but this could really put the bow on the case."

"I don't care! We've got all the evidence to hang him," Callow spat. She got up to leave. To even suggest she talk to Hodge after everything he did … was *insane*.

Callow pushed past Jedediah with Marcus in tow.

"He said he'll tell you about Carmen," Jedediah said calmly.

Callow froze. She turned on a dial.

"He said he'd tell you why."

Callow felt another wave of nausea threatening to topple her over.

"Five minutes. Record it, then leave. Set a timer if you have to," Jedediah said.

Callow looked at him and saw sincerity in his eyes, the way a father might encourage his child with only the best intentions in his heart. She saw Riggs give her the thumbs-up—his *legal* approval. She saw Marcus take two steps toward her so he was just off her right hand, just there as he had always been.

Five minutes of staring the wolf in the eyes. Five minutes, and the bastard would answer the one question that burned so much in her heart. Why Carmen? Was it chance? Or was she chosen? Or was it just a game of chance?

"Five minutes?" Callow questioned.

"Five minutes …" Jedediah confirmed. "But you can't try to kill him."

Callow turned on her heel. "No promises."

CHAPTER FORTY

Callow drew the hospital curtain behind her, her mind running wild with questions. She carried a simple tape recorder and a timer in her rigid hands like religious offerings. She stiffly turned to face the monster in a man's body she was there to meet, her heart threatening to burst from her chest.

Edwin Hodge sat up in his hospital bed. There was a supportive bandage around his neck, and three gauze bandages on his otherwise naked chest. Callow noticed the television had been disconnected from the wall, as had the telephone and the nurse call button. Hodge worked tirelessly to excavate the remains of what looked like vanilla pudding from the bottom of the container, to all the world appearing disinterested in her presence. Callow knew it was an act, though—the one small semblance of control the broken beast before her could exert.

He lifted the spoon into his mouth and made a disgusted face. "Terrible. I asked for chocolate."

Callow stepped forward, scanning the room for knives, sharp objects, even pens. At most, Hodge had the spork he was eating from.

"I cannot move my legs, Special Agent Callow. Even if I wanted to hurt you, it was difficult to hurt you before. Now, even more so."

His voice cut through her hardened exterior. She imagined this was what the Devil himself would sound like—like tipping gravel in a bucket.

She smoothed the bottom of her blouse. "I'd like you to know I'll be recording this interview. You have been informed of your rights and have waived them, am I correct?"

She handed him a card with his Miranda Rights on them and a pen. Discarding the pudding pot, he signed the back and handed it and the pen back to her.

"Of course, Jenny."

His use of her first name made her skin crawl—but then again, that was his intention in doing so. She wouldn't give him the satisfaction of her fury, instead counting down the seconds until his five minutes were up as she set the recorder on the bedside table. "And you agree to speak with me out of your own free will, knowing nothing has been assumed or granted to you in exchange for the information you're providing today?"

"Indeed. I know you must have some burning, *itching* questions for me. Questions which will inevitably lead to my conviction for my crimes. I encourage you to ask them, but you must stay until I've said my piece."

Callow still couldn't rationalize the cold, smooth-talking psychopath before her had been hidden under the flamboyant surface of Hodge the Barkeep and she hadn't realized it.

"You will answer my questions and I will consider staying for yours," Callow said from the foot of his bed. There was a chair behind her, but the idea of casually sitting down and having a conversation with Hodge repulsed her. She stood, because this was *her* show.

"The last question I will withhold the answer to is regarding Carmen Watts," Hodge said coldly, sneering, his voice adopting a slimy, smooth tone. "Ask what you must, listen to my words, and then I will tell you *why*."

Callow felt backed into a corner. Though the handcuffs clinked on Hodge's wrists, she felt as if he was once again one step ahead of her, her every move predicted. Even now, *he* was controlling the playing field.

He winced as he tried to adjust the pillow behind his head, and Callow saw his exterior break. No smile; no sneer or arrogance. Real pain—a real man behind the pain.

She walked to his bedside, standing over him, and slid his pillow behind his head, showing that he didn't control the entire game—and as her fingers folded around the fabric, every fiber of her being screamed at her to hold the pillow over the son of a bitch's face—

She backed away, composed herself, and asked her first question. "How did Marissa Marley escape after you drugged her?"

"She played possum, the little sprite, then stole some poor sap's car and nearly ran you over. I found you both in the alley."

"Did you kidnap and subsequently kill Gwen Hammond and Carmen Watts and later kidnap Marissa Marley with the intention of doing so again?"

"Yes."

"Yes, what?"

"Yes, I kidnapped all three women. I murdered Gwen Hammond and Carmen Watts and later intended to murder Marissa. I injected them all with Xylazine, a horse tranquilizer, to subdue them during the abduction. After killing Gwen and Carmen, I later dismembered them. Individually, of course. Things were quite fun for a while—until they weren't."

Callow snorted. "I should have realized it that day when you wouldn't look at me. I should have read more into Marissa's disappearance right before she was supposed to start working for you. I should have seen the pattern."

Hodge smiled his best salesman smile—a wicked, toothy grin that said, *"I know something you don't know."*

"Special Agent Callow, you never would have known. If I hadn't left you a trail of breadcrumbs, you'd still be at the office, twiddling your thumbs, waiting for the next body to drop," Hodge goaded.

"What about Marissa? You drugged her, but didn't kill her. Why?"

"I had to draw you out of that posh restaurant somehow…" he spat.

His demeanor had changed, flipping in an instant. He was no longer charming, sophisticated, but wide-eyed and tenured in spitting malice with every word. He was a whole different person from the man she'd met in the tavern. He was more of the monster from the loading dock.

Callow felt like she was talking to a snake baring its fangs.

"Do you resent me, Callow? Or do you respect this game we played together, you and I? Do you respect our unique connection?"

Callow glanced at the clock. Two and a half minutes had passed.

"Why Carmen?"

"Do you understand how much we have in common? I had been so lonely, so afraid I would be forgotten … until I met *you*, that is."

"Why Carmen?" Callow said through gritted teeth.

"How interesting was our story, our adventure, which will be told for years to come? The great hunt for the Icebox Killer, and hot on his trail, none other than Senior Special Agent Genevieve Callow—*survivor*." Hodge raised his hands as if worshipping a monument.

"How did you kill Gwen Hammond and Carmen Watts?" Callow asked quickly.

"I removed their eyes, tongue, and ears … in that order. I used a scalpel, sharpened to a perfect edge. I used a meat cleaver to remove their hands and feet, and I used belts as tourniquets to ensure they didn't bleed out from their extremities."

"You'll fry for this …" Callow snarled.

"Sounds a lot warmer than an ice chest …"

Callow paused a moment, holding back every urge to leap over the bed and reach for his throat. She realized he probably wanted that, though; to be released from his awful existence, for surely no human could be so evil without losing a piece of his soul. And to be soulless in this world was a lonely existence …

Callow was beginning to understand why legacy was so important to Hodge now. All of this—the fear, the slaughter—was the mark he would leave on the world.

Hodge didn't have anyone to share memories with, no family or friends, and so he forced his memory to live on in the minds of others. In the most disturbing of ways, it made wicked sense.

With the discovery of how Hodge's mind worked, Callow only had one question remaining.

Hodge sucked innocently on a straw from a box of apple juice. She chuckled.

"I don't recall saying anything witty," Hodge replied.

"Oh, I'm laughing *at* you. '*Sounds a lot warmer than an ice chest.*' How clever. I think you're confused by what I meant when I said you'll fry for this. What I meant was, you'll spend the rest of your lifetime in a six-by-six cell, waiting to die, your memory fading as someone else bigger and bolder takes the limelight. You'll scream your dubbed name from the rooftops and be ignored, and the prison will only remember you by your prisoner ID number. You'll wither away in obscurity. And then, when your day comes, the day you will be released from your agony, they'll stay your execution.

Again and again. You'll die in prison, alone, cold, and *forgotten.*"

Hodge placed his hands flat on the table. "Time's almost up, Special Agent Callow."

"What is your obsession with me? Why me?"

Hodge leaned back in the bed, almost relaxing. He rested his cuffed hands on his belly like a wise man about to tell a tale.

"Because you understand me, Callow, and I understand you. We are alike in so many ways—in ways others can't understand. We shun relationships, but crave to feel something. We prefer to be alone, yet we seek out company. What I do hinges on what you do, and vice versa. We are not just connected, but uniquely similar. Would you like to know why I chose Carmen? A stroke of luck—one which I am eternally grateful for because it led me to you. Our meeting was fate. Carmen had to die to make it happen. Such is the problem with our world. You cannot exist without me, and I *shall* exist to counter you. This is the burden we bear. Good and evil. Light and dark. And we will always be *so very alone.*"

The timer beeped and Callow smacked it. Marcus and a uniformed officer were already barging into the room. Marcus wrapped his coat around her shoulders.

Her hands were numb, and a solid lump formed in the back of her throat. Callow sniffed hard and then allowed her fingers to interlock with Marcus's.

As Marcus led her away, Callow turned her back on the room—on this chapter of her life. She turned her back to the past, where Carmen's death was still a mystery. She turned her back on the nightmare that had plagued her for months on end, comforted in the warmth now radiating from her partner's hand into her own.

She stopped in the doorway. "You're nothing but a memory, Hodge. And you're wrong. I'm not alone."

"Oh, Special Agent Callow! I'll be far from forgotten—as long as *you're* still around."

She started to close the door, then stopped. "I have just one more question."

"There's always another …" Hodge said, his hands folded neatly in his lap.

"In the park. Did you lie about the scream, then wait at the bench, just to speak with me?"

Hodge smiled his sharp, toothy grin. "I suppose that is the million-dollar question, isn't it?

She peered into the hospital room—empty, clinical, and lonely. There were no more threads to tug; no more questions left to answer.

As Kennedy would say, she wasn't about to go down that "wild goose *hole.*"

Want to read about Callow and Oakley and the events at Red Mud River? Just flip the page.

FREE BOOK

Building a relationship with my readers is the very best thing about writing. I send newsletters with details on new releases, writer-life, deals and other bits of news related to my books. And if you sign up to my mailing list I'll send you something I think you'll like, my thrilling novel *Red Mud River - A Callow and Oakley FBI Thriller.*

Tell me where to send the book by visiting www.
davidviergutz.com/freebooks

HOW YOU CAN HELP

Did you enjoy this book? You can make a big difference.

Reviews are the most powerful tools I utilize for gathering attention for my books. As much as I wish I could, I can't load the newspaper with massive ads or slam the subway with posters.

At least, not yet.

But I *do* have something more effective than that—and it's something major NYC publishers wished they could get their hands on ...

My committed and loyal cohort of readers.

Honest reviews of my books help other readers to know what to expect.

If you enjoyed this book, I would be eternally grateful if you could take a few minutes of your time to leave a review. (It can be as long or as short as you'd like)

Thank you!

DAVID'S CATALOGUE

To see an entire list of my titles, simply head on over to www. davidviergutz.com

I write a lot of books and my catalogue has grown too large to list them all here. I write horror, crime thrillers, dark fantasy and more. Head to my website to check out the covers, read the blurbs, and start your next page-turner.

ABOUT DAVID VIERGUTZ

David Viergutz is a disabled Army veteran, a law enforcement veteran, a husband and a proud father. He's also a storyteller, an author of thrillers and horror novels that will keep you on the edge of your seat.

As a teenager, David would often be found dragging a backpack full of books to class, leaving his textbooks behind. He was always captivated by the worlds that authors like Nix, Tolkien, King and Patterson created, and he dreamed of one day creating his own.

Years went by and David found himself serving his country in the military, and later in law enforcement. The experiences he had during those years were both thrilling and terrifying, and they left a deep impression on him.

One day his wife sat him down and gave him the confidence he needed to start putting his imagination on paper. From then on, his creativity knew no bounds and he poured his heart and soul into his writing.

Now, David weaves tales of pulse-pounding realism and nightmare-inducing horror where his years in uniform have given him an unparalleled understanding of the criminal mind. Take the plunge and start reading David's thrilling crime novels and terrifying horror adventures.

This book is a work of fiction. All of the characters, organizations, and events portrayed in this novel are either products of the author's imagination or are used fictitiously. Sometimes both.

Published by DV Publishing, PO Box 1602, Burnet, TX 78611.

www.davidviergutz.com

DEDICATION

Written by a cop about cops.

I dedicate this book to those who wear the badge. I respect your sacrifice, big or small. I am proud to walk the beat amongst you.

Printed in Great Britain
by Amazon

22111520R00179